IN FOR THE KILL

Larson knew he wouldn't get specifics from her. But what he did get was invaluable. She had seen something. And whatever it was, it had so traumatized her that she was suppressing it. Moreover, and this pleased him most, she was fragile. By the time the prosecution called her to the stand, he would know exactly what buttons to push to utterly destroy her.

Guilt. Blood. Bodies. In that order. He had come to Niki Crawford hoping to find out what she'd seen. He was leaving with something far better.

He had struck pay dirt.

GUILTY

BY

CHOICE

PATRICIA D. BENKE

AVON BOOKS ◆ NEW YORK

GUILTY BY CHOICE is an original publication of Avon Books. This work has never before appeared in book form. This work is a novel. Any similarity to actual persons or events is purely coincidental.

AVON BOOKS
A division of
The Hearst Corporation
1350 Avenue of the Americas
New York, New York 10019

Copyright © 1995 by Patricia D. Benke
Back cover author photo by Kira Corser
Published by arrangement with the author
Library of Congress Catalog Card Number: 94-96553
ISBN: 0-380-77566-2

First Avon Books Printing: June 1995

AVON TRADEMARK REG. U.S. PAT. OFF. AND IN OTHER COUNTRIES, MARCA REGISTRADA, HECHO EN U.S.A.

Printed in the U.S.A.

RA   10 9 8 7 6 5 4 3 2 1

For my mother and father

Acknowledgments

My deepest gratitude to Sue Lasbury and Doctor Abigail Dickson, who so unselfishly gave their professional advice and personal support.

And to Ray Cameron, a special debt of gratitude for his insight and humor. He will be missed.

Perhaps the only true dignity of man is his capacity to despise himself.

—GEORGE SANTAYANA

PROLOGUE

Judith Thornton stands outside the bedroom where her daughter sleeps cocooned in blankets surrounded by stuffed animals. In the next room her mother lies asleep on her back, breathing noisily out of her open mouth, wrists bent inward, clenched in a Parkinson grip around the rolled washcloths permanently stuffed in the palms of her hands. Judith Thornton, deputy district attorney, mother to her daughter, now mother to her mother, remembers she needs to go to the grocery store. The nightlight above the baseboard at her feet casts random patterns of black and amber onto the walls. Straddling darkness and light, youth and age, life and death; her identity was such an elusive matter.

There is a word to the housekeeper and a quick run through the mist to the car, rain coating her glasses. When she returns home, so much work still remains to be done, cases to be looked at. But for now the drive to the store is a welcome break from the responsibility of the incessant flow of decision-making.

It has taken most of her thirty-seven years of wanting, demanding the right to make decisions to realize there is no triumph in the right to decide. She had already learned by experience about the unpredictability of it all. Minor decisions with such catastrophic outcomes. Weighty decisions with results so much more insubstantial than one might expect. She had seen that so clearly so recently when she made the most serious of all decisions. Or so she thought. After the stroke when her mother could no longer swallow, she had been given the power to decide whether there would be a feeding tube. *Put it in,* the doctor said, *and your mother will live. No tube and in three weeks at most she will die.* And struggle all she dared over the decision, in the end all the agonizing was worthless. Absolutely worthless. There was no tube. And months later her mother lives. Swallowing pureed food but still alive. Still sitting in the garden in the afternoon.

As the rain begins to fall now harder on the car, it occurs to Judith Thornton that maybe in the end it's only each choice that's important, that reveals what's inside you. In the end maybe you just have to do what's right, right then. The rest was just chaos.

PART ONE

THE
CHOICE

1

A fine late-night mist covered the windshield of Niki Crawford's car. She didn't want to be parked out here like this. It was Friday and it was late. She'd been off duty for hours. But there she was, still in her park service uniform, cold and alone, sitting in the dark in her car at the side of the frontage road. She was telling herself, over and over again, that being here made no sense, and she was a person of good sense, of symmetry, of logic and discipline. At least Niki Crawford was a person who thought she was in control—of her life, her career and, except for the past week, her imagination.

She figured she'd been sitting in the car for fifteen minutes, maybe longer; not wanting to start up the motor and leave, not wanting to get out and do whatever it was she had come out here to do. She should be at home in bed reading, not waiting for some figment of her imagination to come to life. She flinched as she realized she'd been biting the side of her mouth.

It wasn't dedication to her job that had brought Niki to the frontage road tonight. It was fear and need. Fear that she had neglected a responsibility, and need to understand and dispel the uneasiness which had consumed her these past several days.

She hadn't planned on mist or rain. She had no jacket with her and her uniform was short-sleeved and cotton. If she left the car to explore, she'd get sick for sure.

Dammit, why hadn't she planned this better?

The answer was simple. She hadn't planned it at all. She was there on impulse and instinct.

She wanted to leave. But if she did, the image would still be with her, the image of a curly-haired blond little girl in a red print dress and a tall man with dark brown hair. She'd seen them walking in the rain toward the river five days earlier. They had been maybe one hundred feet away as she'd rounded the curve.

The sight of them hadn't been particularly unusual. In her first year as a park officer she'd seen lots of people walking from the road toward the river, even in bad weather. This time, though, there had been something different, something sending up a signal telling her that this wasn't quite right. Something cautioning her to stop. Or wave, or honk the car horn.

But it had been raining, and the timing had been all wrong. The scene had emerged suddenly, like a photograph flashed in front of her in a pocket between the curves in the road. To respond would have required immediate action, but the rain, a drizzle moments before, was pounding noisily on the car. She knew she would get wet and probably embarrass herself chasing down some man and his daughter. She'd resisted her intuition just long enough to round the next curve.

Then it was all behind her, erased by the rhythmic ticking of the windshield wipers.

She hadn't gone back. It had been a quick, simple decision. And now the scene kept repeating itself in her mind without her knowing why.

What she had seen had been keeping her awake at night, and when sleep finally came, she dreamed about the little girl running from the river's edge, alone, her dress wet and muddy.

What Niki had seen—a man, a little girl—was perfectly normal, wasn't it? But if it was so normal, why did she have such a bad feeling about it? She could find no explanation. She could remember nothing that would explain this feeling.

There were just little things, little fragments, that pulled the whole pattern of the scene slightly off center.

And something else. What *was* it she had seen?

Maybe it was the incongruity of the ruffled dress against the man's dirty blue jeans. Maybe it was that she couldn't see the man's hands, or maybe he was walking too fast, too close to the girl. Niki searched her mind for specific things she might have seen the man do that were wrong. She could remember none. Absolutely none.

But there was something and it had to have been important. Oh, God, why hadn't she stopped? How could something as insignificant as rain keep her from checking on the welfare of a child?

On the windows of the car, moisture was condensing from her breathing. It was getting uncomfortably humid, but Niki was cold in the stickiness of her clothing. She wouldn't have ever come here tonight if she hadn't seen the evening-news report of that little girl—the Solomon girl—who'd been missing for almost a week. She'd seen other pictures of the missing child, but the photo on the television screen of a girl in a red dress looked familiar.

It couldn't have been the child she'd seen.

It couldn't have been.

Niki found herself trying to take a deep breath and discovering she couldn't. There wasn't enough air in the car. She tried again, unsuccessfully. She needed to get out. To breathe. To see for herself. To prove to herself she was wrong. Of course she was wrong. Then she'd go home and curl up in bed and be able to sleep.

If she'd been a stranger to San Diego, getting out of her car at this time of night in the middle of so much September darkness might persuade her that she was in the middle of nowhere with miles of vacant land in all directions. But she was in Mission Valley, an area characteristic of San Diego's checkerboard pattern of intense urbanization separated by wild canyons and open space. The valley, a narrow one-half mile or so across, with steep rolling sides rimmed by residential communities, ran for miles. Through it the San Diego River meandered.

Despite the growth around it, the river—and much of the area immediately adjacent to it—had been left untouched by state and county highway planners, which allowed a greenbelt of native California grasses, shrub and wildflowers to mix naturally with the sycamore and eucalyptus trees planted by the city park services. Until recently, there had been no organized effort to transform the river area into city parkland, but there was also no effort to dissuade the public from using the riverbanks for fishing and hiking.

As Niki got out of her car, the wind picked up, whipping the leaves of the eucalyptus trees lining the road. From behind her rose the intermittent sound of traffic on Interstate 8. Overhead to the west, Freeway 805 intersected 8, careened upward toward the sky and then curved north over the river and valley toward Los Angeles.

The field that lay before her was an unlighted pocket along the frontage road, which ran parallel to and between the river and Interstate 8—an ignored patch of land whose current function was providing shelter to the coyotes displaced by the valley's development.

Niki flipped the switch on her flashlight, which she had brought with her, thankful for the light. Her steps were tentative, accompanied only by the sounds of crickets chirping and ice plants crunching under her heavy boots.

As she stepped through the tangle of vegetation that was getting progressively thicker, she followed what she estimated was the path the man and the little girl had taken across the field to the river.

Niki was halfway to the river when the heavy mist turned to a gentle rain. She stood for a moment, listening, as a peacefulness settled over the place and the smell of newly cleansed foliage and earth drifted up to her. Then, as suddenly, the calm turned to a downpour. If there was a reason to go back, this was it. But it wasn't enough now. She forged ahead faster and faster, running toward the river and the shelter of the trees along the bank.

As she neared the water, a feeling of dread overtook her. *Someone, something, was following close behind her.* Then, just like that, it all stopped: the dread, the rain, the feeling of being pursued. But what replaced it, there in the clearing under the trees, was the nightmare she'd had more than once.

The air was filled with a horrible foul odor that overpowered the familiar smells of the decaying mulch and the mud. She recognized it. She knew the sickeningly sweet stench associated with dead things.

Something dead was close by.

The odor didn't frighten her. She worked outdoors. She'd dragged dead animals from hillsides and burned-out terrain. But the smell forced knowledge on her that she didn't want, wasn't prepared for. Her steps slowed.

She saw a doglike form, frozen momentarily in a toothy grin before its flight; then her mind began absorbing the physical fragments of death suddenly surrounding her.

Movement—hers—was directed involuntarily by sight and smell. She was spinning in slow motion. Her flashlight made wild patterns on the ground as its beam leaped from the mound of red cloth to the handless, footless limbs to the things—the bugs—moving in the mound of red. There was a face or what was maybe a face; *yes, it was a face;* but the tongue was blue and sticking out and it was *too long for the face.*

Niki's body was going limp. She found herself sitting on the wet ground, moving quickly backward, crablike, powered by her hands and feet, her bottom scraping the ground.

What followed was a void.

Then Niki was beside her car on her hands and knees, not remembering flipping herself over or what had happened or how long it had been between there and here. Her arms were badly scratched. A sharp pain ripped through her back. She'd bumped into things, but she couldn't remember what. She pulled herself up, using the handle on the passenger side of the car. Somehow she found enough strength to open the door and crawl inside, instinctively hitting the button that automatically locked the car doors.

Niki's hand was immediately at the ignition, her only thought to leave as fast as she could. Should she call the police? Of course she should. But what if they wanted to know—and they would want to know—why she was out by the river in the dark at eleven at night? She would have to tell them the truth. The truth. What was the truth? That she'd seen this child perhaps moments before her death? That she had seen the man who killed her and she'd had a chance to stop the overwhelming horror of this? That she'd ignored every one of her instincts and now the child was dead?

She didn't have to call anyone. She could go home. Yes! Go home and deal with this in her own time, in her own way. *Oh, God, though, the child was out there.* She had seen her. She had seen the coyote. Someone, somehow, had to know.

Niki made a right turn just before reaching the entrance to Interstate 8 and headed toward the closest motel within a mile. It was a relief to see the white glow of a telephone booth at the side of the motel office.

Niki groped in the glove compartment for a quarter before remembering the public emergency line was free.

"Ah, I want to report a body . . . a dead body. Off Interstate 8 at the frontage road . . . in the field under Freeway 805. A lit—little child. It's a girl . . . it was a little girl."

The emergency operator's voice was terse and dispassionate.

"Your name, please?"

There was a long pause as Niki breathed heavily into the mouthpiece of the phone. She hadn't thought about having to give her name.

"Ma'am, what is your last name?"

Niki opened her mouth. A noise came out, not resembling any word. She knew she had information the police would want, would need. But try as she might, she found herself unable to do what she knew should be done.

She hung up the receiver. By now the pay-phone number had automatically appeared on the operator's computer screen, giving the location from which the call had come. Niki realized she needed to leave immediately.

Later, alone in bed in her apartment, still unable to

sleep, the torment would begin anew as the horror of what she had seen clawed at her.

There was suppressed deep inside her the knowledge that all of her compassion and caring, all of her responsibility, had for one moment come up against something else, another part of her she'd only guessed was there, and that other part had prevailed. Without clearly understanding it, she knew she had been all that had stood between order and chaos, sanity and madness.

But it had been raining.

And now her mind, unable to absorb the magnitude of the consequences of her decision, continued erasing from her memory everything she had seen.

The emergency operator grimaced. She'd been cloistered for six hours in the computer room of the downtown fire department on Front Street, eleven miles south of Mission Valley. The station served as the central location for the city's emergency call system.

This was not her normal shift. Hers was earlier. There had already been two crank calls tonight. She'd sent the paramedics off to an unchaperoned teenagers' pizza party and the police off to a four-year-old practicing hitting 911 just like his preschool teacher had taught him to do. Then there had been a variety of calls reporting traffic accidents. Those she had just transferred over to the highway patrol.

This could be another crank call.

Possibly.

Probably.

There was no identification given. And the location described was sketchy. Still, the woman at the other end was doing a pretty good job of acting distraught. Her speech was accelerated. And, hell, the victim was supposed to be a child. The operator's gut told her this was another case where she should err on the side of action. False alarm be damned.

She called the police dispatcher.

"I've got a possible homicide. The phone number is a Mission Valley motel. That's 25131 Hotel Circle. Caller reports a child's body in a field adjacent to Interstate 8 and 805."

The nearest police car was at that moment parked on the 805 overpass above Interstate 8. With help from the overhead lights in his car, Officer Mark Chin was filling out a two-page accident report, his fourth in two hours, and wondering why southern Californians were incapable of driving in even the slightest rain without slowing to a crawl and running their cars into one another. The dispatcher's call interrupted what had otherwise been a routine rainy night.

Mission Valley was his beat. Within minutes Chin, his shoes wet and rimmed with mud, was standing just off the frontage road at the field. He'd been dispatched only to drive by and investigate, but that directive allowed him a substantial range of discretion. He could stay in his car and drive by, drive by and stop, or get out and take a look around.

It could have been a crank caller, or some well-intentioned person with an active imagination. Why head into that wet, black pit out there based on such flimsy information?

But Chin never had a chance to change his mind.

As he stood undecided, a flicker of light caught his eye in the trees beyond. He saw it again through the shrubs parted by the wind. Then again. Aided by his flashlight, he began to follow its intermittent beacon. By the time he got to the trees, his hair was coated with beads of rainwater.

The officer's eyes focused on the child's protruding

eye and her twisted body before he noticed the lighted flashlight lying next to the body. Its beam had beckoned him.

Back at his car, he radioed for help, lots of it. Then he waited alone in the dark, wondering aloud whether there was anything he should do. As the first officer at the scene, he had temporarily become the field commander. His mind ticked away the list of responsibilities: secure the area; protect it. It would be at least thirty minutes before the homicide team arrived. He tried to isolate the factors that might change in that time. The last homicide investigation he'd worked on in the rain was in Imperial Beach on the oceanfront. As the tide had come in, it had washed away the evidence before the homicide team or the photographer had arrived.

Chin decided to check the riverbank to see if it was anywhere near overflowing into the area near the body. It too might wash evidence away. The rain and wind had surely caused havoc enough with the crime scene, so they didn't need to have the San Diego River hit one of its high watermarks and overflow. He radioed the dispatcher to have someone get a weather report and run down a forecast on the height of the river. For the moment, he was convinced he'd done everything he could to assure that the area hadn't been tampered with by either God or man.

Detective Pike Martin knew who it was as soon as the phone rang. No one called him this late at night except the watch commander. The call meant there was a homicide, and more specifically, that the investigation had rotated to Pike's homicide team, one of six in the city. The commander was brief.

"Pike? We've got a kid. It's a biggie. They think it's the little girl that's been missing for a week. Grab a cup of coffee on the way. This may take a while.''

"Where'd they find her?"

"Mission Valley. The frontage road at 805 and 8.''

"I'll be there.''

Pike had been a detective with the San Diego Police Department for twenty-five years. A short, surly man with a long, leathery face and puckish mouth, he'd worked it all—minor drug busts to the worst murders. They'd put the permanent furrows in his forehead and left him with seizures of rapid-fire blinking, a peculiarity which even in his most seemingly controlled moments involuntarily betrayed a rising level of emotion. He was blinking as he hung up.

Pike's routine was second nature. He would put on his yellow jacket with POLICE emblazoned in bold black letters across the back and front and be off. If he left this late, he probably wouldn't be home until morning.

Pike checked the stove burners. They were off. He threw away the pizza box and tossed the beer cans that had been sitting on the television tray since the six o'clock news. He cupped his hands around his mouth, breathed out and sniffed. He reached into his pants pocket for his breath mints, popped two into his mouth and chewed them.

Outside, the sky had begun to clear. Pike was on automatic pilot, following a police protocol that did not vary. From homicide to homicide, body to body, it was identical.

He wondered how long the little girl had been dead. If it was an hour or less, there was a good statistical chance they could find the murderer. The one sure thing was, there was a body—homicide teams don't roll unless there's a death. Even when the police have a person they know is going to die, homicide won't roll until he does.

As Pike neared the field, he could see six or seven police vehicles and the communications van, a large Ford filled with floodlights and evidence-collection devices. The evidence technician was standing nearby.

Pike was the last of his group to arrive. He located his team just off the frontage road. The field commander at the scene, Lieutenant Charles Harris, would brief them once, simultaneously.

"It's a child, a little girl. It looks like it's the kid that's been missing, the Solomon girl. She's been out here a while. There are no witnesses to anything. Nine-one-one got a call from a disturbed female who reported seeing the body. She didn't identify herself. Wouldn't ID herself when asked. Officer Chin saw a beam from a flashlight we think was left by whoever called 911. So we have nothing but the body. You're starting from scratch on this one, and with the rain, we need to take all the precautions we can to preserve the scene. The body's about three hundred feet straight ahead near the river."

Harris turned to the team sergeant, Mike Abrams. It was their responsibility to decide together how they would proceed and which members of the team would perform which tasks.

Permeating all directives was the mind-set, a silent understanding that every murderer leaves something behind. It might be microscopic—some shred of fiber, a tiny piece of paper, skin under the victim's nails, a characteristic laying out of the body. Or it could be big—a tire track, a weapon. Their job, their challenge, was to find it. Because it *was* there.

In most homicide cases, Abrams's rule of thumb was to search the area within throwing distance of the body. This case would be treated very differently. His orders were clear and direct.

"First thing we need to do is light this whole place

up good. Everything from the road to the river. Pull the light van up. Let's move the cars. I think we can drive them just off the road and use their headlights to hit the grass here. If the van's not enough, call the light rig in.''

The "light rig" was the fire department's mobile light unit. It could be called in when the police van's standard quarter-million and half-million candlepower lamps and generators weren't enough to do the job.

Harris turned to Abrams. "How are you going to divide 'em up?" He was referring to the homicide team, whose members would be dispatched to a variety of responsibilities from carrying out the lighting to taping around the perimeter of the scene.

Pike's responsibility was always the same. He was designated ''evidence detective'': usually the most senior detective of the team and the most methodical, the one who loved the monotony of sifting through acres of detail. He would be the only member of the team permitted to immediately enter the inner perimeter around the body. If he chose, he would accompany the body to the morgue for the autopsy.

Within minutes, lines of shiny yellow plastic tape were strung from the shrubs and trees, warning repetitively in bold black capital letters, POLICE LINE DO NOT CROSS.

The scene secure and stabilized, Pike and the evidence technician, Gregg McDonald, entered the perimeter. They walked as if they were in a minefield. One step, then pausing to examine the placement of the next step. One misplaced boot could destroy the only existing evidence.

The halogen lamps should have cast a clear white light, but in the emerging fog their effect was an eerie glow, interrupted by a row of blinking blue-and-red lights atop the police cars lining the frontage road.

Police officers looking for evidence walked silently around, zombielike in the eerie glow.

And so the intense search for clues, for evidence, for the guilty, began in the area surrounding the body. Pike looked down to his right. Directly before him was a footprint in the wet dirt, a fresh one resembling that of a small person, perhaps a woman.

"Be sure we try to get a casting of this," he said, pointing to the footprint as he pulled his handheld tape recorder from his jacket pocket and began making a record of his observations.

"I arrived at the scene at twelve-ten A.M., comma, and located my homicide team, period."

He completed the preliminaries for the tape, verbalizing each comma, each period, each quotation mark and exclamation point. The tape would paint a picture of the scene and the body, and preserve his personal impressions. Whatever else he might feel about the death of this child, his first obligation was to find the evidence that would lead to her murderer. And so he would push aside the revulsion and suppress the knot in his stomach.

She was an item of evidence now.

Pike and McDonald circled the body as Pike continued:

"Body appears to be that of a female child ten to twelve years of age, period. Age approximate, period. Clothing has noticeable ripping or incisions running the length of the skirt area, period. Arms tied behind back and one hand appears to be gone by animal activity or removal by cutting, period. Decomposition significant and bloating substantial, period."

The litany went on and on. Pike, his recorder still running, turned to McDonald.

"Looks as if she's been out here what, maybe five days?"

There was a pause before McDonald answered. Pike knew the time frame was hard to gauge. Decomposition starts fast after death, depending on the environs, temperature, moisture and animals.

"It's hard to tell, Pike. There's still a substantial amount of gas in the body; the odor is very strong. No mummification yet. I'd guess, and it's just a guess, about three days or so."

Pike continued, recording in excruciating detail the condition of the body.

Back on the frontage road, Abrams was intercepting a reporter who'd picked up the story on the police radio band. If this was the Solomon kid, the place could become a zoo very fast. Abrams was glad the homicide team had arrived at the scene first, an event not always predictable. His job for the moment was to keep the reporter contained. In exchange for up-front information and periodic briefings, the reporter agreed to remain at the road and the communications van.

When Pike and McDonald were done, they signaled that those who needed it could have access to the area around the body. The photographers quickly began a systematic visual recording of the immediate scene. The pathologist bagged the victim's arms in plastic to preserve any evidence that might be on them. As he was finishing up, an officer ran toward Pike and McDonald.

"Captain McDonald. Family's on the way down. Someone called them."

"Jesus Christ." Pike threw his arms up in the air. "Preserve the protocol and do everything you have to do to keep them away from the body." He was shaking his head. "Are you sure?"

"I think so. We think someone from the press called 'em and they've called the dispatcher."

Pike searched for the pressure points at his temples.

The bushes around him suddenly began to shake. A wild-eyed woman in a pink nightgown with a green wool coat over it burst out of the shrubbery. A tall, bald man in black wire-rimmed glasses was half hanging onto her raglan sleeve. They instinctively headed for the lights and, with officers in pursuit, lunged past Pike and stopped.

A long, shrill scream punctuated the night. The woman had made a positive identification.

Officers rushed to the couple. Despite the sudden turmoil, the deputy coroner, who had arrived to examine the scene, had not deviated from the task of recording his own observations.

Pike looked up at the sky. The rain was expected to break during the night. It was a calculated risk, but he would recommend to Abrams that they complete their superficial search and come back in the morning. The crime scene, including the child's body, would have to remain intact and undisturbed for the remainder of the night. Absent a real downpour, the scene wasn't going to change all that much, and leaving everything as it was until morning guaranteed they'd have natural lighting, the best possible light. Better the wait than the potential loss of evidence in the dark.

He glanced toward the couple, now sitting on the ground, almost under the yellow plastic tape separating them from their daughter's body. They were holding each other, sobbing. Pike squatted next to them.

"Mr. and Mrs. Solomon?"

"Please, tell me this isn't happening. Make this stop." The woman pleaded with him for the impossible.

Pike knew nothing was going to stop, not the helpless grief, not the search for the cause of the grief. There would be no quick end to this. No funeral for crying, screaming, letting out all the pain and then moving on with life. This was the beginning. The beginning of a process as unpredictable as the girl's death and capable of twisting the lives of everyone in its path. And now, of all the ironies, his responsibility was to assure that the tortuous process was successful. He would sift the evidence. Pursue these grieving people for every bit of information they could give him. Locate and convict the killer. And if he didn't find the murderer? The child's death would follow him forever. Another file not closed. There was something unacceptable in that thought.

"Mr. and Mrs. Solomon, I'm sorry. I'll have one of the officers drive you home or to a friend's or relative's house. There's nothing anyone can do out here tonight. We'll arrange to have a social worker speak with you tomorrow and help make funeral plans for Kelly."

He was hoping he would not have to explain that the body would remain outside all night. Or that the police would not offer the simple dignity of covering her remains with a blanket because it might cause a transfer of vital evidence, a fiber, a drop of the killer's blood, to the blanket.

"See that Mr. and Mrs. Solomon are driven home now or wherever they want to go, and be sure they aren't disturbed by anyone on the way out."

Pike and the officer helped the couple to their feet, and the officer gently took the woman's arm, leading her toward the road.

Abrams gave the order to complete the cursory search of the area from the body to the road, then wrap it up until morning.

By 2 A.M. the area was still, the prevailing sound the now diminishing rain. In the darkness, a tarpaulin balanced precariously on metal rods. Kelly Solomon's body lay beneath it, undisturbed and uncovered as a young police officer in a yellow rain slicker stood watch, his back to the tent.

Six hundred miles in three days. Robert Dean Engle had zigzagged northward across California, his compulsive need to move impelling him first from San Diego to Bakersfield, Salinas and Monterey, then south again, pausing in Riverside. He was still awake and pacing. Another sleepless night to remember what he had done. What a mess he had left.

The motel room smelled just barely clean—pine disinfectant covering the smell of old cigarette smoke. He wrote quickly, in a frenzy. His brown hair barely touched his shoulders. His writing was interrupted only when he rose and strode back and forth across the length of the brown shag carpet. He sat and rose, paced, sat again. The stress of travel was not what kept him awake. It was, instead, a profound need to disgorge the knot deep inside and relive what he had done—an explosive tension urgently awaiting release, finally spilling out onto the paper.

September 13

Today I stepped on a snail and squashed its shell. I could hear it screaming a very angry kind of scream. I laughed. Then I felt so sick and awful about it. It's funny I can't feel bad with my captives. They're EXCITING. The last golden one was SO very good. And MUCH nicer than any of the others. Even right before the last moves she made, when I know the hurt was at its highest BEST, she was nice to me. She was more noble than those screaming insects and bugs. I told her so again and again when the teeth were biting and biting at her. Only her eyes were sad, pleading. But she stopped that too when I told her to and I whispered to her that I could not stop until she was dead. I think she understood. She sat on my lap and cried. She UNDERSTOOD. I told her that bitch who saw us wouldn't help her or she would be dead too. I told her nothing could help her. Nothing can stop the BITING.

Engle grunted with recalled satisfaction. Not quite like the real time, but good. He felt—what was it?—not powerful. *Adequate.* He felt adequate. It was so good to feel adequate. He stretched his arms and continued writing.

This room is a hole. I was going to check out of here, but I've decided to stay for a couple more days because I can HEAR them in a fenced yard not far from here. I can SEE them playing in the morning. I have picked a spot on the side street with a very good view. But I've made no final choice YET.

Engle rose and walked more slowly now to the bed, diary in hand. He slipped it under the pillow, exchanging it for the slip-joint pliers he kept there. He pressed the tool against his cheek, running it gradually down the length of his body to his waist, then back up again to his mouth, releasing his breath on it, savoring it. His tongue darted in and out. When just the right amount of moisture was spread on the metal, he rubbed it against his T-shirt. Polishing it as one would a precious jewel. Then he held it up to the light, opening and closing, opening and closing its jaws.

"My alligator. Biting. Biting."

Engle yawned, replacing the tool under the pillow. He would sleep now, happy in the peaceful, comforting solitude of adequacy.

By nine the next morning the rain had stopped. Kelly Solomon's body was gone, removed from the frontage road turnout by the coroner's office.

Pike and Abrams had conferred earlier, weighing the alternate search methods available. They had examined aerial photos taken by the police department helicopter and concluded that the terrain and vegetation would lend themselves to the technique requiring a long line of people walking through the area in unison. So intensive was the inspection of terrain using this method that it was referred to as a strip search, after the most personal of physical body searches.

A telephone call to the police training academy downtown had produced thirty-nine young cadets, all volunteers, each hoping against the odds that some kernel of knowledge retained from a forensics class would result in his small portion of the line discovering the critical piece of evidence. A disturbed mound of dirt might produce the murder weapon, a clump of weed, a cloth fragment or a drop of the assailant's blood. At the end of the turnout, a comb of human hands moved across the earth, parting the grasses, probing the soil.

Pike occasionally used this strip-search technique of having the members of the line move at arm's length from each other. For this particular search, Abrams had insisted on tightening the line, bringing the students in shoulder to shoulder, then lowering them, crawling, at ground level on their hands and knees.

The turnout had been divided into a grid pattern of six parts, roughly equal in area. Pike would twice take the line through each part while a second unit dragged the shallow river. At the perimeter of the turnout, a third unit collected mostly an assortment of cardboard fruit-juice containers and soda cans—garbage, they called it—each item handled as if it were the one that would reveal the identity of the murderer. The rule for the scene was to avoid touching anything until it was properly photographed and its location and position noted and measured. There was no special protocol for moving the items other than to be guided by the knowledge that the most critical period in preservation of all evidence, fingerprints in particular, was during initial handling and removal of the item from the crime scene to the lab.

Within three hours they had collected fifteen aluminum cans by carefully placing an index finger in the pour hole, the position least likely to disturb existing fingerprints, lifting each can without touching its sides and placing it in a separate brown paper bag marked with the date, the collector's name and the exact location where the can was found.

2

While the search had been under way, Niki Crawford slept. The radio alarm had sounded for work at six-thirty, but she'd turned it off and gone back to sleep.

When she woke up, not refreshed, but dragging from a fitful night, her struggle began anew to identify some reason why her life had taken such a terrible turn. She had lived obediently, studied hard, graduated and found a job whose greatest discomfort was that she had to deal with the crass language of her mostly male coworkers. Her life had a peaceful symmetry in which good thoughts *always* prevailed and evil was ignored. No, she had not invited this.

She had done nothing to be punished for.

3

Judith Thornton watched her six-year-old race down the fifty-foot hallway. This morning Elizabeth was a blur of fluorescent pink and green in Nike shoes and Guess jeans, a walking trademark of yuppiedom and an island of color in what had been two years of personal turmoil.

Soon after Judith and her husband, Steven, had moved from their small house to the six-thousand-square-foot home in one of San Diego's exclusive residential areas, there had been one traumatic event after another. Whatever the causes, and there had been more than one, her marriage had fallen apart. Steven carried away his possessions in the new apple-red Miata she had hoped might slow his restlessness. Her belief that they were dealing with a midlife crisis was dashed when he appeared one evening for visitation with Elizabeth and calmly announced his intention to marry the young woman who had been hired as his paralegal. It was all so trite, so common.

Soon afterward, her mother had come to live with her. But within a year Judith's mother had begun to show increasing signs of multiple infarct dementia, an inexplicable and continuous series of strokes that had left her mute and quadriplegic. She now required a full-time aide.

Suddenly Judith was officially one of the generation she'd been reading articles about—the sandwich generation: taking care of children and elderly parents at the same time.

All of this would have been enough to shake the foundations of a young child's life. But Elizabeth had been spared by Judith's determination to keep the child's life on its own track, not on hers.

Now, as Elizabeth ran through the house to organize her backpack, Judith took a few precious minutes to organize her own agenda for the morning. She had been a deputy district attorney for eight years, hired, it was said, right out of Stanford Law School, only ten minutes after the district attorney and his chief assistant had interviewed her. No one doubted the story. She was a thin woman whose strength of character and poised self-confidence showed through her auburn-haired, tomboyish beauty. Brusque and at times painfully forthright, she was that rare combination of aggressive, skilled trial technician and legal scholar. She could stop an adversary in mid-sentence with the icy stare she had come to be known for, a look that could bring even the most vigorous of arguments to an abrupt end.

It was seven-thirty. Her trial call wasn't for an hour, and she had only one heavy-duty offender in court this morning, charged with robbery by use of a firearm. She'd offer the defense six years, the maximum prison term for the robbery, and drop the two years that could be added on for the use of the gun. It was a good deal. She expected the defendant to take it. He was heading for a life prison term anyway on an unrelated homicide.

The six years he'd get on this case was next to meaningless. He'd serve it concurrently with the life sentence. Everyone knew this. She could deal with him quickly; and although the public might not understand the expediency or even agree with it, the plea would avoid a useless trial that would cost thousands of dollars in scarce resources only to end up with the same prison sentence she was going to get this morning for next to nothing.

Coffee in hand, Judith stepped into her mother's bedroom. She was surprised to find her awake, staring at the ceiling. The older woman had been sleeping much later into the morning these past three weeks.

"Good morning, Mom."

Her mother's eyes immediately closed.

She did that all the time now. Smiling at visitors, shutting Judith out. Someone told Judith that this happened when daughters stopped being just daughters and became caretakers.

When it first began happening, it was painful. But Judith had conditioned herself to ignore it, preferring to believe it was her mother's way of releasing her to go about her business; an act of love, not of rejection; an interpretation far more consistent with her mother's nature.

"See you this evening, Mom. Your nurse is here . . . Jean's here. Have her help you pick some of the flowers. They're all still blooming." She kissed her mother's forehead and left the room.

Judith remembered how her weekday mornings used to be before she realized the magnitude of her mother's medical condition. She would help her into the bathroom and let her sit on the toilet as part of the morning routine. Most of the time it yielded nothing. After fifteen minutes or so, Judith would knock on the door, maybe open it a crack, and there would be the questions, almost by rote.

"Ready, Mama?"

No answer.

"You want to get up or sit a while longer?"

Still no answer. The conversation was all one-sided.

"Okay. A couple more minutes and I'll check on you."

Some mornings her mother would "rotund," the doctor's term for staring into nothingness, talking to no one in particular and generally ignoring the world around her. Judith would look in and there she would be sitting, maybe in her rayon, pink-flowered mumu, itching her thighs.

"I'll get up."

She made her statements without looking at Judith.

"Scrambled eggs today, Mom. And I've got Tabasco sauce. Elizabeth's ready. Time's up."

What she had meant was that her patience was gone and she wanted to get her mother out of the bathroom so she could move on to her own tasks of seeing that six-year-old Elizabeth was ready, and getting on with a hectic day of trial work. The routine would continue. With her mother still sitting on the toilet, Judith would lift the nightgown over her head and slip on a fresh one. It was during one of these wardrobe changes that Judith had first noticed her mother's body beginning to deteriorate. The suddenly wrinkled arms. The weight loss, and then the prominent cheekbones. But she still had enough physical strength left that she could cooperate and even help as Judith moved her about.

"Ready, Mom? Mom?"

Her mother's only response was to turn her face to Judith and stare. For a time Judith had thought this was some game she was playing, and being unsure of how to deal with it, Judith felt frustration well up inside. But when the doctor bluntly told her that her mother's mental capacity was utterly incapable of any such calculation, Judith realized she'd been silly.

Her outstretched hand would lock her mother's in hers.

"And one . . . two . . . three . . . up!" Turning her mother slowly, Judith would become a human shoehorn and, with her mother's body leaning into her, slip her into the wheelchair she'd pulled up next to the toilet. Sometimes her mother needed to say something, her brow knitting as if she were deeply worried.

At these times, usually what emerged from the depths of her mother's mind made little sense. Often she would ask, "Who's the owner of this house? The man who was here?"

Judith would do her best to explain. "I am, Mom. Remember, Steve and I bought this house two years before we divorced. Mom, you've asked this before. I own it."

Her mother's eyes would be on her, demanding a different response.

"No, that tall man," she would insist. She'd mentioned the tall man so many times that Judith had frequently believed her mother might really be able to see what she could not. Sometimes as she made such statements she would turn to look out the bathroom window. "He's lost a cat too. I saw him outside my bedroom window, near the street, near Walworth Avenue, looking for it." Walworth Avenue was in Pasadena, one hundred and thirty miles north in Los Angeles County. Her mother's first house was there. It was the home Judith had been raised in. Mentally, her mother had gone back to the 1950s, to when Judith's dad was alive and she was raising Judith. Judith thought at times that if she simply moved her mother back to Pasadena, they'd all be fine; they would all be in the same reality.

On those mornings Judith would be looking at the clock. If she finished her mother's breakfast by seven-fifteen and hurried to have Elizabeth ready for school by seven-thirty and at school by seven-forty-five, she was able to make it to her office by eight. Her life used to run pretty consistently in fifteen-minute increments.

Eventually the morning bathroom routine gave way to bedside care, and as her mother's brain continued to shrink, her speech stopped and with it her tales of the tall man. The more ill her mother became, the less there was for Judith to do. With her mother's last stroke, she had become quadriplegic, and Judith had to give up being a physical caregiver. She hired Jean, a gentle day nurse, who arrived each morning at seven and stayed until Judith returned home.

So now there was a new pattern in Judith's life. And it included time for ponytails and cups of coffee in the morning. Her mother's body was still there, still cared for, but the woman who was her mother was somewhere deep in Judith's memories. Judith was not yet willing or able to summon the memories. If she did, she would have to confront how much of her mother had already died.

The phone rang as Elizabeth appeared with her red-and-blue backpack and headed for the garage. The caller was Judith's secretary, cautioning her not to make any unscheduled stops. The district attorney's chief assistant, Lawrence Farrell, had telephoned personally and left a message for Judith to call or see him as soon as she came in.

* * *

Reynard Way was a direct-surface street route from the Mission Hills district of San Diego, where Elizabeth attended school, to the courthouse building downtown; it was a two-lane roadway winding through a mélange of graffiti-splattered houses, apartments and small businesses. For a long time the graffiti artists—Judith hated that term but still involuntarily thought of them as such—had confined their signatures, their tags, to the walls of the street overpass and the vacant buildings. RINO. FLYER. PUPPET. WORM. For several years their tags were generously scattered around, but never on inhabited houses. Never on occupied businesses. There was an ethic of sorts that made them just barely acceptable. Then suddenly there were new tags—ones she didn't recognize. And they were on everything. Homes. Shops. Even delivery trucks sitting in driveways overnight were fair game. The dignity of eight full blocks had fallen as the verbal litter began making its way closer to the downtown high-rise section of the city, marking a turning point into a new mean-spiritedness, an open and angry defiance she hadn't perceived before.

This morning someone tagging as Thee Dude had crossed out all of Flyer's tags and signed his own in red above them.

At the second stoplight, Thee Dude had defaced an entire row of newspaper racks. But Judith Thornton quickly surrendered her consternation over the newest vandal of Reynard Way as her gaze moved from his writing to the headline pressed against the glass cover of one of the racks. The proclamation, in bold print, directed her attention to a story all of San Diego had been following: KELLY SOLOMON FOUND DEAD!

She brought her car to an abrupt stop at the curb, found the necessary quarter in her wallet and, leaving the engine running, retrieved a paper. Even before returning to the car, she had cast her eyes quickly down the single column of print under what was obviously a school photo of the dead girl. The story was short and sketchy. The body had been found in Mission Valley. At their doorstep.

The court-personnel parking lot was nearly empty when she arrived. Only the cars of District Attorney Parker Hunt, his chief assistant, Lawrence Farrell, and the public affairs officer were parked, with diagonal precision, next to one another in their reserved spaces.

Judith's first stop was the message desk, where the secretary handed her a small pile of pink slips. On the top were three messages, all received within the past thirty minutes, from Farrell. All three were marked "Urgent." Judith took the messages, quickly glancing through them.

"Can you get Mr. Farrell on the phone? Tell him I'm in and will be right up. I need a few minutes to look through these and check my desk."

"Mr. Ellison's been looking for you too, Mrs. Thornton. He needs some information on that last prostitute murder."

It was not unusual for a prosecuting office of the size and sophistication of the San Diego district attorney's to investigate as well as prosecute major crimes.

Ellison was one of the four trial deputies assigned to the Major Crimes Homicide Task Force, which Judith supervised. She had mixed feelings about the string of murders Ellison was helping piece together. The investigation was significant, and it had plugged the task force into state and national information data banks while generating nationwide publicity for the office. But her investigators had stumbled onto evidence of possible sexual relationships between several police officers and two of the prostitutes. When the prostitutes had later turned up dead along the freeway, the task force personnel, Judith included, had promptly been removed from the mainstream office geography of the sixth floor to the current fifth-floor location adjacent to the investigative arm of the office.

The move downstairs was all for legitimate reasons of internal security. The nature of the investigation and the possible involvement of law enforcement in crime required the utmost security, sensitivity and control of paper and communication. But the move had been a reluctant one for a district attorney used to keeping his most sensitive matters within his own yelling distance.

Judith's thoughts of the investigation were interrupted. The phone was ringing in her office. It had stopped by the time she got to her desk, but the first of her three lines was blinking. The buzzer followed. It was her secretary. Farrell was on hold.

"Larry, I just got in. I saw the paper this morning."

"That's why I'm calling, Judith. The Solomon case is being assigned to the task force, if you can stand all the excitement down there."

His voice was deep, clear and deliberate; humor was delivered under a veil of cold sarcasm that opposing counsel found so intimidating but which juries found so endearing.

When Farrell had hired her, there had been an instant bonding between them—he, the experienced trial attorney; she, the new and promising protégé. She had spent her first year following him around, talking to him about his cases, sitting in the back of courtrooms listening to him. She had seen the jurors watching him at the prosecutor's table even as the defense attorneys were parading in front of them. And his faith in her potential had paid off. Hers had been a quick, successful rise through the ranks. Like all new deputies, she'd been given the "gobblers"—the turkeys, the cases that couldn't be won. But she'd won them. She'd been an instant star, a woman with a reputation. Her reward had been an advancement, and then, shortly after her separation from her husband, she'd been offered the directorship of the newly created task force. At Farrell's urging, she'd accepted. Now Farrell was offering her a chance to work on what could be the most significant case of her career. She tried to keep her response as measured as his offer.

"I think we can use a little excitement down here."

"Fine. You're going to need to get geared up pretty quickly. The press is already jumping down our throats, and frankly, we don't have a whole lot yet to give them."

"Go ahead and send down all the paper you've got on it so far, as well as the police reports. Do you know who's assigned from the police department?" As was customary, the police investigators would be joining the district attorney's prosecution team.

"Pike Martin."

"Pike Martin . . . if he's who I'm thinking of, I've worked with him. But it was a long time ago. Isn't he the guy who got into hot water a year or so back in the Randolph case? Didn't he keep some evidence from the defense attorney that would have shown the guy's client wasn't guilty?"

"He was *alleged* to have withheld evidence."

"Are you sure you want him on the Solomon murder?" Judith asked. "If we were to make an arrest and end up in trial, I for one would not be interested in dealing with a rogue investigator."

"Pike's about the best there is," Farrell snapped back. "We looked hard at what happened in the Randolph case."

"And?"

"And we decided there were extenuating circumstances. Pike's wife had left him and taken their kid. Then the kid got hit by a car. We gave him the benefit of the doubt. It was a tough time."

"Did the child die?"

"On impact."

Farrell had hit a sensitive nerve. But she wasn't giving in just yet.

"Convince me."

"Look, Judith, Pike's a process guy. That's how he sees the system. And who's to say his view's not worth some consideration. There's a bunch of hoops you've got to jump through to the golden ring."

"That kind of investigator scares me. They make mistakes while they're concentrating on going through the hoops at just the right angle."

"Okay, look, if you don't want him, I'll have the chief assign someone else." This was only mock agreement. She knew the ploy. She wanted to hear more.

"I didn't say for sure I don't want him, did I? What else does he have going for him?"

"Judith, so far this is a circumstantial evidence case. There's not much out there pointing to anyone's guilt. It may stay that way. It isn't going to be a slam dunk. And if the case is a weak one, every challenge to every piece of evidence is going to be critical. If one evidentiary card falls, the whole house'll cave in. You're going to need an investigator like Pike to hold the pieces together."

"Well, I know he's good. . . ."

"Like I said, he's about the best. He's a bulldog. If he gets his teeth in, he won't let go until there's blood all around. And it won't be his or ours. I just have a feeling about this one, Judith. It's a gut feeling, but I think we need him."

"How about his emotional tie to the case? A little girl's dead. His daughter died. Can he stay objective?"

"Do we want him to be objective?"

"I do."

"I don't."

In situations like this, Judith usually acceded to Farrell's viewpoint. Not today. Not on this case. But she was ready, perhaps, to compromise.

"How about this, Larry? I'll trust your instincts on this and take him on. But I'd like a backup on him from the start."

"How about Mike Abrams?"

"I don't know him. Has he worked with Pike before?"

"They're partners on the same homicide team and they've been friends a long time. It was Abrams who saved his hide in the Randolph case."

"Swell. You're making me feel better and better all the time. Okay. We'll see how this works out. But if he gives me any trouble . . ."

"I'll come get him myself. But you won't regret it. . . . There's just one more thing, Judith. I'll be joining the task force as personal liaison to the district attorney."

This last political statement, devoid of any hint of apology, was not entirely a surprise. For months there had been persistent rumors that Hunt was about to retire and that he would be endorsing Farrell as his successor. Farrell's direct involvement in the Solomon case could

contribute to that happening, at least by way of publicity
and photo opportunities. It would keep Farrell in the
public limelight and hopefully in the minds of the county
supervisors deciding who should fill the D.A.'s spot until
the next election, when the incumbent, whoever it was,
would have a tremendous advantage over any chal-
lenger. Judith's name had also been mentioned in news
accounts of the story. But she'd chalked it up to over-
zealous reporters scanning a field barren of female con-
tenders.

"Who's going to try the case if we arrest someone?"

"In all honesty, Judith, it hasn't been decided yet.
We'll cross that bridge when we need to. At this point
your unit's directing the investigation through arrest. All
I need for now is updates, and if there are any big
breaks, I need to know about them before the press does.
Any press releases will be handled directly out of Parker's office up here."

She was uneasy, not knowing whether the conditions
of regulation were due to a lack of confidence in the
task force—in her—or to ego and political imperative.
When she didn't immediately respond, Farrell continued.
"Don't worry, Judith, there won't be any interference
with the unit."

Despite her visceral irritation with having someone
looking over her shoulder, she wasn't worried. Farrell
hadn't advanced to his current position on ego alone. To
be sure, he was the consummate politician, but he was
also a dedicated public servant. It would be completely
out of character for him to sacrifice a prosecution for
personal gain.

"I'm not worried, Larry. I'll let you know what happens with Pike."

When Farrell was off the phone, Judith wrote a formal

request to the police department for their investigative assistance on the Solomon case and placed a call to Pike Martin's office, leaving a message saying they should meet as soon as possible.

4

The ebb and flow of the paper in his office was Pike's measure of how a case was going and how quickly it was winding its way through the system. On the big ones, the paper would trickle in, grow, peak and, sometimes within an hour of the disposition of the case, disappear.

Since the finding of Kelly Solomon's body, a mound of paper had quickly been growing on Pike's desk, spilling over onto his side table. And so the flopping of paper hitting his desktop didn't startle him.

Pike turned away from the aerial-photo enlargement of the field, which covered the wall above his credenza. It was Abrams, delivering yet another file, another brown envelope.

"Mike, your timing's good. The Solomon case landed with the Homicide Task Force. Thornton's asked for a briefing this afternoon. What do we have that we didn't have last night?"

"Nothing. Between the rain and the animals, whatever evidence there may have been at the scene has probably long disappeared. There's nothing within a three-hundred-foot perimeter of where the body was found.'' Abrams pointed to the file and took a seat on the opposite side of Pike's desk. ''Take a look. It's item eight.''

A two-page report on the crime-scene evidence was faceup in the file. The list of items recovered wasn't long. It said far more about the character of the area than about the cause of death or the identity of the murderer. Under his breath, Pike began reciting:

''Six bottles: four beer, Coors, one broken; one Coke bottle severely scratched; one Perrier. One steel rod. Fifteen cans of assorted types, Coke, Pepsi, beer, all empty, some various stages crushed. Two tennis shoes in men's sizes, unmatched, one Nike, one unknown. One sock, white with blue-and-red stripes at top. Old newspaper, *San Diego Union*. One railroad spike. Two syringes. One thirty-six-inch metal rod. Two condoms.''

Pike gave up reading aloud after the first page and quickly scanned the remaining page. The items listed were things of the homeless, the hiker and the addict.

''We don't have a hell of a lot here. The cans and bottles, have they been run for prints?'' Pike asked.

''It's in the works. The lab's been letting everything dry out. They might pull something, who knows, but don't hold your breath. Some of the stuff's been out in the heat for months, and now we've got the rain on it all. If they do pull something up, chances are we'll get so little it's not going to help us. Or we'll get something so old and dilapidated no judge will let us use it. But who knows? Miracles do happen.''

They might get lucky. Both men knew that fingerprints preserved at anything near forty degrees Fahrenheit and fifty-five percent humidity could last indefinitely and be lifted for analysis years after the imprint was made. Pike was familiar with cases where forensics had been able to develop and lift prints from metal containers in storage for eight years, and from papers after as many as thirty years.

"The autopsy report's in the file too, Pike, along with the toxicology results. I haven't been through them yet. I just glanced at the photos in the envelope there. We've got eighty-six black-and-whites from the scene and the autopsy."

Pike pulled the four-page autopsy report.

"There's no official cause of death," he observed. "Let's see . . . let's see." He quickly located the significant findings. "There's severe trauma to the skull and ribs, some fracturing not caused by animal activity. A pliers-like instrument was used on her, nipples pinched and partially pulled away from her body. Viselike marks on chest. Broken capillaries at the throat. Sperm discovered in vaginal area. Blood alcohol level was .03. That's about two or three cans' worth of beer for a kid her size. Actual cause of death—unknown. Suspected strangulation. She was raped, beaten and strangled, not necessarily in that order."

Abrams was listening, sorting the crime-scene photos into piles, each relating to a separate area of the body.

Pike continued reading aloud, switching to the toxicological report. "Wait a minute." He paused. "We might have some evidence showing the order of things here. There's a lot of inflammation around the wounds in the chest area, and there's hemorrhaging with intact red blood cells showing beginning infiltration of neutrophilic leukocytes. That means her body was reacting to the injuries and there probably was a time interval between most of these injuries and death. It should interest the D.A. It's her evidence some real serious physical abuse happened before death. Pull the photos on the chest and back area. Let's take a look."

Abrams handed Pike the photos.

"Hey, will ya look at these," Pike said, setting four of the photos out in a row. "Forget the vise marks for a minute. Look at these black, semicircular marks on her chest and back. The autopsy report says . . . let's see . . . their cause isn't conclusive, but the coroner says they have the appearance of heel marks. What kind of force do you think it would take to put heel marks like these on someone's body? Look at them. They're deep. Straight in. It would take some long, strong legs and a sharp heel. Anything on our evidence lists that could cause these?"

"Nothing."

Pike took his fluorescent green felt-tip pen and circled three of the semicircular marks, then rose and pinned the picture onto the three-by-four-foot corkboard on the wall facing his desk.

"I've got seven more torso photos and four close-ups," Abrams said as Pike took his magnifying glass in one hand and his marker in the other and began circling what he felt might be important evidence.

They spent the next forty-five minutes looking at the photos and comparing them with the observations in the coroner's reports.

Judith had read the full autopsy report before her first meeting with Pike. She had also reviewed the autopsy photos containing Pike's highlighting of the strange semicircular marks on Kelly's torso. Several of the torso photos she had thumbtacked onto the corkboard on the wall to the right of her desk.

Her initial conversation with Pike was personal and easygoing, far less tense than Judith had feared it might be, given her earlier concerns about his investigative skills. Following their review of the evidence collected, she turned to the identity of the perpetrator.

"Pike, can we talk profile here? Who, or what, are we looking for?"

"With the condition our guy left the body in—rape, torture and mutilation—he's a sadist. He's probably picked up distorted sexual training. Maybe bunked in with Mom and whoever and never quite got the hang of what normal relationships were supposed to be like. As far as what we're looking for . . . if he fits the standard, he's a white male between the ages of thirty and forty. He has no skills and no friends. He's a loner incapable of loving anything and he's filled with anxiety. He could kill a kid like this Solomon girl and go to work the next morning as if nothing happened. Instead of playing tennis to relieve the tension, he murders. Walk on any downtown street and you might walk right past him. Go out to dinner at a burger joint with your kid and he might be sitting at the table next to you, eating a hamburger."

"Where does that leave us?"

"We find him before he does it again. Right now I think we need to identify whatever tools he may have used to torture the girl. We've got those circular gouges on her body, and there's nothing we've found in the field that could have caused that damage. It's possible whatever he used on her he's still got. The two might give us an idea of where to start looking. Maybe we have a mechanic. We need an idea of what the tool might look like."

"What's the lab given us so far?"

"Nothing yet. They're running everything through for prints now."

Somehow this wasn't enough. There had to be some other explanation.

"Pike, I haven't been at this job long, but I don't remember ever having to deal with this kind of crime against a child. Violence, yes. Mostly robbery, theft, murder. But most of them are object crimes. Someone needs money. Someone's angry at a wife or a neighbor. Not this . . .'' She searched for a term. "Random violence. You know, people in the wrong place at the wrong time. People who kill for no reason. You used to be able to know how to protect yourself and your kids from it. But you can't anymore.''

Pike rubbed the day-old growth of beard on his cheeks.

"I have a theory. I mean, we've got a sadist here for sure, but we've created a good environment for it, don't you think?'' Pike grinned, obviously having thought this through at some point before their discussion. "Last I looked at our stats, San Diego was the sixth largest city in the country. We've got just over a million people and over two million in the county. Thousands of these folks are just bursting with the cowboy ethic we all get spoon-fed from infancy. All that shit about freedom and individualism and land of opportunity. They come with their guns drawn, ready to take on the whole world, and they run right into a wall of thirty-story high-rises and end up on our street corners holding signs saying they'll work for food. They come down here to strut their stuff and they find out no one wants to see them strut or see their stuff, ya know?''

This was far from the kind of analysis Judith usually started a homicide case with, but she understood what he was saying. You didn't face the criminal justice system day after day and not see the American cowboy ethic run amok.

"The Old West and the city don't mix well. But why Kelly Solomon?''

"Why not Kelly Solomon? Some of these macho cowboys who can't make it go home. Some go to college and chase the girls up and down Montezuma Road over at the state college. But the sadist cowboys—the ones already sick, and that's what we've got here—the tension just keeps growing and growing inside. There's a time limit on how much tension sadists can take. When the pressure gets to be too much, they just explode at someone. Then they can relax for a while. Until the pressure gets too high again. It's a predictable cycle in most serial killers.''

''You think we've got an urban-cowboy maniac here?''

''I'll bet money.''

''Pike, I wasn't sure if our working together was going to work out okay, you know?''

He couldn't have known the origin of her apology. She was just a prosecutor advancing a vote of confidence.

''It'll work out. I want him as badly as you do.''

It wasn't true. He wanted him more. Much more. And Judith knew it. She knew it from the way he was blinking at her when he made the statement.

After she'd gone, Pike reexamined the list of items found at the frontage road turnout. Should he call the lab? He always felt like an interloper there. He never forced himself into its procedures. While the lab and he dealt with putting the pieces of the same puzzle together, the lab did it with twenty thousand square feet of finely tuned state-of-the-art machinery and computer equipment, staffed by a force of fifty-five. All of which was entitled to deferential treatment. Curiosity, however, finally overcame him, as he knew it would, and he reached for his phone, punching in the lab extension. Leland Henrickson picked up at the receiving end.

Henrickson was a nationally recognized fingerprint expert whom Pike many times had said he would take dusting for prints with a paintbrush and cigarette ashes over someone with state-of-the-art equipment but less ability.

"I've got what looks to be a couple of partial prints from two of the cans collected at the crime scene. That's about all I've got. We're not sure yet how clean they're going to be. The prints may or may not be any good. I'm testing them now."

Henrickson was nonchalant. A partial print was not much to get excited about, especially partials from a crime scene. They were never perfect. The cans would have been handled over a period of time, so there were probably layered prints. Maybe layers on layers. And considering the circumstances of the cans' physical location and exposure to the elements, the prints would be even more difficult to deal with.

"Mind if I come up, Leland? I'd just like to take a look at them."

"Fine. We've got them in process now."

"You sure I won't be interfering?"

"You will, but come on up anyway."

Room 432, the fingerprint processing department, faced the elevator lobby. It was uncluttered, lacking test tubes and microphones; to the unschooled eye, it resembled a storage room more than a criminology lab. Against the south wall, two rectangular tables were covered with items found at the field. In front of each was a label taped to the table, telling the date and, as specifically as possible, the exact location where the item was found.

At the north wall, Henrickson stood poised over a twenty-gallon glass fish tank. Inside the tank a beaker of warm water, a beer can and a strip of metallic paper sat side by side.

"That's a poor excuse for an aquarium, Leland. Mind if I come in?"

"Pike, good to see you. So far so good. It looks as if we're going to have a good, tented-arch pattern from an index finger."

Tented arches, loops, double loops, plain whirls. The terms had no special meaning to Pike. They were all patterns of impressions made by ridges on the ends of fingers and thumbs—all different from person to person. But to Henrickson they were as good as portraits.

"Come on into the light room."

Pike followed Henrickson into a small adjoining room and watched as he placed a long popsicle stick into the pour hole of a Coke can sitting near the laser-light machine. Henrickson handed Pike a pair of orange-tinted glasses and turned out the overheads.

"Take a look." In the fluorescent orange glow of laser light, Pike could make out smudge marks on the can.

"We have a good partial right here near the upper rim," Henrickson said, pointing to a spot near the top of the can. Pike lowered his head toward the object while Henrickson rotated the can ever so slightly.

"We've got the other can in with the superglue now and we'll follow with this one."

The men returned to the fish tank in the processing room.

Leland lifted the top and poked the stick through the can's pour hole. "It's done."

He showed the can to Pike, who took the stick and ran his finger over the fingerprint, which had been transformed into a hard white marking.

"Where were these cans found?"

Henrickson pointed to the beer can Pike was holding.

"That one there, about a hundred feet from the girl's body, inside a brown lunch bag with some junk-food wrappers in it. That's probably why the print's still there. This second can was found nearer the frontage road. From what I can see under the light, it's a thumbprint, whirl pattern. The prints are from two different individuals. Neither belongs to Kelly Solomon.''

As he spoke, Henrickson placed the soda can into the fish tank, along with a new metallic strip he peeled from its cover.

The strips he was using contained the same glue you could buy in the supermarket to fix broken china. Its forensic qualities were discovered quite by accident when one of the manufacturers of the superstick glue began to notice dirty smudge marks on the inside of the plastic bubbles holding the glue tubes ready to be shipped to markets. In trying to figure out how to get rid of them, they discovered the smudges were fingerprints developed by glue fumes when the tubes leaked. The manufacturers discovered that if the glue was placed in a tank with a cup of warm water to provide moisture that could adhere to the amino acids on the prints it would polymerize the acids. The prints would turn to hard white plastic in fifteen to twenty minutes. They could then be dusted with black charcoal and prints lifted from them as many as three times. ''When we're through here,'' Henrickson said, ''we'll photograph them, then get them into the computer.''

It wasn't as easy as it sounded. They wouldn't be able to simply feed the partial print into the computer.

Once the print was lifted from the superglue print, it would be turned over to an examiner who would photographically enlarge it to a five-to-one ratio, place a clear, transparent overlay on the enlargement and finish drawing the print: filling in the print pattern; carefully establishing its core, axis and center; ultimately creating a geometric grid pattern with X and Y coordinates. The entire print pattern would then be reduced to a one-to-one ratio and fed into the computer network. They would run the print through the local computer data base of something like three hundred thousand prints of known offenders and arrestees, then through the state Remote Access Network base of over a million known prints. If the print on either can belonged to a person whose prints were in either data base, and the computer was allowed to reach down far enough, they might get an ID. From start to finish, the process could take as little as four hours—fish tank to identification.

5

xxxx xxxx xxxxx xxxx xxxxx xx xxxxxxxx x xxx x
xxxx xxxx xxx xxx xxxx xxx xxxxxxx xxxxxx xxx
xxxx xxxxxx xxxxxxx xx xxx xxx xxxxx xxxxxxx xxxx
xx xxxxxxxxxx xxx xxxxx xxxxxxxxx xxxxxxxx xxxx xxx
xxxxx xxxxxxxx xxx xx xxxxxxxxx xxxxx xxxxxxx xxx
xxxxxxx xxxxx xxxxxxxx xxx xxxxxxx xxxxx xxxxx
xxxxx xx xxx xxxxxx xxxxxxx xxx xxxx xxx xxxxxxx
xxxx xxxxxxx xxx x xxxx xx xxxxx xxx xxxxxx xxxxxxx
xx xx xxxxxxxx xx xxxxx xxxxxxxx xxxxxxxx xx
xxxx xx xxxx xxxxxxxx xxxx xxxxx xxxxxxxxxxx

The small chapel of St. Sophia's Syrian Orthodox
Church was awash in pink and white—tea roses and
baby's breath. Cascades of them, draping the small white
casket, hiding its pier. On the altar, sprays and baskets
of wildflowers and lilies testified to an outpouring of
anonymous community support.

Deborah Solomon, her face covered by a thin black
veil, sat next to her husband in the first pew, directly
in front of the white casket. There were whispers
throughout the chapel that the night before, she had
come to the funeral home with Kelly's favorite books
and favorite music. She had read to the girl in her
closed casket while the second movement of *The Nutcracker* had played gently in the background. The
voices, in hushed reverence, whispered that Kelly's
ballet shoes, the ones she hadn't yet worn, had been
tucked into the casket, the funeral director giving only
lip service to laws forbidding such things. There were
whispers that Kelly's mother had been there until midnight.

Pike Martin, who had been seated in the rear of the chapel, had heard the whispers and watched as the woman allowed herself to be helped into the mortuary's black limousine that was parked behind the hearse; unbearable grief made her powerless to do anything other than follow its object. Pike had broken one of his hard-and-fast rules. He did not attend the funerals of victims whose deaths he was investigating. Over the years he had consciously stripped away all but the necessary functions of his job. Absorbing the grief caused by the tragedy of the crime was not a necessary function. And it diverted his energy.

But he was carrying the morning paper, periodically reexamining the article about the dead girl. As the hearse and entourage left, he read it again.

Killer Stills the Music Forever
Kelly Solomon Services Set Today
By Jon Kolker

On Saturday mornings, when nine-year-old Kelly Solomon practiced her ballet lessons in the small blue-and-white house in Mission Bay where she and her father and mother lived, the neighbors could open their windows wide and breathe in the ocean air and hear the strains of Tchaikovsky.

Today, Kelly Solomon will be buried, the victim of a vicious and unsolved attack.

"It's a tragedy, a horrible tragedy," a close friend of the family said yesterday.

"If you are looking for another name for this beautiful little girl, call her joy and love," her teacher at Fairmount Elementary School added. "She had a knack for making friends and for making everyone feel part of her group in whatever she did. That's why she was popular with everyone.''

Three days before she was kidnapped, then brutally killed, she had been chosen to dance the lead role in her dance-school production of *The Nutcracker* ballet, set to begin practice in October.

''Kelly's mother and father are heartbroken,'' said family friend and spokesperson Linda Benard. ''Her mother is just devastated. Kelly and her mother were very close.''

Kelly's ballet teacher said the girl had a ''God-given talent'' to interpret classical music through dance. ''[She] was a star. She was a joy, a real dream student. I will miss her. We'll all miss her.''

Spokesperson Benard said Kelly's parents have asked that any persons wishing to may send donations to the Kelly Solomon Scholarship Fund, in care of Fairmount Elementary School. Kelly's funeral will be held at 1 P.M. In St. Sophia's Syrian Orthodox Church, Mission Bay.

Pike scanned the people still milling about at the curb. They consisted of mourners and the curious who'd read the same article he had. He looked at the faces of those who were on the fringes of the crowd, hoping to see someone or something unusual. It was not uncommon, he reminded himself, for a sadist to stay close to the victim in some way. But he had a feeling this was not one of those easy cases.

Something stirred deep within him, a pain he had been trying very hard to avoid after he'd reread the newspaper article.

Whatever it took, he would find whoever had caused this.

6

It had been two days since Kelly Solomon's funeral. The newspaper articles had stopped. What was left now was the tedium of forensics—microscopically examining every piece of evidence collected at the crime scene.

When the phone rang, Pike expected it to be Farrell or Judith. One of them had called each day for an update on what, if any, new leads had been discovered. This time it wasn't the D.A.'s office. It was the lab. And this time there was something positive to report.

Pike let the mouthpiece of the phone slip under his chin as he scribbled on the yellow lined notepad.

"Hold on, Leland. I want to be sure I've got this. Spell it. E-N-G-L-E. Robert Dean Engle. Date of birth, August 12, 1959. When we run his rap sheet, we'll get a good picture of the guy. Let me know if anything else develops up there. And thanks." Without letting the receiver drop back onto the phone, he punched in a four-digit extension.

"Judith? It's Pike. I'm glad I caught you. We got an ID off a print from a beer can we picked up at the park turnout. It doesn't mean a whole lot at this point. We've found its owner, a Robert Dean Engle. E-N-G-L-E. I'm going to run his name and see if he's got a rap sheet. If he does, we'll send it over to you. I'm here all day. If you want to get together, I can be there.''

Pike reset the receiver and looked around his office. The mounds of paper were growing taller. He had successfully sorted it all into neat stacks, general topics. Contacts, reports, press clippings, his notes. All he needed was one bit of good, solid information to pull it all together. Maybe this was nothing. But Engle was in the computer, and there was a reason for it. Perhaps he was a government worker who had been routinely fingerprinted when he was hired. But then again, maybe, just maybe, he was their guy.

The Major Crimes Homicide Task Force briefings, particularly those in the investigative stages, were always held in Judith Thornton's office. Today the general practice yielded to the addition of Farrell as liaison to the district attorney. The group of four assigned investigators and Judith Thornton gathered in Farrell's conference room. Farrell himself conducted the briefing.

"As most of you already know, we have our first real lead, a partial print from a beer can found near the location of Kelly Solomon's body. It belongs to an individual named Robert Dean Engle, a registered sex offender sentenced in August '77 on a 647.6.'' Section 647.6 of the California Penal Code dealt with misdemeanor child molestation, the upshot of the offense being molesting or annoying a child under the age of eighteen. Neither the number nor even the name of the offense told much about the facts of an individual crime. This one could have been pretty minor. Maybe the guy had opened his shirt and scared some kid with his hairy chest, or had mooned a family through a car window.

On the other hand, it could have been a plea bargained down from a charged crime that was far more serious than the misdemeanor. They'd need the crime file so they could look at the charging documents and sentencing report filed by the probation department.

"He served a six-month term in county jail as a condition of probation, then was released . . . let's see . . . February 1978."

So far, not so horrible, Judith thought. Probation. He could have been sentenced to a maximum thousand-dollar fine and a year in jail. He was likely a first-time offender, because a second 647.6 would have required a mandatory prison term.

Farrell continued. "It gets better. He got another offense in April 1979. Another child molest, but this time it was a 288 and he had an ADW added."

Suddenly all the warning signs were there. ADW. Short for "assault with a deadly weapon," one of the offenses added to aggravate a sentence for some other crime. In this case, it was aggravating a sentence for a lewd and lascivious act toward a child under the age of fourteen.

"This time he went away on a plea bargain to simple kidnapping. He . . . uh . . ." Farrell's voice dropped. "He spent his time at Atascadero."

Judith recognized the drop in Farrell's voice. It happened frequently when discussion turned to Atascadero State Hospital.

"Larry, was he part of the MDSO program up there?" she asked. The program she was referring to was a controversial experiment which had placed mentally disordered sex offenders back into the community for treatment and cure. It had been an abysmal failure, suspended when offender after offender reoffended, some committing the most heinous crimes seen in decades.

Law enforcement throughout the state was still playing catch-up as one after another of the program participants was picked up on a new offense. Indeed, the list of graduates was beginning to read like a Who's Who of the state's most notorious child murderers.

"We haven't confirmed yet if Engle was part of the Atascadero program, Judith."

End of discussion. Farrell chose not to pursue the question, even though Judith knew his feelings ran deeply on the topic. He had often expressed a desire to see the full list of men who had been released through the program, as well as their subsequent criminal histories.

"His ADW was dismissed. He was a perfect angel up there, because he was paroled in September of '79."

The investigator next to Judith leaned toward her. "Why wouldn't he be an angel? He didn't have any kids up there to distract him."

Farrell continued, oblivious of the chatter.

"He fell under the state's new sentencing laws on that one. Kidnapping carries a five-, eight- or eleven-year sentence. He received the five-year sentence. When they calculated his time off for good behavior and subtracted it from his sentence, along with any work credits, he'd have spent about two years confined. So it could have been real bad to start with, before the plea bargain and sentence credits. He's still on parole."

The investigator next to Judith spoke again, this time to himself. "Some sentencing system. Makes you want to throw up."

His words had been audible. But Farrell continued, neither acknowledging nor contradicting the comment.

"We're waiting for the files on the '77 and '79 offenses. Records is pulling them now. We'll have an even better idea of the guy's history when we get the full psychiatric reports. His parole officer will be here at three P.M." All releases from prison on parole were conditioned on a waiver of Fourth Amendment search rights. A parole officer could search Engle's residence at any time with or without a warrant. It was always useful to have the parole officer along. But on a case like this, if they could get a search warrant, they would.

"We've got an address for Engle out in Lakeside. Pike, we're going to ask you to go along with the parole officer. You know what we've got on our hands here. Handle it appropriately." Appropriately meant carefully.

The comments and questions immediately began to pummel Farrell from around the room.

Someone asked the question in everyone's mind.

"Can we peg this guy to any other missing children?"

"Not now, but we're checking. My gut feeling is that the common elements between Engle's prior crimes and finding that print so near Kelly Solomon's body are too close to be accidental."

"Do we have any shrink reports on him right now?" Pike asked. Then, without waiting for a response, he continued. "I'll bet the '77 and '79 crimes are identical or close to this one. The guy's probably got a history of mental illness going back to kindergarten that gets worse by the year. Seen it thousands of times, and not just in child molest cases." Pike stood up. He couldn't sit anymore. He needed something in his hands. A report. A file. A photo. He wanted to take off in some direction, and was waiting for someone to tell him which way to go.

Farrell opened a manila file. Not much was in it. It was clean and uncreased. By the time of the trial, the file would be four inches thick, dog-eared, dirty and coffee-stained.

"Here's a picture of our guy. Pass it around, then

hang onto it, Pike, so you can take it out to the guy's apartment with you," Farrell said, handing the three-by-five-inch black-and-white photo to Pike.

"Did the computer give us any other names?" someone asked.

Pike responded spontaneously to the question. "We ran the print for all prospects and came up with a list of twenty possibilities. Engle's name came back number one on the list. Statistically speaking, he's the guy who owns the print, but so far as our case is concerned at this point, he's just a bad actor who drank a beer out in a Mission Valley field."

Judith had intercepted the photo as it made its way around the table. It was a full-face shot. Engle looked to be somewhere in his late twenties to mid-thirties. Dark, below-earlobe-length hair; short mustache; slight smile.

But there were the eyes.

Sometimes with even the worst serial offenders, there was nothing showing. Then there were the Robert Engles. His eyes had that look in them. Distant. Detached and wild. It was a look Judith recognized, a look that caused a reaction in herself she trusted. His was the face she avoided late at night in convenience markets. If she saw it, she left. If she saw it in a suspect, she dug in and covered every step, every possibility he was involved.

As she studied Engle's face, a secretary entered with the D.A. files on Engle's prior offenses. About thirteen inches of file. By sheer weight and measurement, they had a heavy-duty offender on their hands.

Farrell pulled an envelope marked "Confidential" from the thicker of the two files and began to read to himself, leaving his colleagues anxiously eyeing his reactions. He was reading the probation officer's report, a concise summary of prior criminal history and current sentence.

Farrell shook his head. It was a well-what-do-you-know-about-that shake.

"Looks like our guy's a drifter. He's worked carnivals, rodeos, anything that moves. On that '79 offense, the one he served just the two years on, it seems he was arrested after some guy saw him stop his car near a school and talk some young kid into getting in. The man thought it was kind of strange, trusted his instincts and followed them to Engle's apartment, then called the police. When the unit got there about seven minutes later and broke down the door, they found the kid on her back on the floor and Engle sitting on top of her with a metal bar across her throat; both were clothed, him laughing, her frightened. No rape. He said they were playing, but talk about sheer luck. If that guy hadn't followed them, she'd be, who knows."

Judith's attention shifted to Pike, whose face began to redden, anger clearly rising.

"And the motherfucker's out in two years? Two years!" Blinking rapidly, Pike spit the words out, forgetting for the moment, or perhaps not caring, that the D.A.'s chief deputy was present.

"Take it easy," Farrell said, reading quickly through the trial reports. "It looks like the kid's parents wouldn't let her testify or she'd have been too traumatized. We took what we could get on it. But if you're all wondering, our office's preliminary decision is that when he is caught on this one, he's facing the death penalty this time."

"One child too late," Pike offered.

"At least one child too late," agreed another officer.

As soon as the meeting adjourned, Judith cornered Abrams.

"Pike flew off the handle. If he gets too close to the case, I need to know. You're his friend, Mike. See if you can keep him buttoned up before I have to talk to him. We can't afford any mistakes on this one, especially with Larry out on a limb politically and the press watching every move."

Lakeside. Pike and Judith had exchanged knowing looks when Farrell said the name.

The city of Lakeside was on the outer eastern edge of the county, twenty minutes from downtown San Diego, yet it could have been mistaken for a rural Western town. The annual rodeo was advertised all year long on the marquee over Oak View Avenue. The most likely visitors from San Diego were those seeking inexpensive auto-repair work from the small shops whose owners could live comfortably in the rural community.

By late afternoon Pike, Abrams and the parole officer were walking up the cracked asphalt driveway of the Lakeside Carburetor and Engine Rebuilder's shop. Two apartments, including Engle's, were above the shop.

An elderly woman in an oversized black sweater was hosing down the dandelion-infested grass strip at the front curb. She saw them and moved slowly into the middle of the short driveway. She smiled broadly as they approached.

"Good afternoon, ma'am. I'm Pike Martin from the San Diego Police Department. This is Detective Abrams, and Mr. Thompson here is with the State Parole Department."

"Are you here to see unit A?" she asked, absent-mindedly ignoring Pike's police uniform.

"No, ma'am, we're here to see the man who lives in apartment B above the shop. I believe his name is Engle—Robert Engle."

"Yes, 'tis, but he's not home jist now. Gone ta Redding. He'll be back day after tomorrow, he said. His is a fine apartment too; real good condition."

Pike felt a sudden sinking feeling in the pit of his stomach.

"Why? Is he going someplace?" he asked.

"He give me his thirty-day notice—jist like the law says he got to. Goin' east, he says. Doesn't like the smog comin' down on us like in L.A."

"Ma'am," Pike began, "can we ask you a few questions?"

"Why, sure, I don't mind."

Pike held his photo of Engle out about a foot in front of the woman's face.

Her reaction was immediate. "That's Bobby."

He held out a second picture, this one of Kelly Solomon, and asked, "How about this photo? Ever seen her?"

"Well, no, not as I can remember."

"Ever see Mr. Engle with any little girls?"

"No. But I know he likes kids. He bought this bike for his little niece."

"Is it here?"

"No. I never saw it. He only said he bought it."

"Did he tell you what color bike, ma'am?" the parole officer inquired.

"Why, no. But he said it was for her birthday, I think."

"You're sure that's all he told you about the bike?"

"I'm sure."

"Mind if we look around, ma'am?" Pike asked.

"It's okay with me, Officer."

This casual reference to Engle's having a bike at the same time as the Solomon girl's disappearance was so strong a lead, Pike could taste it. He could feel the muscles in his neck begin to tense. It was one of those leads that screamed, *You're right on the trail! You've got the right guy!* But it had meaning only to the investigation. Its usefulness stopped there. It got you going even faster, but in itself it meant nothing. It had almost no evidentiary value, because all that had happened was that Engle had said the word "bike," and the girl's "bike" was still missing.

"If Mr. Engle calls, ma'am, please don't tell him we stopped by, okay? This is official police business."

She nodded at Pike. "Nosirree, I won't. Why? Did he do somethin' wrong?"

"We're investigating his possible involvement in a crime. That's all we can tell you. But we strongly advise you not to confront him. If he comes back, please call this number." Pike handed her his business card, and the men conducted a cursory look around the building in case the bike was there. It wasn't.

On the way back to their car with the parole officer in tow four feet behind them, Pike and Abrams began reviewing the events of the past several days. They agreed Engle was probably about to leave town, do a rabbit on them. They called an officer to stake out the apartment and placed a priority search-warrant request with the district attorney's office. There was one more thing Pike wanted to do. Before returning to San Diego, they spent an hour cruising the nearby streets and alleys and checking the commercial trash bins in the neighborhood on the off chance a bike had been trashed.

The following morning Pike had the search warrant signed and in hand as he, Abrams and a team of twelve police officers drove back to Engle's apartment. The warrant was specific and limited to what they expected to find that might be tied to the crime. It authorized the officers to search all parts of the house and containers in the house for numerous items, including implements of restraint, tools, children's clothing and photographs of children.

Although Engle was not there, the officers followed their usual practice and covered all the doors. Pike knocked four times and shouted, "Police officers. We are here to serve a search warrant." He knew no one was inside to hear him, but their bible, the California Penal Code, required that they knock and give notice of their purpose to occupants before entering a residence. The search was going to be by the book even if at times it approached the nonsensical to an outsider. Rather than break the door open, Abrams asked the landlady to use a spare key to open it.

Pike wasn't sure what he expected to see when the door opened. The room was dark, smelling heavily of dust and cigarette smoke. Pike would have guessed the apartment would be messy. But it was neat. The bed was made. Not a dirty dish in the sink.

"Have some of the boys check those desk drawers in the bedroom for an address." Abrams reminded his team it was a priority that they locate, if possible, mail addressed to Engle at this residence. Establishing he lived here would help make him responsible for what they might find.

Pike conducted a cursory walk-through. During the examination he looked under the bed and pulled out a black typewriter case. He shook it, producing what sounded like the shuffling of paper inside. Opened, the case produced hundreds of photos of young children spilling onto the floor, along with several mementos, a crucifix and a heavy, three-inch-wide metal horseshoe.

"Jesus. Look here. Look at these, Mike."

Abrams and Pike fingered through the pictures. They

appeared to be mostly of young girls between the ages of five and ten. Many of the photos were of nude children, some showed groups of young children, and others were simply pictures of children outside at play.

"Think we can find Kelly Solomon in here somewhere?" Abrams asked.

"We might, but I wouldn't feel real confident discounting any of the photos. She might be in one of them, even in the background, and I wouldn't know if I was staring right at her. We need to get someone who knew her to look through these. Someone who'd recognize the back of her head."

7

As the thick layer of Los Angeles smog turned the sunset a rusty orange, the blue Toyota slowly wound around the curves of the San Gabriel Mountains, forty-five minutes from Engle's motel room. He was searching for the place. He had been there twice in two days and so had some familiarity with the area. This evening he was extra proud of himself because he was able to drive directly to the location. The road there ended abruptly at a metal gate. On the other side, more of the same scenery—shrubbery, oak trees and a dirt road just big enough for his car to pass on. The NO TRESPASSING sign posted on the gate virtually guaranteed they would be alone. He had broken the combination lock on the gate yesterday. It still hung loose.

Engle got out and walked around, looking for some indication that there were others in the area. There was no one.

He stood in the roadway, hands on his hips, looking toward a large oak tree a hundred feet or so away.

"I like this. Yes. Behind that tree'll do just fine. And if the light is good, I might even get a picture first."

8

Deborah and Abe Solomon had agreed to examine the photos found in Engle's apartment. The viewing would take place at their home, in familiar territory, so that they wouldn't have to exert any more effort than was absolutely necessary. Because the photos found in Engle's apartment were evidence, chain-of-custody protocol dictated they be examined under the strictest of controls. Pike had checked them out of the evidence locker and would return them immediately after the Solomons were through looking at them. He tucked the box under his arm and rang the doorbell.

The woman who answered the door was at once recognizable as Kelly Solomon's mother. She was not the wild woman he had seen at the turnout the night the body was found. Nor was she the desperate woman mourning at the church. Up close, Pike could see she was a tall woman with finely chiseled features, smooth olive skin and soft brown eyes. Her straight black hair was drawn to the back of her neck and tied with a pale blue silk scarf. She had a relaxed, refined look. He supposed she might be Italian or Spanish. Only the ashen pallor of her face and her hollow eyes hinted of the despair she had experienced this past week.

"Mr. Martin. Come in." Her voice was barely audible as she opened the screen door separating them and gestured for him to enter.

The house was comfortably furnished in bold green-and-red floral prints. A dozen photos of Kelly were set on the fireplace mantel. One in particular caught his eye. It was of the girl in a red tutu and toe shoes.

Deborah Solomon noticed his attention had focused on the picture.

"That was taken last year, when Kelly was in her first recital."

"It's a very nice picture."

"Do you have any children, Mr. Martin?"

He hesitated.

"No. I haven't just now."

She'd missed it.

"It's a shame. They can bring you such joy." Tears began falling down her cheeks. It had happened fast. She'd given no warning signs to him.

"Mrs. Solomon, I'm not going to take up any more of your time than I have to. We appreciate your taking the time to look at these photos."

"I should have told you . . . I hope it's okay . . . you'll have to excuse my husband. He's not been very well. If you think we need him, I can go upstairs and . . ."

Pike understood.

"No, it's all right. If we find anything important, maybe we can get you to see if he can give us a few minutes."

"Thank you. He just felt that . . ."

"It's okay. Really."

"Well, where would you like me to look at them?"

"How about that round table I saw in the living room?

You'll be able to move the photos around better there.''

Pike pulled an envelope from the breast pocket of his jacket. In preparation for the meeting with the Solomons, he had also prepared a photo lineup. He'd had the county jail pull photos of six men who closely resembled Bobby Engle. These photos, to which Engle's had been added, making their number seven, he now spread in a row in front of the woman. Each had a number assigned and printed on the back.

"Have you ever seen any of the men in these pictures?"

She closed her eyes and shook her head.

"Take your time. Look again."

Slowly she picked up each of the photos. "No. I'm certain I've never seen any of them."

Pike collected the photos and put them back in the envelope.

"Is he in there, Mr. Martin, the man they think . . . took Kelly?"

"I wish I could tell you, Mrs. Solomon. I'm not at liberty to discuss the pictures."

There had been only curiosity in her voice, not enthusiasm. This was going to be hard on her. Pike knew that. He was certain she had never before seen photos of the kind she was about to view.

"Now, I've got a pretty large box of photos here. I'd like you to look through them and tell me if you recognize anyone. Study them, one at a time. It's going to take a while. Maybe we can let you have a break every ten minutes or so, just to keep your mind fresh."

Pike hadn't told her the box contained the photos found in Engle's apartment. As good police procedure dictated, he had kept the directions brief, giving her no names of suspects, no descriptions, no hints of any kind as to what she was going to see.

She began systematically examining them, one at a time.

Pike could see her discomfort show periodically. She frowned, grimaced, looked away. Once, as she held the photo of a girl nude from the waist down, she wept.

Thirty minutes into the examination, halfway through the photos, Deborah Solomon gasped. Pike moved quickly to her side. She was staring at one of the pictures.

"Oh . . . my God."

Pike looked over her shoulder, realizing at once that the fully clothed, smiling, freckled youngster in the photo she was staring at was not Kelly. He could tell that it had been taken at Mission Beach; its landmark roller coaster loomed in the background. For the moment, Pike assumed the woman's gasp had nothing to do with the photo.

"Can I get you something, Mrs. Solomon?"

She looked up at Pike.

"The little girl in this picture is Tara, Kelly's best friend, our next-door neighbor. I don't understand. Kelly was with Tara the morning she disappeared."

Pike lifted the black-and-white photo from her immobile hands.

"It's been cut in half, Mr. Martin. What does this mean?"

She was right. Someone had ripped away part of the photo.

"I'm not altogether sure exactly what this means. You're certain this is your neighbor?"

"Mr. Martin, Tara and Kelly lived next door to each other all their lives. They were as close as sisters."

Pike marked the photo on the back with his name, the date and the name of Deborah Solomon. He placed it in a brown envelope he'd brought along in case any of the photos proved to be valuable evidence.

The pace of Deborah Solomon's examination of the photos quickened. Like Pike, she expected Kelly's picture was the other half and was in there somewhere. But after twenty minutes more, she'd finished. No photo of Kelly was found in the collection. But she knew. Deep down inside, they both knew it had been there.

"Do you want me to look at them again? I will."

"If I thought it would do any good, I'd say yes. But it seems to me your examination was pretty thorough. And please don't think that because you didn't see Kelly in there, the search wasn't helpful. You know it was."

"I hope this doesn't sound awful to you. I wish Kelly's picture had been in there."

"It doesn't sound awful at all. Not at all. It's very important I talk with Tara as soon as possible."

"I can call her mother right now."

Within minutes Deborah Solomon had called next door and arranged to send Pike over with Tara's photo. As he was about to leave, she turned to him, venting the frustration of combined disappointment and relief.

"The bastard who took all those pictures did it, didn't he?"

"Mrs. Solomon, I can't think of anything as stressful as this last week's been for you. I promise we'll keep you posted on what happens with this. I can assure you we'll check out the photos completely, starting with Tara. And we'll find him, Mrs. Solomon. We will find him."

A few minutes later, Pike was sitting with Tara Markham and her mother in the living room of their home.

"Tara, can you tell me anything about this picture?" he asked.

"This was the morning Kelly and I went to the beach

on our bikes.'' Her voice fell. She looked quickly at her mother and back at Pike. ''A man asked us if he could take our picture for a contest. He said we could win fifty dollars, maybe. He said Kelly was going to be pretty in it and she could have her picture in a magazine. Kelly, she was really excited, but some woman came up and asked about the pictures he was taking, and he left us there.''

''When did this happen, Tara—can you remember?''

''Yes, sure. It was the morning we couldn't find Kelly. It was the last time I saw her.''

''Did you see the man again?''

''No, I didn't. But I know that's the day. Look.'' She held the photo out to Pike. ''See, the roller coaster's going. It had just opened. I was only there once, with Kelly.'' She looked at her mother again. ''I haven't been back since.''

''Tara, do you recognize the man you talked to that morning in this group of photos?''

Pike set out the same photo lineup on the coffee table that he had earlier displayed for Deborah Solomon.

''I don't know. Two of them look like the man, but I'm not sure.''

''Take your time, Tara.''

''This one.'' She pointed to number three. Pike held his breath. Number three was Engle. ''And this one. And him.'' Numbers one and six. His odds plummeted. Still, she'd picked Engle first and quickly. That accounted for something. That would be usable evidence. He scribbled Tara's name on the back of the photos she had selected, indicating in what order she had pointed to them.

Back in his office, Pike returned the evidence to its locker and rough-typed his report, carefully noting the number of photos examined and what Tara and Deborah Solomon had said while they were examining them.

When the report was done and delivered to the typists, he phoned Judith Thornton. The first order of business now was an arrest warrant, which would direct any peace officer to take Engle into custody immediately.

For a warrant to be issued, the district attorney would have to file a formal complaint charging Engle with a felony. That would be the easy part. While the evidence was not strong at this point, the prospect of his flight from the area and his possible contact with Kelly on the day she disappeared would be enough to tilt the scale toward issuing the complaint now.

Pike's conversation with Judith Thornton resulted in the expected. A complaint for murder would be filed against Engle, and with the warrant for his arrest would come an all-points bulletin. But even these steps, as aggressive as they were, might prove futile. Engle had all the traits of a random killer. He had no attachments anywhere, and there was no way to predict when and where he would move or how far he would go. For the moment, all they could do was stake out his apartment and pray he came back to San Diego.

9

Engle was dreaming. He was five years old again in the big house outside Houston, the two-story one with the white cotton Cape Cod curtains that got sucked out the windows when the wind picked up. In his dream, he was in his bedroom. At first out of focus and in half-light, his mother's contorted face became more clear. She was screaming at him.

"Where is it? Where did you put it?"

He gloated. Let her scream, he thought.

"I didn't see it. I don't know where it is. Honest." Oh, he was the perfect one. There was nothing to lose because she would never, never find it. She would never know he hid it.

"You little pissant! You've got it—I know you do." She stopped haranguing him and looked toward the bedroom door. He heard it too. The front screen door downstairs had slammed shut. He could see her face. She wanted to hit him. He knew that.

"If he leaves, you'll pay for it!" Her voice was a veritable screech as she ran from the room. He could hear her feet thumping down the stairs.

In his dream, he saw himself move to the window and stand behind the billowing curtain. Mama was in the front yard chasing after Steve. Again. What was it he'd been telling her? Bobby didn't have to read his lips.

"It was that jerk-off kid of yours." He was saying that. He always called him a jerk-off kid. That worthless moocher. Bobby would make her choose again.

Bobby looked under the bed. The shiny red metal toolbox was still there. The wrenches were still in it. Steve needed to get it back so he could work on his car. From downstairs came the sound of squealing tires. He'd be back. He always came back.

But now, hold on. Bobby looked out the bedroom window at the scene unfolding below. There was the little girl from next door. Tina. Tina. Tattletale. She must have seen him and the red box when he took it from the garage to the house. Yeah, she'd asked him what he was doing with it. Now she was pointing at the upstairs window. At him. This was going to ruin his plan. Mama wouldn't choose if she knew. She wouldn't have to. There would be hell to pay.

He could undo it! There was still time! Bobby grabbed the metal box and raced down the stairs to the garage. If it could go back before she came in . . .

But the timing was bad, bad, bad. His mother was coming through the garage door just as he was putting the toolbox in its place near the lawn mower, about to make his getaway.

Her hand grabbed his right ear and pulled hard. There was indescribable pain. She dragged him back over to where he had put the box. Her free hand lifted the lid and removed something skinny. Then she dragged him into the house. He couldn't remember what she was yelling; it had happened so long ago.

But he remembered that while she was yelling, he was being dragged past the tattletale. She was just a foot or so away. Watching it all. But a little too close. As his mother pulled him, he reached out. His fingers sank into her blond curls. They were a sight! Mother screaming, pulling Bobby. Bobby screaming, pulling the screaming tattletale. Even after she freed herself from his grasp with much help from Bobby's mother, there were thick strands of her blond hair twisted around his fingers. Whatever else happened after that, those last moments, even though filled with justifiable fear, brought a rush of satisfaction.

Then there was his mother's voice again.

"I'm going to teach you a lesson you won't ever forget! Pants!"

He knew the order and what was expected, and he complied. She was going to hit him. Fine. Fine. Fine. So what? He wouldn't let her know he felt anything. But wait. This wasn't right. Steve's pliers were biting—biting at him, at his private parts; she'd told him never, never let anyone touch him there; why, why was she doing this? Ohh . . . He had never felt such pain. She threatened; her face was there in front of his. It looked like a face in a Christmas-tree bulb. She would do it again if Steve didn't come back. Remember *that* while you are crying there in bed, he told himself. Ohh, he wanted Steve to please, please come back. . . .

Bobby awakened in a sweat. His dreams had always been trips in time. Random stopping points. Backward. Forward. Forward and backward every night. The luminescent numbers on the clock told him it was 2:32. It would be nice sometime to sleep through the night. He wished he knew how. He shifted onto his side.

Sometimes at night he wished he were dead. Sometimes he fantasized about killing himself. He lay in bed watching the patterns from the headlights of passing cars move across the motel room wall and he remembered Steve had come back and married his mother. What was it she had told him? "Now you have to listen to Steve." He slipped into a tentative slumber again. He could see his infant half sister laughing. His mother was laughing. Steve was laughing. Steve never made him laugh.

"There's the doe. And the fawn. Doe's yours. Point. The gun, shitface, the gun. Not your finger. Jesus, you are dumb. Right. Shoot. Shoot!" He felt the tears rolling down his cheeks.

"I ca-ca-can't."

"Fuck, I'm glad you ain't no son of mine. Here." Steve grabbed the rifle, placed the butt at his shoulder and pointed it for him, pushing his head down to the scope. "There. There's the shot, now pull the trigger . . . easy, easy. Good! You bagged her!" Even in his sleep he could smell it, the blood.

He remembered the doe, her neck twisted, her head immobile, her eyes following him as Steve repositioned him and the rifle, and he pulled the trigger again, putting an end to the animal's misery. . . .

Bobby awoke with a start, his body shaking. It was finally morning. For a while he was in peace. But by seven-thirty he felt the need to drive around. Maybe one more look, a little more planning, and tomorrow he would hunt. He'd been thinking he'd leave directly for Colorado. There was nothing in San Diego for him. The owner of the apartment could give his shit away for all he cared. It wasn't worth much. And there was his one rule: never, ever backtrack. San Diego would be backtracking.

He had carefully tucked his writings away between

the mattress and box spring of his bed. He didn't want to pack his diary just yet. There was one more entry he would have to make.

After dressing, Bobby drove to a convenience store for a cup of coffee and a doughnut. He had fifty-four dollars. He'd need to get a little job pretty soon to tide him over.

At his corner, he parked and waited. It was eight-twenty. Ten minutes until the bell.

Then suddenly there she was. The sight of her came as a total surprise.

There!

Dressed in blue.

Blue jeans.

Blue blouse.

Oh, my!

She was walking past him, right near his car.

Bobby slid over to the passenger seat. She was so close! If he wanted to, he could reach out and touch her. His breathing quickened. Every instinct in him told him, *Do it now! Call her over!* But there was another voice: *Easy. Easy, now. Not yet. Not here. Too close to the school. Be patient. Tomorrow is soon enough.*

He watched as she crossed the street in front of his car. This had been an excellent choice.

The surprise had almost caught him off guard. It had been so tempting. Had he wanted to carry her away, he could have. He watched as she disappeared into the cage area where the other children were playing.

Bobby drove around aimlessly throughout the day, returning to his room for an evening nap. Seeing the girl had made him uncontrollably restless. He had driven past the school three times in the afternoon, and at 10 P.M. he couldn't resist the urge and returned again to the corner where she had come so close to him. His voice told him he didn't need to go back again. That he should rest now because he would need all his energy tomorrow. He didn't listen.

Many times—too many to remember—Riverside Patrol Officer Edward Parelli would sit for hours waiting for the expected to happen. It was part of the job. Stakeouts. Arrests. Serving search warrants. Waiting for the D.A.'s decision to charge. Waiting for the trial and then the sentence.

Only this time he was in the right spot at the right time, and it all just unfolded in front of him. The unexpected. Tonight, as he sat in the parking lot with the taco between his teeth, a truck, a blue Toyota, caught his eye, passing right in front of him. He finished the bite and threw the rest of his lunch in the bag as he began to follow at a cautious distance, in the Toyota's blind spot. As he followed, he awkwardly pulled his clipboard from under the seat and smashed back the memos to those dated a week or so earlier. He found the one he wanted. A yellow all-points bulletin. Murder. The license plate matched. The vehicle description matched.

Parelli radioed for backup units. Then he closed his eyes for a moment and saw a hand pinning the detective badge on his uniform.

Outside the motel, Riverside Police Sergeant Jack Fletcher and a team of fourteen officers had been staked out since 11 P.M. They'd moved in, supplementing Parelli and the six officers who had tailed Engle, then watched the motel to be sure their guy didn't slip out unnoticed.

The SWAT officers had spread out in an accepted

pattern. Four covered the motel room door. Three covered the window at the back of the room. The remaining seven officers were staggered throughout the parking lot, including two at Bobby's truck.

At 11:30 P.M. there was a knocking at the motel room door. The thought that it was the police never occurred to Bobby. He didn't connect the sound of the hovering helicopter with anything associated with himself.

"Yeah. Who's there?"

"Mister, do you have a blue Toyota?" The voice had a sincere sound of urgency.

"Yes, I do. Why?"

"There's someone out here trying to break into it. Hope your radio's not gone yet." It was a ruse, a trick. But the law allowed it, particularly when the suspect might be violent.

"I'll be right there," Engle yelled, pulling on his pants, leaving his chest and feet bare.

Six steps out the door, he was surrounded by police officers, all pointing their rifles in his face. One booming voice, screaming, reached him.

"Hands on your head!"

Bobby complied.

"Get on the ground. Down! Down!" Hands were pushing him hard to the asphalt.

"Spread-eagle! Spread 'em!"

His legs were kicked apart, his arms pulled up hard behind him and cuffed in cold, cutting steel. A hand was pushing his face against the pavement, scraping the skin on his cheek and nose, contorting his mouth. Someone stepped on his leg; it was no accident. If they'd just shoot him now, it could be over; he'd be out of pain. There were feet all around him, some running. He was vaguely aware of the helicopter spotlight overhead.

Lights were coming on in the motel, and he could see the shoes of people running everywhere.

Two strong sets of hands reached under his arms and pulled him to his feet. A face appeared directly in front of his. The voice yelling directions earlier belonged to this face. The man was reading from a small card.

"You have the right to remain silent. Anything you say can and will be used against you in a court of law. You have the right to speak with an attorney prior to any questioning. If you cannot afford an attorney, one will be appointed for you. Knowing these rights, do you wish to give them up and speak with us?"

"No. I want an attorney."

The officer's jaw shifted.

"Notify San Diego. We've got their man."

From some distance away an officer began to yell. Bobby knew they must have found his writing. And his pliers—his alligator. His beloved alligator.

But they'd never find his snake.

He didn't even know where it was.

The telephone startled Pike from a sound sleep. He looked at his wristwatch. Two o'clock. In the morning. He'd been slumped in the armchair in front of the television for over two hours.

His stomach was sour, probably from the barbecued ribs he'd had for dinner. He was in no condition to look at bodies or blood now. Maybe he'd get lucky and the homicide would be a clean one. Maybe a strangulation. Fat chance there was of that. Not at this hour. It was a gunshot or a stabbing. Had to be.

"Pike here." He massaged his face. "Where's the body?"

"In jail." He recognized Abrams's voice. "Stop

mumbling and listen up. It's good news tonight. We got Engle.''

"We got who?'' Pike was still shaking off sleep.

"Wake up, Pike. The name's Engle—remember our boy Bobby Engle?''

"Oh shit! Engle!'' Pike was suddenly there, his mouth puckering, his eyes blinking. "Where? Who got him?''

"Riverside picked him up. A patrol officer spotted him.''

"No shit! Do they want us to come get him?''

"Sorry to spoil the excitement, but no. They're bringing him down first thing in the morning.''

"Has he been questioned?''

"He didn't want to talk. All discussions terminated.''

"Did they find anything of the Solomon kid's on him?''

"Did they ever. They got a diary that details every scream. The son of a bitch was stalking the next kid. And they got a tool, a pliers of some kind. I can't wait to get my hands on it.''

"Where'd they find the stuff—his car?''

"No, in his motel room.''

"Motel room? Who issued the search warrant?'' It was a routine question. He expected a routine answer.

"I don't know if there was one.'' Abrams was so matter-of-fact, it crossed Pike's mind this was a prank.

"C'mon. You're joking.''

"It's too early in the morning for jokes. I can't verify a search warrant.''

"Ah, no . . . Jesus Christ.''

"Don't get wild on this, Pike. It's been pretty chaotic up there. Give them a few hours to get their shit together. I'll be in at seven.''

"Are you sure there's no warrant?''

"No, I'm not sure. So there's no use churning yourself over this until there's a reason to. Try to get a few hour's sleep. We've done one hell of a job. The guilty scumbag's behind bars."

"Shit," fumed Pike. "For now, he is."

10

Through the closed door Abrams heard a string of obscenities. He recognized the angry voice. As the telephone receiver slammed, Abrams entered and found Pike at his desk, beads of sweat trickling the length of his jawline.

"Was that Riverside?"

"Yeah, that was Riverside. Some rookie officer with shit for brains went through Engle's motel room during the arrest and grabbed everything he could get his hands on. Including that diary and the pliers. The officer who grabbed the stuff's only been out of the academy four months. It happens, but Christ, why in this one?"

"Weren't they briefed beforehand?"

"How the hell do I know?" Pike replied. "There's no sign of a search warrant. I still don't know if there was a telephonic warrant in progress." The usual search warrant might take days to obtain, but a telephonic warrant could be obtained by the district attorney's office over the phone in a matter of hours from one of the duty judges.

"We're trying to verify, but if we get no verification

there was a warrant, the search may be illegal and we've got one hell of a problem with anything they found in that motel room.'' Pike wiped the sweat from his temples.

"It's just a goddamned piece of paper. A piece of paper, signed by a judge, telling me I can go into a place and get the things listed on that piece of paper. What the hell difference does it make if I go in before I get the piece of paper and the judge says afterward, 'Yes, there's enough reason to have gone in for the stuff'?''

"Pike, you've done a thousand search warrants. You know why you get them. You get them because that's what the law says you have to do. If you didn't need to get them before you went in, you'd be going in without thinking why you need to and probably not caring why you need to.''

"But do you know what's in that diary, Mike?''

"Strong evidence.''

"Strong? Hell, it would put the dirtbag away for the rest of his life.''

"Pike, you know goddamned well that what they found in his room doesn't matter. It's how they got it.''

"You know what we've got so far in the case, Mike? We ain't got shit. If that search is bad, nothing those officers found can be used as evidence against Engle at trial. Jesus, so far, it's the only solid stuff we've got.''

"Where'd they arrest him? Inside or outside the room?''

"Outside. They fed him a line and when he came out they popped him.''

Abrams had been hoping for a clear arrest outside the motel room; it would be easier to uphold the search without a warrant. But if the ruse had been used to get Engle outside in order to search his motel room, it would still be a struggle to uphold.

"Did Engle make any statements?'' Abrams asked,

hopeful the arrest itself might have yielded a usable admission of guilt.

"Yeah. 'I want my attorney,' " Pike said, grim-faced. "We've asked for the written reports and Riverside's supposed to be sending them down today. They're going directly over to the D.A." He rubbed his eyes.

"You get any sleep since yesterday?" Abrams asked.

"Yeah. Some." Pike reached into his pocket for a wrinkled white handkerchief and ran it over his still sweaty face as he searched for the words to explain his frustration. "I don't know. It didn't ever seem to be so hard to do the job."

"That's because it never was this hard to do the job," Abrams said.

"Is it me? Maybe I'm just getting old."

"It's not you, Pike. No one trusts us anymore. So we've got rules everywhere, and if you don't follow them, you've got a problem."

"And good sense be damned?" Pike asked, more as an exclamation than a question.

"Sometimes, yes, I guess it follows. But that doesn't change the fact you need a search warrant to get into someone's house."

"I don't understand that academy talk, Mike. I only want to do my job. And I can't."

"Don't let it get to you. Just think how a rookie feels. You're still too young and there's too much we've got to do. I look at it like it's bound to happen like a life cycle, this business of chasing crime . . . it just naturally grinds you down around the edges. Then it grinds you down on the inside. Then you retire. . . . Let it go for now. There's nothing we can do even if there was a screw-up by Riverside. You—we—can't keep it all under control all the time. The D.A.'s announcing the arrest this morning. We can take a hard look at it when we find out which deputy D.A.'s been assigned. C'mon. I'll buy you a cup of coffee.''

Parker Hunt was a six-footer; a two-time national swimming champion whose body had more recently settled heavily into middle age. Still, though his gait had slowed and he had added an unnecessary inch or two around the midriff, there was a residual grace to his movements. It showed in the way his arms swayed when he walked and in the way his body maintained a straight-arrow posture when he turned.

Following a short career in public relations and an even shorter career as a lawyer with the San Diego City Attorney's Office, Hunt had joined the county district attorney's staff. He had started his work there in the early seventies, when the office was so small that everyone could go to the cafeteria for coffee and sit around one of the eight-foot-long tables. By the nineties, the office had spread to three full floors of the courthouse building. On occasion, staff visiting from one of the floors would not be recognized by the receptionist and would be asked to identify themselves. The office had grown with the county population until its staff, like the court's, was crammed into every available office space but was still grossly under the number projected as necessary, given the county population.

After a successful trial career, Hunt had run for district attorney. He was the best possible candidate for a moderate Republican county—a soft-spoken, conservative Democrat who was tough on crime. He had won the election handily and quickly established a strong middle management with his ace trial attorney-turned-chief assistant, Lawrence Farrell, as its cornerstone. With the iron-fisted Farrell overseeing the charging and trial functions, the office reputation had soared. And Hunt, reaping the reward of his own sound management judgment, had run unopposed in three successive elections.

Hunt owed his political fortunes as much to his alter ego Farrell as he did to the political climate of the time, and in the eyes of all save the most inexperienced of court observers, Farrell was his undisputed heir apparent.

And though it was Parker Hunt who made the policy decisions affecting the office, the trial deputies understood who was in control of their lives. Farrell was. It was he who decided which deputy got which case, who got the high-profile trials and who worked misdemeanors and for how long. He knew the mechanics of the criminal trial forward and backward. He determined when to charge, what to charge and whom to charge with the crime. And although it was also he who got to handle the highest of the high-profile cases, he was the one most likely to win them. In the eyes of many, by the end of Hunt's twelve years in office, Farrell had emerged as the more powerful of the two. Yet he used his powers first to the benefit of Hunt and the office. He knew the strengths and weaknesses of his trial deputies as well as he knew his own, and he assigned them to their tasks accordingly and without favoritism.

His dedication was unchallenged. Indeed, if you wanted to spar with Hunt on almost any issue, you needed to get through Farrell first. And that was no easy task. Many careers had taken an abrupt nosedive because their owners had challenged office power and the route leading to it.

When word raced through the office grapevine that there had been an arrest in the Solomon murder the previous night, everyone, including Judith, believed Farrell would handle the Engle trial. And when she learned that Hunt wished to speak with her before the press conference announcing the arrest, she assumed it was to inform her that Farrell would be introduced as the trial attorney on the case.

That morning, Hunt personally greeted Judith at his secretary's large mahogany desk and escorted her into his spacious office. He extended his arm, motioning for Judith to have a seat in one of the two cobalt-blue accent chairs placed in the corner of the office used for informal conferencing. He took a seat in the other chair, his heavy frame awkwardly out of place for its delicate bent-arm design.

"You probably know by now that we've made an arrest in the Solomon murder case. We're pretty sure this is our man. The press doesn't know yet."

He handed Judith a file. She opened it and glanced at the single-page document that would be filed in court. It was an amendment to the complaint filed when the arrest warrant had been issued.

"Look it over, Judith. We think the facts in our case will support a death penalty charge."

Judith silently read the amendment. It alleged the murder had occurred during rape and torture of the victim, two of the limited situations which permitted the imposition of capital punishment in California.

"When will the new complaint be filed?" she asked.

"Riverside picked him up last night. We've got a press conference with law enforcement here at ten o'clock. We'll file afterward. I'd like you to be at the press conference, Judith. I know the task force has been handling the investigation in the case, but I'd like you to personally handle the trial."

This wasn't what she had expected. As she searched for the right words to respond, Hunt seemed to be reading her mind.

"I realize your expectation might have been otherwise, and if you don't think it's something you want to handle, let me know now, because in about half an hour I intend to tell the press who the trial deputy is going to be.''

''We'll do it, of course.''

''Not we. You. This is going to rest on your shoulders alone, Judith. If you think you need a second chair, we can assign one of your task force deputies along with you. But I think any reassignment of a second deputy will have to be temporary. Your resources down there aren't going to allow two deputies to take a year off, if it's necessary, to try Bobby Engle. And frankly, the case is so sensitive that I'd prefer the responsibility to rest in one person's hands. What do you say?''

Her response was controlled and measured, masking the rush of excitement. ''What time's the press conference?''

''I can count on you?''

''I'll do the best I can. Any support services the task force can lend would be appreciated. One of the things I know we need already is a run on the computer system to see if we can match Engle up with similar crimes in other states.''

''Whatever support you need, you've got. Just ask. And, Judith, you know as well as anyone that there's a pecking order around here. There may be some bruised feelings. I trust you can handle it diplomatically.''

She was afraid to ask whether he was referring to Farrell.

''I think I can handle it.''

''I know you can. Come on up a little before ten so we can get the introductions out of the way.'' He grinned. ''We're expecting a crowd.''

Judith walked back to her office on a cloud. Along the way she passed Farrell's open door. He was at his desk, but waved to her as she glanced in. She dared not mention the new trial assignment to anyone just yet. Hunt had handed her the Engle file, but not the ball game. That was still his.

Judith hadn't been in her office more than a few minutes when there was a knock at the door.

It was Farrell. "Can I come in?"

"Sure. Just getting ready for the big press conference."

"I wanted to say good luck with the Engle trial, Judith. You'll do a great job. I'll be staying on—as liaison to Parker. And if there's anything I can do to help, let me know."

She wasn't sure at first how to react. He knew. He'd known before she had. Obviously her assignment to the trial had been discussed between Hunt and him before Hunt had handed the file off to her.

Farrell smiled. "See you upstairs at ten."

Jon Kolker was late for the press conference and he was frustrated and angry. He'd planned to spend the morning researching his upcoming series on the death penalty in California. Then, in the middle of his telephone conversation with the deputy attorney general who was heading the state's capital punishment team, his editor had dropped a note in front of him, asking him to get down to the district attorney's office ASAP for some dumb dog-and-pony show. He'd have been right on time if he'd been able to find a parking space nearer the courthouse.

As far as Kolker was concerned, this was just another example of the newspaper trying to screw him. Andrews—his editor—had agreed, when Kolker left the police beat to take on the job of legal affairs writer, that he'd do the big-picture subjects like the death penalty series and Hap Yarborough would continue to cover the routine courthouse cases. But for the tenth time in four weeks, Hap had called in sick or hungover. And now he—Kolker—was stuck with the courthouse beat too. He was sure this was some routine piece of crap this morning. Not even a press conference. Probably a press availability for the photographers. He hadn't been to a real press conference in almost a year. The kind where you got to ask a question and maybe a follow-up. Rumor had it Hunt might be retiring soon. No such luck today. His death penalty series would just have to be put on hold.

Mumbling to himself, huffing and puffing up the Union Street-entrance stairway into the long corridor that led to Hunt's office, Kolker remembered this was supposed to be the week he'd sworn to give up smoking, begin a jogging routine and, for as many days as he could stand it, skip the two-martini lunches at Mario's.

"Sure—and maybe go back to church, make an alimony payment on time and win the Pulitzer Prize."

Well, the big five-o was a month away. Maybe he'd take these challenges up then.

Outside the D.A.'s office, he spotted the television cables taped to the gray marble floor. Through the frosted glass door he could see the glare of the lights.

"Must be a shortage of fender benders on the freeway and lost-dog stories to get these guys down here."

After all, giving a criminal justice story even a modicum of serious treatment was going to require more than a minute and a half. Oh, well, there was always the bright side. After the D.A.'s ego got massaged, maybe he could sneak in a question or two. Hunt had once or twice answered questions Kolker had shouted at him on his way out. He sure wanted to ask about Hunt's rumored resignation, and whether there'd be a quick appointment to the spot. Yeah—and if he could get someone to speak on the record, he could get back to the office by lunchtime.

Kolker was relieved to see that nothing had started. The camera crews were still adjusting their lights and microphones. They looked efficient and skilled enough, but these TV guys sure as shit never knew what questions to ask. Their minds worked with the same depth as their medium.

Already lined up behind the D.A.'s desk was the usual cast of characters. For the press conference, Hunt chose to sit in his brown, high-backed leather chair rather than on the low, tweed-covered typing chair he found more comfortable. It created a striking setting, Hunt at the center of his polished mahogany desk. Behind him were a navy blue wall of West's California codes on walnut shelves, the United States and California flags at each corner, and the seal of the County of San Diego, hanging on the wall directly behind him above his head.

Flanking Hunt on the right were his chief assistant, Farrell; his personal press officer, Tobias; and Judith Thornton. On the left flank . . . now, this was interesting. Two unexpected players. That airhead Sheriff Ted Murray, the cowboy of the North County, whose skill on the horse was matched only by his inability to speak three consecutive understandable sentences. And Police Chief Neil Bradley, whom Kolker had tangled with five years ago when he was covering the police beat. And at the very end, some police chief from somewhere else. It looked like—He squinted. Riverside.

Hell, maybe there was a real story here after all.

The press conference itself was more subdued and comfortable than most, since it was being held in Hunt's personal office. The location emphasized its importance. Kolker could remember the office opened to the press on only two previous occasions, the first when Hershel

Traak had been arrested. Traak, an unemployed drifter from Arkansas, had been sought for a string of coed murders in San Diego and Los Angeles counties. He'd strangled six young women in their dormitory beds before being caught climbing into a first-floor dorm window in search of his seventh victim. Unfortunately for him, it was the cafeteria window. A night security guard, finding his gun unnecessary, had grabbed the nearest object, a griddle, and hit him over the head with it, knocking him out and making the citizen's arrest of the year.

The second press conference had been held to announce that Traak had been killed during a fight over cigarettes while awaiting trial in the county jail.

Accidents of timing and fortuity of coincidence. Such were the forces by which victims were frequently chosen and then vindicated.

Hunt's slight gesture into the air with his right hand brought the room to complete silence.

"Ladies and gentlemen, I've called this press conference to announce we have arrested an individual in the murder of Kelly Solomon." There was a rustle of paper as notebooks opened. Hunt graciously waited for a moment to allow them to adjust to the serious nature of the notes they were about to take. "Through the outstanding joint efforts of our law enforcement agencies and our advanced forensic technology, we have arrested an individual, Robert Engle. He is thirty-five years old and a resident of Lakeside. He has a prior criminal history. This morning Mr. Engle will be charged with a capital murder in the first degree. He's being held without bail. The director of our Homicide Task Force, Deputy District Attorney Judith Thornton, will be handling the trial. We're not going to be taking questions. I know there are a lot of them, but you will all shortly be receiving a full press release, and we hope to have a recent photo of Mr. Engle for you by the end of the day." With that, Hunt rose and left the room with Farrell, allowing the remaining participants to speak what was on their minds.

Kolker cornered Judith as she was about to exit.

"Can I talk to you for a minute, Ms. Thornton?"

"Jon Kolker, isn't it? You're on the courthouse beat?"

"I'm subbing this morning for Hap. But I've got this series going on capital punishment, and this Solomon case fits right in. I was thinking during the conference, such as it was, that I might want to follow the case from start to finish. What do you think about that?"

"From start to finish? Capital cases are never finished. I haven't got a whole lot of time, but come with me for a minute if you want."

Kolker followed Judith through the back hall, down the staircase and into her office.

"You want some coffee?" she asked.

"No, thanks. It's too early in the day. You can drink too much of the stuff."

"There's a lot worse you could drink, and it doesn't land you in a courtroom."

Ignoring Judith's comment and the office chairs, Kolker leaned against the side of her desk.

"Can you give me the scoop on this guy Engle?"

"Are we off the record?"

"Yes."

"Can I trust you that nothing's going to be printed that will lead back to me?"

"Nothing."

"Well, we haven't got a lot on the guy. He's a drifter with a record of child molest."

"You think he's the one?"

"We wouldn't have charged if we didn't think so."

Her answers offered no more information than was

necessary. Like most experienced deputy D.A.s, Judith Thornton had a natural distrust of reporters. And like most experienced reporters, Kolker regarded prosecutors with a healthy skepticism. But the two had a mutual respect for their need of each other; hers, to see complicated stories correctly condensed into a few paragraphs that could be quickly and easily understood; his, to gather enough good information to report correctly.

"Can I give you a call later, maybe, when the trial gets started?"

"I don't mind at all."

"If I can switch gears here for a moment . . . There's talk in the corridors that you might be one of those next in line for D.A. You want to comment on that?"

"Not really. The fastest way to circulate a rumor is to release it on the second floor of the courthouse."

She hadn't mentioned Farrell. Maybe it was the competitor in her. The last thought surprised her. Her aspirations to the office were not so well formed. She was not even sure the D.A.'s spot was something she would ever want. There was a lot of power in it, but she'd be removed from doing what she loved best—trial work—and heavily into what she didn't like—paperwork.

"Is the D.A. spot something you're interested in?"

"I never discount anything. But it hasn't been offered by anyone, so I haven't had to think about it."

"Would you accept if it was offered?" he asked.

"It hasn't been offered."

"Yet?"

"Yet."

"Any other names being discussed that you know of?"

"Yes. In fact, Farrell has also been mentioned."

She felt better having said this.

"There's never been a woman in the spot, has there?"

"No, there hasn't."

"Maybe being a woman would help your chances?"

"Oh, I don't know. Maybe. But I'm not really interested."

"You'd be good." He switched gears on her again. "Getting back to Engle for a minute . . . how can I get some information on him? I'll bet he's got quite a history. Any recent or real serious prior child molests you know about? I'm especially interested in how a guy like that could be out walking the streets."

Should she be honest? She glanced at her watch. She knew what she wanted to say.

"Blame the legislature. Don't look at my office. And don't look at the courts. Go back to the seventies and look at what the legislature did then. They were on a roll up there in Sacramento. They wanted the folks back home to applaud how tough they'd gotten with the criminals. What they did, though, was turn 'em loose. Shocker, huh? And you're asking *how,* of course. Well, let me tell you. It used to be, the judge would look at a criminal and say this is an assault on a kid and you're sick. The law says you get a term of one-to-fifteen years. You go up for fifteen. Now the judge doesn't get to do that. He gets to pick from a choice of three prison terms—say one, three or six years. If the crime's mitigated, take one, and if it's aggravated, take six. If you don't want to give reasons for choosing the sentence, pick the mid term—three years. Then take time off for work credits. It's just a damned mathematical calculation. That's how I can best explain why Engle was loose on the streets. His release was due to a math equation. But that's not what the public wants to read, Mr. Kolker, and it isn't what reporters like you want to write, because it's too hard to complain about a legislature that changed the law fifteen years ago. Of course, you can handle it all very simply. He's not guilty, Mr. Kolker, until he's proven guilty in court.''

Kolker had been writing at a pace as furious as her monologue. When she had finished and he had written his last word, he looked at her calmly and shook his head.

"Whew! You are one angry person, Mrs. Thornton. I'm supposed to be the skeptic.''

"Can we cover that another time, Mr. Kolker? I've got to get over to court and be sure the complaint against Engle's been filed. I think you've got enough there in your notes to get you started and keep you busy for a week or two.''

"Maybe we can kick it around over a drink sometime soon.''

"Over coffee.''

"You can count on it.''

She was relieved when he left. If Engle was guilty, she had no reasonable explanation for what he was doing loose on the streets, at least none that made any sense.

Judith spent the remainder of her morning reviewing her files on Engle. By eleven o'clock the full reports from Riverside had been received. After examining them, she called Farrell.

"I think I ought to let you know up-front that we're definitely going to have a problem with the search up in Riverside. I haven't spent any time looking at the cases yet, but there was no warrant. There's a diary with incriminating evidence on the Solomon case, and a pair of pliers that might have been one of the murder weapons. They are devastating evidence and we stand to lose them both. You'd better take a look at these reports, Larry. I'll send them right up to you.''

"If it's as bad as it sounds, I'd appreciate your keeping it under wraps for now, Judith. Tomorrow Engle's going to be arraigned and counsel's going to be appointed. His attorney will be onto the problem sooner than we want. Don't you worry about handling the press on this when and if the shit hits the fan. Refer all press inquiries up here. We'll handle them directly out of Parker's office. Let us be the buffer for you on that one. With what you're describing, the newspaper editorials are going to dump on everyone. Just handle the legal challenge as best you can, and don't be afraid to get real aggressive on it. I want Riverside's reports on my desk as fast as you can Xerox them.''

"I'm going to spend the rest of the day in the books and talk some strategy with my investigator," Judith said. "We'll do an internal memo for you by tomorrow, and maybe we'll have a better idea of what we're up against."

"Maybe it'll all go away." By the tone in his voice, he knew it wasn't going to happen so magically.

Immediately following their conversation, the search-and-seizure law books in the central library of the office began to find their way into Judith's office.

Everyone had his own research technique. Judith worked in piles. Cases directly related to a legal issue she was working on had their pile, while the various related issues had their own. Her objective was always to absorb the entire area of law involved to see how the pieces fit together, how the parts related to one another. She would sometimes spend days erecting towers of casebooks, surrounding herself with them, little yellow-and-white tags protruding from each book marking the cases she'd found. The tags were inscribed with her short, cryptic notes about the importance of the case or some passage in it. When the cases in the piles began to cross-reference one another, she would feel that the first part of her job was complete. She had the beginning and end of her analysis, and all she had to do was to figure out how the center pieces fit together. This she did by going back and analyzing each of her piles of cases. If she understood the whole and its parts after that, she could deal with the law even if it was adverse to her position.

But by midafternoon the end process had yielded no feeling of personal satisfaction. Six piles surrounded her. Some of the books were open, some closed. She'd gone to lunch and come back, only to find that her initial conclusion hadn't changed. She'd read and reread the police reports from Riverside. There'd been no warrant, telephonic or otherwise, for Engle's motel room. Based on her reading, she'd concluded that neither the pliers nor the diary—nor anything taken from the motel room, for that matter—could be included in evidence. In her opinion, everything had been seized illegally, making it all inadmissible.

Judith reached for the phone and dialed.

"Pike? Judith Thornton. I've looked at Riverside's reports. I called the officers supervising the SWAT team. There's no warrant and it's a problem. I don't think the pliers and diary are admissible. That doesn't mean we can't try to introduce them. We have a judgment call to make here."

"What kind of judgment call?" Pike asked.

"We have a case from Cal Supreme that's going to be a bear to overcome. We can try to introduce the evidence and maybe succeed if we've got the right judge. Then where are we? Suppose we do get a judge who's smart enough—or crazy enough—to get around the case law, and Engle's found guilty and gets the death penalty. He has his automatic appeal to Cal Supreme. You want to guess whether they'll stick to their own case law? It's not that old a case. If we get a reversal from Cal Su-

preme, we're looking at a second trial for our Mr. Engle.''

"So you want to start this right out, Judith, by excluding everything?''

"No, that's not what I said. I want to see the lay of
the land before we commit ourselves to shaping our entire case around the evidence taken in the motel search.
For now, you write up your reports to include what was
found in the motel and continue to develop every one
of your leads. Tomorrow Engle will be entering his plea
and having counsel appointed. We're going to need
everything we can get our hands on after that to squeeze
past the preliminary hearing if that evidence is excluded.''

The preliminary hearing would follow soon after the
plea. It was the hearing at which the court would listen
to the evidence the People had and decide if there was
enough to send Engle to trial for the crime. If it decided
there was insufficient evidence, the court would dismiss
the charges. And Engle might walk out the door. To be
sure, all that was needed in order to send him on to trial
was for the judge to find a reasonable suspicion Engle
had committed the crime. It wouldn't require a finding
of guilt beyond a reasonable doubt. That standard would
be applied at trial if he was bound over. But even with
the less demanding burden of proof on the People, Pike
knew the preliminary hearing would be difficult. Without the evidence found in Engle's motel room, all they
had was a fingerprint on a beer can, a picture of Tara
from Engle's Lakeside apartment and maybe the landlady's word he had a bicycle at some point in time near
when Kelly Solomon had disappeared. These items put
Engle in areas where Kelly had been. But alone they
proved nothing more than incredible coincidence of time
and place. Guilty verdicts were not won, the death sen-

tence was not imposed, on incredible coincidence. Without the diary and the pliers, the evidence wasn't even enough to force a plea bargain out of Engle. Any good defense counsel would push it to the wall.

"I'll send over my analysis, Pike. If I find some easy way out, I'll let you know—but don't count on it. Tomorrow we'll see who's going to be appointed to defend Engle. That'll tell us what type of firepower we're going to be up against."

By the time Judith had started for home, the sky was threatening more showers. Her route took her down Adams Avenue, past her grocery market, and gave her a chance to pick up the few things on the list she'd been carrying around in her purse for two days. When she emerged from the store, the ground was wet and cars were covered with water drops. She'd missed the rain. She always felt cheated when it rained while she was stuck inside some place and couldn't see it.

Judith pushed the shopping cart sideways toward the trunk of her car. Even in the subdued lighting of the parking lot she could see the scratches and dings beginning to appear on her car. Hardly had she taken the key from her purse when a figure appeared from the other side of the vehicle. Her first observations were directed to the man's hands. She had a stomach-in-the-throat feeling—her brain shifted her body automatically into alert, commanding her heart to race, her lungs to breathe more deeply. The smell of the wet asphalt was suddenly more intense.

Judith's eyes ran the length of the man's body. His hands were clutching the handles of crutches. He had only one foot. Her alarm turned to cool evaluation of the circumstances. The true level of danger was less than her body had prepared for.

"Excuse me, ma'am." What followed was garbled. He tried again.

"Excuse me, ma'am. Can you help me out a bit with some money for groceries for my family?"

Judith thought about ignoring the request, but decided to respond in a way that might terminate any further conversation. "I'm sorry. I don't talk to people who approach me at my car at night."

"I know, ma'am. That's why I said, 'Excuse me.' I don't mean you any harm."

He was putting her on. The sentences made no sense.

"I'm sorry. I just don't talk with strangers at night at my car."

The man stared at her for a moment, then ambled off.

"I mean, c'mon," she muttered to herself. "One foot and crutches. I could have beaten the guy to a pulp."

Judith loaded the groceries quickly into the trunk, noticing out of the corner of her eye that the man had walked past a couple crossing the parking lot and he hadn't stopped them. Had she looked like a soft touch? She thought back to the time she'd seen her father leave the car to hand a five-dollar bill to a man sitting on a corner curb. But that had been in a different time, a different world. Back then, you could act on an immediate, unanalyzed desire to help a fellow human being for no reason other than it looked like he needed help. Except, in her memories there was no such compassion in her. Not in this city, not at night. What a skeptic she'd become. Maybe the guy had starving kids. She'd prosecuted too many criminals. Her view of life was becoming tainted.

Maybe it was just San Diego. It had grown so fast. And somewhere in the growth there were people being lost. People wandering around with no identity. Like that man in the parking lot.

For a minute or two her mind was at rest as she drove. She was surprised when her thoughts turned to Kolker. She liked him. She liked talking to him. It had been a long time since she'd just sat and talked to anyone about her own feelings about things. She was, for a moment, sorry she didn't drink.

Without being sure exactly why, right then she made an abrupt left turn at the Mobil station into Kensington. It was one of those parts of the city built up in the early 1900s, when the average house had gone for five thousand dollars. The same house today went for three hundred thousand or more.

She drove down familiar streets—Marlborough, Middlesex, Edgeware—named by a Canadian developer with a love of English places. The architecture of the houses was inconsistent, a hodgepodge of Swiss chalet, California bungalow, mission—all with thick stucco walls that you could scrub the hell out of without worrying about wallboard coming off in your hands.

Kensington had a village atmosphere she had always liked: the little library in the park, the palm-tree-lined streets and small shops bordering the homes. There was a sense of place here.

She slowed her car in front of one of the two-story Spanish colonials so common to the area. The light in the living room was on. It looked the same, the house she and her husband used to live in before they moved to the house on the one-acre lot. It struck her this was the third time in as many weeks that she'd made this detour.

11

The following morning Judith watched as the calendar deputies for the public defender's and district attorney's offices took to their respective tables in Department 8 of the Municipal Court. While all cases moved through the Municipal Court first, the felonies were tracked through their own arraignment department. There, the court would sort through the cases calendared, taking pleas, setting bail and appointing counsel for the indigent.

The calendar deputies stood, each with two-foot-high piles of criminal files. As each case was called by the clerk, they pulled the pertinent file. There usually was not much to do other than follow the directions already written right on the file by those in their offices who decided what plea bargain, if any, could be given to each defendant. If the plea was acceptable to both parties, it could be taken and the defendant given a date to return for sentencing. If there was to be no plea of guilty, the court would appoint an attorney as needed and set the case for a preliminary hearing.

It was not unusual for the calendar deputy for the

defender's office to request that the plea itself be delayed.

"The People of the State of California versus Robert Dean Engle, case R 019354." Engle's was the last case called.

Judith stepped forward. "The People are ready on the Engle matter, your Honor."

The public defender rose. "The defense would like to continue Mr. Engle's arraignment, your Honor, until he has had a chance to speak with whoever is going to be appointed to defend him. I've spoken at length with him this morning and I can represent that he understands this request."

"Mr. Engle, you have the right to have the complaint against you read in court today. You have the right to enter your plea to that complaint today and to have me appoint counsel for you. Do you understand those rights?"

"I do, Judge."

"And do you give up those rights?"

"I do, Judge."

"Mr. Engle, this is my last day in this department. I am here only for two months; then I rotate out. I rotate out tomorrow. A new judge will be here when you return. Do you object to that?"

"It's okay with me, Judge."

"I'm going to set this matter over for seventy-two hours. Let's take a look at the appointment list and see who's available."

The public defender was quick to respond. "Your Honor, the public defender's office has culled through its list and, assuming it is okay with your Honor, Harley Bennett has agreed to represent Mr. Engle."

"Mr. Bennett is a class-five attorney, is he not?"

Class-five attorneys were those most experienced in

trial work. On a scale of one to five, only those graded as a five were authorized to handle capital cases.

"He is, your Honor, and some."

"Mr. Bennett is appointed. Please notify him of his next court appearance. I am assuming the district attorney has no objection?"

"None, your Honor."

Now Judith knew what she would be up against in court.

The best.

PART TWO

THE TRUTH

12

━━◆━━

The walk from Harley Bennett's office in the public defender's building on Third Avenue to the courthouse and jail complex at First and Broadway was a short one. Bennett had agreed to defend Bobby Engle, but not without mixed emotions. Even though it was a big case, his approaching celebrity status carried a heavy price. The district attorney's asking for the death penalty meant the case would probably chew up six months to a year of his life. Even to a dedicated defense attorney like Bennett, that was a long time. His three pending murder trials would have to be kited off to other attorneys. His home life would certainly suffer more than it did already. Luckily, his children were off to college, and his wife had long since adjusted to a husband subjected by his own design to horrendous work hours and stress.

It was 7:30 A.M., early enough that the downtown mix of homeless panhandlers and mentally ill was still pressed into the service doorways and entrances of any building offering shelter and safety. Huddled stiff and hollow-eyed, some shoeless, in frayed blankets and trash bags, they would be gone by nine, pushed off to sleep and beg at the city square outside Horton Plaza's shopping center by the janitors whose jobs were to hose down the entrances of their urine, before the wave of suits and high heels converged on the courthouse. Lately, a line of homeless had been forming outside the courthouse doorway at the close of the business day, attesting to the collective belief that if there was one edifice which would offer protection from the insecurity of the dark, it would be that which housed the halls of justice.

So far, no one had approached Bennett. No hand had touched his shoulder. No dirty-clothed, unshaven, red-eyed man had interfered with his slow, deliberate stride. For that he was grateful. He used to feel sympathy for the city's homeless street people. But in the past several years their number had grown, and they had become a more aggressive lot, pursuing, yelling and swearing, even striking out at those who declined an invitation to contribute. The debate went on as to whether it was the fault of the relaxed attitude of the city leaders toward the homeless. Point the finger at whomever, they were no longer just migrants following the warmth of the Sunbelt. They were, increasingly, society's castoffs. Some of them were on drugs; others were alcoholics; some were just down on their luck. But a hefty percentage was the mentally ill, for whom society had made no provision and who a decade ago would have violated even the most minor of laws and found themselves lost in the jails and prisons for indeterminant periods of time. In layered clothing, they stood on bus benches, yelling to invisible crowds, searching the trash bins for anything usable or edible.

Bennett had seen pity for the wretched around him turn to dismay, and from dismay to resignation. Disdain loomed on the horizon. Imperceptibly it inched forward with each new crane in the city skyline, each new hotel complex, each glass tower. Dirt and glitter mix poorly.

Around him, carefully planned, newly constructed office buildings of pinks and grays stood in stark contrast to the washed-out tan concrete of the courthouse and the intermittent stench of poverty and illness clinging to it.

The court complex was the product of decades of lack of planning, poor planning and diminishing governmental resources, a combination which guaranteed the buildings would not be adequate to handle the ever-increasing demands being placed on them by San Diego's rapidly growing population.

To the west, towering over everything, were the five hexagonal glass towers of the thirty-story, multimillion-dollar Emerald-Shapery Center, its rooftops trimmed in green neon visible for miles in the night sky. He'd read the pamphlet—three hundred seventy-five thousand square feet of office, retail and hotel space whose rooms offered panoramic views of San Diego Bay, the Pacific Ocean and Mexico.

Like most court regulars, Bennett had adjusted to the court's steady deterioration: elevators that regularly broke down, poorly circulated air, sewage pipes that periodically leaked onto desktops, asbestos-lined ceilings. He was convinced that one day it would all fall down about their ears or be condemned by the health department and bulldozed away.

The lack of physical comfort was only part of what disturbed him about the deterioration of the courts. The condition of the courthouse had become a symbol to him of the decline of the justice system itself: a decline of its power, its respect.

Sometimes he could convince himself he was exaggerating the court's ill health, but events around him increasingly pointed Bennett in the opposite direction. He wished he had the time and energy at the end of the day to try to create some kind of plan that would deliver the judicial system to the idealistic state envisioned by the framers of the Constitution, but even Bennett, the bar's Defense Attorney of the Year 1988, winner of the 1989 Golden Gavel Award for Trial Advocacy, was powerless in the face of such decay.

Inside the courthouse door, Bennett bought a cup of coffee and carried it outside and across the street to the jail. He might have to wait anywhere from thirty minutes to an hour and a half for the guards to bring Engle down.

He hadn't met Engle yet. The first interview with a client was usually short, even when the crime was as serious as capital murder. This was not by design. He simply had nothing yet from the police or the district attorney—no police reports, no forensic results. All he had on Engle was a copy of the complaint issued by the district attorney's office, setting out the charges filed against him, and an office memo informing Bennett he had been appointed to defend Engle.

At the outer window, he handed his county ID card to the deputy sheriff and took a seat on the wooden bench nearest the entrance door to the jail. Forty-five minutes later, his identification card was exchanged for a plastic clip-on ID tag. He heard the familiar scraping and clang as the giant metal double doors slammed behind him, one at a time. Then the search was on for an empty conference room—no easy task, given the small, cramped rooms that were used constantly. By day they were interview rooms; by night, dormitory rooms. They smelled of sweat and urine and the veiled odor of hate and fear that permeated the entire jail; above it all, a voice was announcing the comings and goings from the first floor.

"Upwell!" Someone was going back up the elevator to the cellblock.

"Downwell!" Someone was coming down. From the corner of his eye Bennett caught the new admittees—naked, lined up for the white-glove test, a body-cavity search of the rectum performed by a rubber-gloved individual; hence its name. Even the hard-line prison inmates making return visits found it humiliating and repulsive. Yet despite common knowledge of its existence, it continued to yield all manner of contraband—balloons of heroin to packs of cigarettes. He could hear the guard yelling, it seemed at the top of his lungs.

"There are a few simple rules here! When you are passing or standing by others, especially me, keep your hands in your waistband! Don't talk. Walk in a single line. There will be no signals, no homeboy signs! Clothes—push them to the front now! Turn around and put your hands up on the wall and let me see your left foot. Bend over! Don't panic when the heroin falls out next to you! Okay! Okay! Oops, sorry, don't touch—let the deputy get that! Okay! Now! Pick up your clothes and move out into the next room—single file. Let's go!"

In his twenty years of practicing law, Bennett had never found any single word to adequately describe the county jail. The closest he'd gotten was "abysmal," but it didn't quite capture the smell.

Bennett had always trusted his viscera when it came to his impressions of people. Twenty years' experience in and out of courtrooms and jails had given him enough of a view of humanity's range to allow him to size people up intuitively. A trusty's voice boomed. "Downwell! Robert Engle!"

The young man led into the conference room was no addict, no motorcycle-riding cruiser. His face was narrow and egg-shaped with high cheekbones, and his straight brown hair was combed back and away from piercing brown eyes. His mouth was thin and taut. He reminded Bennett of a snake, ready to strike.

Bennett stood, handing Engle his business card.

"Mr. Engle, my name's Harley Bennett. I'm a deputy public defender. I've been appointed to represent you."

Engle eyed him warily, awkwardly extending his hand. He was prevented from doing so by his handcuffs. Beside the cuff on his right hand, Bennett could see a yellow wristband. All wrist identification bands were color-coded. Yellow. Engle was a problem of some kind, either medical, psychological or security. As Engle took the seat that he was motioned to at the table, Bennett saw the letters KS imprinted on the band, shorthand for "keep separate."

"Call me Bobby," Engle said.

His teeth were yellow, cigarette-stained, his breath fetid. Long fingers displayed dirty fingernails he began to bite as soon as he sat down. Bennett could not fault his appearance. Inmates had limited access to anything that could be sharpened to a point, and that included toothbrushes. Showers were taken weekly, not daily. Bennett was always amused to see squeaky-clean inmates depicted in movies. His clients usually didn't look or smell acceptable until they were "dressed out" for court appearances.

"Bobby, do you understand the charges against you? They're the most serious there are. Murder with special circumstances. That means you could get the death penalty."

"Yeah. They're saying a kid was killed and I had something to do with it."

"No. They're saying a kid was killed and you murdered her."

Bennett used the word "murder" purposely. Engle had no visible reaction to it.

"We can talk about the offense itself some other time

if you want. There are a couple of things I need to cover with you right away."

"Like what?" Engle inquired defensively.

"Like don't bullshit me or lie to me. If you do, you're wasting my time and my investigator's time. I don't like wild-goose chases. And if the D.A. catches you in a lie, it's all over. If there's something you don't want to tell me, tell me you don't want to tell me. I can deal with that. Second, I don't know if you've admitted anything about this offense to anyone or even talked to anyone about the case. But I'm telling you, from this point on I don't want you talking to anyone, and I mean anyone. There's only one person you can trust. Me. You talk to the friendly guy in the next cell, you decide things are dull and you feel like bragging about your experiences, pick some other topic. Because I can assure you the guy in the next cell is interested in only one thing—himself. He'll run right to the D.A. and sell what you tell him for a deal. And for a conviction on you, the D.A. will deal. Do you have any questions so far?"

Engle didn't answer. He stared stonily at Bennett.

"Bobby, are you understanding what I'm saying?"

"Sure am."

"Is there anything you want to ask me?"

"Not really."

"Your arraignment was continued so we could connect. Today I just wanted to introduce myself, see if you have any questions. Do you understand the arraignment is the time for you to tell the court how you're going to plead?"

"Yeah. That guy in the courtroom explained it all to me."

"You mean the deputy public defender?"

"Uh-huh."

"I need to look through the police reports, Bobby, and review the forensic results, and then we'll meet again before the arraignment. By the way, are you under the care of any doctor or psychiatrist?"

Engle shifted uneasily and hooked his elbow over the back of his chair, his body leaning into the table.

"I'm not crazy, Bennett."

"Who thinks you are?"

"The shrinks you're going to have take a look at me."

"Bobby, don't concern yourself with what any psychiatrist might think. They can give you false impressions, especially if they're trying to draw information out of you that you don't want to give. Have you ever been seen by any psychiatrist before?"

"Yes. Two skinny women. I didn't like either of them, so I spent all my time talking to myself."

"I'll need to find the reports they made. Was it in the last year they saw you?"

"Uh . . . no. When I was arrested way back."

"Okay. I'll get it all when I go through your file and pull up your history. Anything else?"

"Any chance I can get out of here?"

"It's a capital case, Bobby. You're being held without bail. The chances of getting you out are nonexistent. I'll try to get back to you tomorrow. Hang in there. It's going to be a long haul. If you need something, you can call me on the phone, collect, at the number on the card I gave you. Don't write to me. Jail security reads everything going out. Okay?"

Bobby was staring blankly at the table. Bennett knew it was no use extending his hand. He gave Engle a pat on the shoulder and checked out at the window, exchanging his plastic card for his own identification card and exiting through the two clanging doors when the signal was activated.

Outside, he took a long, deep breath of fresh air.

13

Bennett arrived at the jail at 8 A.M. the next day, well before the noise level became a factor and before his morning calendar call. He waited patiently for Engle to be brought down, adjusting gradually to the sounds and smells. As he waited he examined a copy of Engle's rap sheet, the official police rundown of his prior arrest record. Given Engle's record, Bennett knew his client would be regarded as a heavy-duty offender. He needed to look at the files of the prior offenses to see how heavy-duty that was.

This morning Engle's eyes were dark-circled. His shoulders slumped and his face looked drawn and fatigued. He moved slowly.

"How are you doing this morning, Bobby?"

"I couldn't sleep last night. Too much noise in the next cell. And I had a bad dream."

"You have them often?"

"Life's a bad dream. And I'm in the center of it."

"Would you like to talk this morning? About the crime you're charged with?"

"You want to know if I did it."

"It would help."

"What if I couldn't remember if I did it?"

Bennett needed to measure his words carefully.

"You mean, would it help your defense?"

"Yeah."

"It depends. Anything you give me will help."

"I remember a little girl's face. And I remember being at my truck."

"Did you do anything to the child whose face you saw?"

"Maybe."

"What might that be? Could you have struck her?"

"I don't really recall anything else."

"But you said you saw her face. Help me out."

"Just her face. It was yellowish, a different color."

"Could you identify this little girl if you saw her again?"

Engle looked wary. "I don't know."

"Bobby, the little girl you are accused of murdering had lots of wounds. Was there a knife?"

Robotlike, he replied, "I remember being mad at her. At this yellow face. And I think I might have hit it with my pliers."

"I have some photos here, Bobby. I'd like you to look at them for me and tell me if you see that face here."

Bennett removed from an envelope a set of ten black-and-white, five-by-seven glossy photos of different little girls and placed them in a row in front of Engle.

"Maybe." Engle's robotlike stand prevailed as his fingers came to rest on each photo. He worked his way down the line of pictures, reciting his reaction the way one might pick the petals off a daisy. "Maybe not," he said carefully. "Maybe, but I'm not sure."

Bennett leaned forward. "Don't bullshit me. Answer my questions," he whispered. Engle's mouth puckered and tightened, stretching into a smirk. He stared at the pictures for what seemed a full minute, then pointed haltingly at the corner of one of them. His eyes were bright and his entire body was taut now, Bennett noted. He turned the photo over for Engle to see the name "Kelly Solomon" printed neatly on the back. It was then that he noticed Engle had become tumescent.

Bennett had been hoping he could believe in Engle's innocence. That belief would inject a formidable level of energy, of electricity, into the case, into him; running his workdays into night into day again. It could turn the will to prevail into a passion to vindicate. There was no feeling like it except perhaps, he had always surmised, the belief on the part of a good prosecutor that a defendant was guilty and deserved nothing less than death. Put those two people in the courtroom toe to toe and you'd see the Constitution incarnate. The stage might have been set with Engle. Bennett knew Judith Thornton was handling the People's case. She would have been a challenge if Engle were innocent. But this would be no struggle for vindication or virtuous principle.

Engle was guilty.

Bennett knew what the psychological tests would reveal. He was defending a parent's worst nightmare: the guy the system let slip through, the guy who should have been caught up with long before this.

But whatever Bennett's personal feelings, they counted for nothing. They would be buried under the weight of his responsibility. He was going to defend a child killer, and to the public, he would be something just below pond scum. A great attorney, maybe, but a shitty excuse for a human being—or at least that was what that woman must have thought, the juror who voted to acquit his last client of child abuse, then walked past them in the hallway, recognized Bennett and spit. Not at his client. At him.

"Bobby, I'll see you tomorrow morning. They'll bring you to court and the judge will ask how you want to plead. We'll be entering a not-guilty plea for you, and we'll get a date for what's called a preliminary hearing. That's when a judge decides if there's enough of a case to hold you for trial. But tomorrow's simple, and I'll see you in court and answer any questions you might have. Do you have any questions for me right now?"

"Will the television people be there?"

"Maybe."

Engle was smiling.

"No smart-alec stuff in there, Bobby, okay? Got it?"

"Yeah . . . I got it."

Harley Bennett noticed line 2 was blinking. The comm line was his direct link with his secretary, three offices down the hall.

"Collect call, Mr. Bennett."

It was Engle. He was breathing excitedly.

"Mr. Bennett, I decided to do something. I need to tell you about it right away."

He'd just talked with Engle this morning. What course of action could he possibly have decided on so early in the criminal process? The authoritative tone in his voice concerned Bennett.

"I'll try to find some time this afternoon, Bobby. It's not going to be easy, though."

Bennett glanced at his calendar. This was a particularly bad day to try to work a lengthy discussion with Bobby into his schedule. After talking with Engle this morning, he'd had a probation revocation hearing in one of the courtrooms at the Stanton Hotel, followed by a preliminary hearing eight blocks away on the third floor of the county courthouse and then an appearance on a restraining order at the family-law building six blocks north of the courthouse. This afternoon's schedule was no better. Two hearings scheduled in different courtrooms at the same time. At least they were in the same building.

Increasingly, the courtrooms were being spread all over downtown. There was no money to build a new, more efficient courthouse, so the court grew where it could afford the rent, expanding into any available space in the city, including old, half-empty hotels and even gyms. No one, not judge, attorney or juror, knew precisely where he might be sent at any particular moment, nor for how long a period of time. New judges who had no permanent courtroom had to move to whichever one was vacant. They were assigned a shopping cart along with their casebooks to facilitate their moves. Only a month earlier, the Board of Supervisors had requisitioned ten new shopping carts for the court.

Engle's request to see Bennett had an air of urgency about it, and despite the difficulty in scheduling a meeting, Bennett's instincts dictated he should make personal contact with his client as soon as possible.

When he arrived at the jail conference room, Bobby was already down and waiting. The lack of daylight had not yet begun to bleach his face of color. But he had an energy Bennett had not seen before.

"Mr. Bennett," he announced, "I want to plead guilty."

Nothing much ever surprised Bennett, but guilty? He had heard of cases where the defendant wanted to die and resisted appellate review after a guilty verdict. But he had never represented a client in a capital case who had capitulated before trial to dying in the gas chamber.

It was out of the question. Bennett hadn't yet

scratched the surface of the offense, the circumstances of its commission and what it was that had driven Bobby Engle to commit the crime. Somewhere in the morass of autopsy materials and Bobby's background lay the answer to the puzzle, perhaps, but he needed more time to ferret it out. Even if Engle pleaded guilty to the crime and even if he admitted the special circumstances charged, there would still have to be a trial to decide if the death penalty applied.

"Do you understand, Bobby, the significance of what you're telling me you want to do?"

"I think so. This is one decision I want to be mine alone."

"I don't think you do understand." There was silence before Bennett spoke again. "I don't know what's brought this about. Tell me."

"I did it. Is that a good enough reason? I can tell you some details—the ones I can remember. How I did it. If the law says I die, I die. If I'm freed, I'll kill people until they catch me again."

"Bobby, it's not that simple, even if you plead guilty. The law punishes—it's supposed to punish—people for what's deserved. But no one, however bad or incurable he is, deserves to die. My God, it's such a violation, a useless, hostile act. Somewhere deep inside you is some good that deserves to be saved."

Bobby's face wrinkled and his mouth puckered. Bennett's first reaction was that he'd moved him to tears, that he'd somehow reached him. He hadn't. Bobby's shrill laughter brought the guards running from the hallway.

"You okay in here?"

"Yes, Mr. Bennett just said something very funny."

Bobby was rubbing his eyes. They had teared up in

his fit of laughter. When he regained his composure, he fliply told Bennett, "You can't stop me."

"I want you to sleep on this, Bobby," the attorney cautioned him. "I advise you strongly not to talk to anyone about this. Do you understand?"

"I'll sleep on it," Engle promised, "assuming I can sleep. But I won't change my mind."

"I'll do everything in my power to prevent you from doing this," Bennett replied firmly.

Their meeting had lasted fifteen minutes. At the end, Bennett emerged, his jaw fixed tightly, his own face drained of color. Although he was going to be late for both of his afternoon appearances, he needed to see the clerk in the criminal presiding department and alert her that the plea the next day would be somewhat complicated.

14

Judge Henry L. Moore was not a person to tangle with in court or on the golf course. He was a short, wiry man who still sported the crew-cut hair style he'd worn in the fifties, when he was president of his fraternity house at USC. His judicial reputation mirrored his demeanor: direct, cutting right to the problem at hand. He could move a lengthy calendar at record speed and leave the bench smiling, unscathed by the frenetic pace it took to keep the wheels of justice turning. Yet if confronted with a challenging legal issue, he had the capacity to immerse himself in the books behind the doors of his chambers and emerge with a scholarly decision. He was a good choice to handle the high-profile capital cases in which conscientious as well as obstreperous attorneys challenged every word, every move, in issues of overwhelming complexity.

As Moore entered the courtroom and took the bench for Engle's arraignment, he glanced quickly at the defense table. Engle had already been brought over from the jail. So far, so good. The defendant was present. No snafus, no miscommunications with the jail.

The news media were all over the courtroom. Moore recognized most of the reporters. Hap was there from the *Star Press*. So was that paper's political affairs writer, Jon Kolker. Moore also recognized the thin, studious young woman sitting alone with tablet out and pencil poised. She was the new political affairs writer for *The Los Angeles Times*. There hadn't been a request to televise these proceedings, but all three major local stations were represented, their field reporters sitting in the front row a respectful distance from one another; hair coiffed, pancake makeup already applied. They were ready for the shoot. They could leave the courtroom after the hearing and go outside to their respective station-remote vans, where, as the Minicams rolled, they would say a sentence or two about what had happened in court that morning. Current film of the defendant wasn't critical. They'd show the file tape tonight that they had shot days earlier, when Engle was first arrested.

It was just as well. Not much was going to happen today, and what *was* going to happen, they wouldn't be allowed to watch. For the press to get hold of any hint of Engle's confession of guilt would be devastating to any future jury selection. It could taint the entire San Diego area and require that the case be sent out of the county for trial.

"Counsel, are you ready to proceed? I'm informed Mr. Bennett wishes to address the court preliminarily."

Bennett, who was seated next to Engle at the defense table, rose. "Your Honor, for the record, I have informed the prosecution that the hearing this morning will be somewhat sensitive, and Mrs. Thornton has stated she will voluntarily excuse herself from it."

Judith agreed. "Your Honor, this matter has been set by Mr. Bennett. The people are making a special appearance to ask that a record be made of all proceedings and sealed for purposes of appellate review. It is our understanding the nature of this hearing is highly sensitive and deals with the possibility the defendant may seek to take action his attorney disagrees with. With those representations, we would request that if this hearing evolves to any other subject matter, we be advised immediately and that we be immediately informed of the date set for any other hearing.''

"Agreed, Ms. Thornton. Let's clear and seal the courtroom, please. And that means the press as well.''

It was one of the peculiarities of criminal law. When the press's First Amendment rights collide with the defendant's right to a fair trial by maintaining confidentiality, the former must yield. Still, Moore never felt comfortable excluding the press from the courtroom. To do so ran against his grain and caused a whole hornet's nest of aggravation in having to sort out the public's right as well as the defendant's. He hoped the press would react mildly or not at all to what was happening.

Normally, a judge might take counsel into his chambers to discuss a matter of great sensitivity. But Moore saw no need for it today. With the D.A.'s attorney gone, no one was left in the courtroom except Bennett, Engle and Moore's courtroom staff. Besides, Moore might want to talk to Engle, and he'd rather do that somewhere other than in his personal chambers.

It took only a moment for Judith to exit and slip down a side stairway. She had no desire to discuss what had transpired with Kolker and his newspaper colleagues, who stood in puzzled excitement in the hallway. As soon as the door closed behind her, the judge leaned forward.

"Counsel, it's my understanding the defendant wishes to enter a guilty plea in this case.''

"Yes, that's correct.''

"Has an offer of some kind been made by the prosecution?" Moore inquired.

"No, Your honor. Mr. Engle wishes to plead guilty to first-degree murder and admit the special circumstances."

"Is that correct, Mr. Engle?"

"Yes, it is, your Honor. I want to plead guilty."

"Mr. Engle, this is highly irregular. Do you understand the implications of this decision?"

"I do, your Honor."

"Your Honor, I wish to speak if I may."

"Certainly, Mr. Bennett."

"My position is simple. As your Honor is aware, California's Penal Code allows a defendant to enter a guilty plea in a capital case only if his attorney consents. As you can imagine, I've had only the most preliminary of discussions with Mr. Engle. As I've explained to him, I have just begun to work on his case, to investigate the murder. I cannot consent to a plea of guilty at this time. In my opinion, it would surely lead him to the death penalty."

"Mr. Engle, what have you to say?"

"Your Honor," Engle stated, "I don't know anything about the law Mr. Bennett is talking about. I don't think it can keep me from telling the court or the whole world that I murdered a kid. No court, no attorney, can keep me from doing that. Only one person should be able to control what I do. Me. Not Mr. Bennett. Not the people of this state. Not you. I have a right to decide my own plea."

With that, Engle folded his arms across his chest. Judge Moore turned his chair away from Bennett and Engle and reached for the Penal Code behind him.

"Mr. Bennett—the section's number?"

"It's 1016, your Honor."

The judge turned his chair again to Bennett and Engle.

"Let's see what this says, Mr. Engle." He leafed through the pages and read silently, gently rocking in his leather bench chair.

"Mr. Engle, on its face, the statute says just what Mr. Bennett says it does."

"If it does, it can't be legal. It sure isn't right and it makes no sense," Engle replied.

Bennett interrupted. "Your Honor, I agree with the court. The statute is clear. The first rule of statutory construction is to follow the plain language of the legislature."

Bennett was purposely catering to Moore's well-known conservative judicial philosophy.

"Your Honor, that law says my attorney can keep me from pleading guilty? If that's true, then why can't I get rid of Mr. Bennett and be my own attorney? I know I can do that, and then I can decide for myself how I want to plead."

Even Bennett was surprised at Engle's knowledge of the law. Either he'd been through this before, which was not likely, or he'd been talking to someone in the jail, which was more probable.

"Mr. Bennett, it appears there are two major questions here," the judge said. "First, can Mr. Engle plead guilty without your consent. Second, whether he is capable of representing himself. Mr. Engle, I'd like you to think about this for a few days. I want you to talk to Mr. Bennett. I can assure you he's an excellent attorney with a great deal of experience. If you want to present a persuasive case to a jury or judge, he can do it for you. I'm going to hand Mr. Bennett a plea form. It outlines everything you're admitting to, what its consequences are and what constitutional rights you are giving up when you plead guilty. Take it with you. Read it, understand it, before you come back into court. Mr. Bennett will help if you need assistance. In fact, I instruct him to go over it with you. I am also giving you this form.'' Moore held up another form with little boxes running along the right-hand side.

''This form outlines what rights you're giving up by representing yourself and sets out what you must demonstrate in court for me to rule you are capable of representing yourself. We'll set another hearing date for day after tomorrow, at eight-fifteen, and consider your requests at that time. I want to tell you I do not enter into this lightly, Mr. Engle. Do you give up your right to enter your plea today so you can think about this?''

Engle sighed and shrugged. ''Okay, Judge. I'll read the forms.'' He turned to Bennett. ''But I won't change my mind.''

It was hard enough to defend a guilty man. It was impossible to defend a guilty man over whom you'd lost control.

Bennett had to get a fast handle on Engle. He needed to know whether the man was hell-bent on suicide or just out to manipulate the system and everyone in it, Bennett included, and perhaps escape by virtue of creating as much chaos as he could. The thought that this action might simply be the product of a repentant man was quickly considered and as quickly dismissed.

Not Engle.

Engle was guilty, and there was not a shred of remorse in anything he had said or how he had said it; there was nothing but self-gratification. For the time being, Bennett had no desire to discuss with him the details of or motivations for the crime. That would come later, and it would have to come from others who knew him better than he knew himself and from experts who could psychologically dissect the man. The most immediate need was to determine what was motivating Bobby's request to plead guilty. Beyond that lay another, personal obligation even more fundamental to the case. Bennett needed to find a convincing reason that the law should spare Bobby's life. It was important not only for purposes of assembling the evidence for trial. Bennett had to persuade himself such a reason existed before he could hope to persuade a jury to spare his client.

15

Bennett wanted two things right now. He wanted to talk with Engle's family and he wanted a psychological evaluation that combined testing and family history. It wouldn't be enough to put a defense together, but it would be enough to get him through the plea stage.

Family history proved scarce except in one respect. Engle's half sister, Penny Reynolds, a marketing executive for a computer firm, lived in Irvine, a bedroom community in Orange County less than two hours north of San Diego.

Penny had agreed to speak with Bennett. He had stressed his need to talk with her was urgent. She in turn assured him what she had to offer would be helpful and wouldn't take long. A meeting over lunch would be sufficient.

They agreed to meet at a mutually convenient coffee shop, close to the office where she worked and just off the freeway. Bennett arrived thirty minutes early so he could review his notes. He left word with the hostess to escort Penny to his table when she arrived.

Penny Reynolds was a tall, poised woman. Her St.

John knit dress affirmed what little Bennett knew about her. She was an articulate career woman who had married well. Yet she displayed no uneasiness in discussing what must have been uncomfortable memories.

"We lived in Texas till Bobby was fifteen. Dad—Bobby's stepdad—was crazy. He finally—mercifully—ran his car off the road into a tree and killed himself. He could be so nice to Mama, but those times were scarce. I don't remember him ever hitting me real bad. But Bobby . . . he treated him differently. He was harder on him. Much harder. If Dad got drunk, he'd get violent. I'd hear him grunting like an animal, hitting and pinching Mom. He'd kick her sometimes. And us too if we got in his way, but especially Bobby. It was like he enjoyed brutalizing that kid. He liked to hunt deer. He'd fire his gun at Bobby's feet. Sometimes Bobby would just stand there with tears running down his cheeks, Dad laughing like it was the funniest thing he'd seen. He'd yell at him to dance. He'd make Bobby go hunting with him, tell him he'd make a man out of him yet. When they'd come back with a kill, poor little Bobby. His eyes would be so red and puffy. You know, I'll never forget—once Dad was so drunk, he took Bobby into the bedroom; you could hear the thuds and whacks. He beat him so badly. It was just inhuman! I ran in finally and there was poor Bobby hung up by his hands on the bedpost. All he could say when I pulled him away was, 'I hate her. I hate *her.*' I thought for a time he was mixed up. But he meant he hated Mama."

"Your mother's dead?" Bennett asked.

"Yes, two years now. You know, sometimes she was right there during the beatings. She'd watch them happening and do nothing."

"Bobby talked to you about that?"

"Yes, he did. I know Bobby loved her. But I confess,

I still can't understand how she could let Dad brutalize us like he did. You know, Bobby would go into his room sometimes and cry and cry. I'd go in and hug him. I'd find him sitting in the dark in the closet. I had my schoolwork. I was a good student. Actually, Bobby was really smarter and more creative, but he couldn't concentrate on school. He didn't have anything to hold onto. Eventually he began stealing. He was depressed almost all the time and was absent a lot from school. Then he just dropped out and drifted a while from job to job. He never had a chance, not from the get-go.''

"Do you think Bobby could kill a little girl?" Bennett asked.

Penny waited a long time before speaking, and then avoided a direct response.

"The thing I remember most vividly about Bobby was, one afternoon he and I and a few of the neighborhood kids were upstairs and we started teasing our old cat, just playful, you know. The cat scratched Bobby and he just picked it up and started twisting its head. Out of the blue. And the look on his face was so awful. Like that cat was all the bad things in the world. My feelings about him changed that afternoon. He definitely had a different side, a side that got happiness out of inflicting pain on others. It was like he wanted to have control over something, even up the sides. He had such anger inside him, really explosive anger. He got hurt so often, I suppose he stopped caring who or what he hurt.''

"I'm curious—"

She wasn't ready to break her train of thought just yet, and ignored Bennett's attempt to refocus their conversation.

"There was another time . . . this isn't pretty, Mr. Bennett. But Bobby . . . he took some kittens, little things about ten weeks old . . . up to our roof in a bag and—'' She stopped, and for a moment Bennett thought she would not finish the story.

"And what?" Bennett asked.

"He . . . he threw them off."

"What?" Bennett said, stricken by Engle's cruelty.

"He . . . threw them off. One at a time."

"But why?"

"To see which one survived."

Bennett fell silent, reflecting on the significance of her memory.

"Mr. Bennett, you were asking about . . ."

"Religion. . . ."

"Are you kidding? He said reason was his only God."

"Are there any old girlfriends who might be willing to testify?"

"Girlfriends? Bobby never had any girlfriends as far back as I can remember. Ever."

"Did he have any serious injuries as a child that might have caused brain damage?"

"Nothing was ever medically diagnosed, but Dad hit him so badly, it wouldn't surprise me if there was some kind of organic brain damage." She laughed. "Every month or so Bobby had an accident. I think he'd broken both legs before he was sixteen. Nothing I can think of, though, that would cause the kind of damage you're talking about. Unless there was something wrong that caused him to be accident-prone. I think he put himself in danger all the time. Once we went to the beach and he wouldn't come out of the waves. He'd gone in too far. He was about twelve or thirteen then. The waves were really high. Mom kept yelling for him to come out. But he wouldn't. Just like—defying the waves, playing with them, daring them. Dad finally went in and grabbed him by the hair and dragged him out, shaking him and slapping him all the way. Bobby was grinning—freezing cold, but so happy with himself, totally defiant.''

''Would you be willing to tell a jury the things you've just told me?''

''I haven't seen Bobby in probably five years, but I'll do whatever I can to keep him from dying, no matter how bad this might be.'' She grew reflective. ''This little girl. Do *you* think he killed her?''

''I think he deserves the best defense I can give him whether or not he killed her.''

During his career Harley Bennett had defended parents with one healthy child thriving in cleanliness while another child starved to death in a filthy bedroom. It could be like that. He had seen the damage selectively struck within the family. The damage leveled at Bobby Engle had indeed been selective and no doubt was the major factor in his demented view of the world.

When he was through defending Engle, people would ask Harley Bennett how children raised in the same family could turn out as differently as Penny and Bobby. The answer, he would point out rather matter-of-factly, was that they lived in the same house but they were not raised the same way. As objectively as he could, Bennett would now assemble the Engle family history and forward it to the psychologist he normally consulted for a read on his clients.

Psychologist Evelyn Cross was a heavyset woman with jet-black hair that she pulled up into a beehive configuration. She'd been practicing in San Diego as long as anyone in the court system could remember. It wasn't the ''Golden Days,'' as she now referred to her practice of two decades earlier. Back then, the police would bring arrestees right to her office as soon as they were picked up, even before they'd talked with an attorney. If it was cold outside, she'd have them take a seat in the sitting room of her office, make them hot chocolate, bring them cookies and talk with them. If she got to them close enough to the time of a murder, she'd usually get an accurate picture of them before they were told not to say anything and were locked away in the psychologically repressive county jail.

But those days had been over for some time. Dwindling funds and suspicious defense attorneys armed with procedural rules had put an end to the days when she could spend six hours at a time with a person, administering a battery of twelve tests, unlocking the secret lives of sex molesters and murderers. Now she was lucky if she spent two hours with an arrestee; barely enough time to give the standard Binet-Gestalt, the Rorschach and the person-tree-house drawing test. She sought relief for her frustrations by shopping at Nordstrom's in Horton Plaza, where she minnowed through the jewelry and scarves, looking for items to add to her extensive collections of both.

No, it wasn't like the good old days, but she could still get a good picture of how a person's brain was working. It made no difference who hired her. She shot straight and played no favorites. That was why Harley Bennett sought her out. If she had enough data, she could give him a clear picture of Bobby Engle before the next court date, and some advice on how he should handle his client.

"Downwell, Robert Engle!"

In the humid, smelly interview cubicle, she set up her tape recorder and readied her pencil and yellow lined notepad. She positioned the two cubicle chairs next to each other at the end of the rectangular table, the one on the right for her and the one to her left for Engle. The tabletop, like everything around her in the jail, had been brutalized, half of its white Formica top pulled or ripped off, exposing the wood beneath.

Engle was delivered to her in handcuffs, which would remain on him. She was permitted to talk to him in privacy, but a guard was nearby. Although she'd had a few close calls, she'd never been assaulted. No inmate would dare to physically challenge her rock-hard demeanor. No, the battle in this room was of a more subtle nature.

"Good morning, Mr. Engle."

"What's so good about it? Have you looked around here?"

She reflected momentarily, then issued a missive of her own.

"You're right. It stinks in here. My name is Evelyn Cross. I'm a licensed psychologist, and Mr. Bennett— your attorney—asked me to talk with you, administer some tests to you too. Can I ask the guard for a cup of coffee for you?"

"No."

"Fine. Let's get down to business, then, shall we? I've had a chance to look at the police reports on the case . . ."

As she talked, she watched in fascination as Engle inserted an inquiring index finger into his right nostril, studied his findings and rolled the product into a pill-shaped object. Suddenly he flicked it toward her, the way one would shoot a marble. It missed.

"That wasn't exactly polite, Mr. Engle. And it was wide to the left."

"What wasn't . . . what did you say? Polite?"

"I said . . . flying snot isn't polite."

She hadn't flinched.

Engle smiled and pulled his chair closer to the edge of the table. She moved hers farther to the right.

"We have a lot of work to do, Mr. Engle, in a very

short period of time. I'd like you to take these three pieces of paper. On the first, draw a picture of a person; on the second, a tree; and then a house on the third.''

She suddenly felt his sandled foot on top of her shoe. As she moved her foot away, his followed. She fixed a disapproving eye on him, lifted her foot and smacked it on top of his.

Engle's response was to draw his legs up onto the chair in a coiled position, his tongue darting in and out of his mouth at her.

"Stop that at once! Cut out this nonsense!" she demanded as she rose and tapped sharply on the cubicle glass with her pencil, finally getting the attention of a guard seated on a bench outside. The man looked surprised as she beckoned to him with her index finger, but he came at once, leaving behind the records he had been working on.

"Will you sit in here until I'm finished with this person? He's not behaving in a civilized way and is contaminating the session with obscenities that are not in his best interests.''

Her low, raspy voice was too authoritative for the guard to challenge her request. He asked no questions, nodded affirmatively and pulled up another chair.

Engle, smiling at her, quickly put his feet back on the floor and began drawing.

It did not take Evelyn Cross long to assess the arrestee. Her telephone call to Harley Bennett followed quickly on the heels of her meeting with Engle at the jail.

"Harley? Yes, hello . . . I have talked with, observed and tested our Bobby Engle. I got your notes on your meeting with the sister and I looked at them too. You have as clear a psychopathic personality as I've ever had occasion to examine. He hasn't the slightest remorse or sense of guilt about anything he does or has done. The personal family profile is there too, but you saw that, of course. Brutal stepfather. Weak, abusive mother. No life rafts anywhere. Another tragedy causing same.''

"Did you get anything resembling remorse from him, Evie?''

"Nothing. He was too busy putting the make on me.''

"I trust you handled *that* all right.''

"I handled it.

"I can work with him for you if you'd like. My opinion is, he *does* want to plead guilty. In fact, he's enjoying this, you know. But he clearly doesn't think much of anyone, including himself. I'd also have them watch him carefully at the jail. Murder like this, sadism, is the act of striking out, but it's also the act of murdering the self. I'll get you a written report on it all.''

"Thanks, Evie. I've got a pretty good idea of what I'm dealing with, and it'll all be helpful if we get to the penalty phase. If he continues to insist on a guilty plea, I just hope I can persuade the judge to reject it.''

"When you get my report and look it over, let me know if you want to talk more. I've got to go. I've got a doctor's appointment in precisely twenty minutes.''

"You're okay?''

"I've got an ulcer. The doctor prescribed some blue pill that cost me seventy-two dollars for twenty-one of them. I can't afford myself anymore.''

Bennett wouldn't need to talk to her again until after Engle entered his plea. Between his talk with Penny Reynolds and Evelyn Cross's interview, he had enough background information on Engle to know the man did want to die and to understand why he wanted to die.

16

Rail-thin and pale, Lydia Dodd was a courtroom veteran with a haircut that looked as if someone had put a bowl over her head and clipped around the edges of her thin, straight blond hair. She had been Judge Moore's clerk for fifteen years. Like any experienced clerk, she catered to his likes and protected him from his dislikes. His strengths she emphasized; his weaknesses she filled in with her own abilities.

This morning she was seated at her desk, next to the judge's bench.

It was eight-forty-five. The judge was in but was uncharacteristically late. He routinely buzzed her comm line promptly at eight-fifteen to see if the parties were ready to proceed. This, though, was not a normal morning. They were beginning another death penalty case. Nothing would be quick, easy or routine at any step of the way.

Clerk Dodd sat patiently with Bennett, Engle and the bailiff, waiting for some sign from the judge. Judith Thornton was still voluntarily absent from the courtroom.

At eight-fifty, the clerk looked up and realized Judge Moore was standing at the open door in the back hallway, waiting to enter the courtroom. She snapped to attention and nodded to the bailiff, who was standing in the well of the courtroom, the area between the bench and the railing beyond which the audience sat. The well was sacred territory into which one came only by first asking permission of the court.

"Remain seated and come to order." Because the courtroom had been cleared for the Engle case, the deputy dispensed with the more formal salutation of "All rise." The courtroom was again sealed, the prosecutor absent. This time the windows had been covered with brown paper to keep the curious and the press completely shut out.

The judge quickly ascended the three steps to his bench.

"We're on the record in the Engle case. Good morning, Mr. Bennett, Mr. Engle. The record can reflect all necessary parties are present. We're here to consider what I understand to be Mr. Engle's request to enter a plea of guilty to the charges. Is that correct, Mr. Bennett?"

"Yes, your Honor, that's correct. And for the record, my position has not changed from what it was at our last hearing. I am opposed to any plea of guilty at this time. I've talked to Mr. Engle at length, explained my opposition to his plea and discussed the facts of his case."

"Mr. Engle? Do you wish to address the court?"

"Everything Mr. Bennett says is true, Judge. And if the court will not let me plead guilty, I want to be my own attorney and I will make the decision to plead guilty for myself."

"Well, Mr. Engle—"

"Judge, it's really simple. I killed that girl. I don't want a trial."

Engle had done what certainly no attorney dared to do. He had interrupted Judge Moore. Bennett could hear Moore's pencil tapping on the bench top.

"Mr. Engle, please do not discuss the facts of your case just yet. The court understands your position."

"I don't think you do, Judge."

Moore leaned forward and pointed his pencil at Engle.

"You are incorrect, young man. I understand you perfectly."

"Then how can you turn down my confession? I did it. Would it help if I supplied more details? I can give you a blow-by-blow description."

Moore's pencil tapping was now audible throughout the courtroom. His clerk and bailiff were looking at each other. Bennett put his hand on Engle's shoulder. Only the court reporter, charged with recording every word spoken, typed on, with no visible reaction to anything being said.

Engle continued. "What is a plea, Judge? Isn't it my chance to get this off my chest? It's my chance to tell you all if I did it. Doesn't the law let me do that? What control do I have over my own life in this courtroom if I can't do that? And how about the mother of that girl I killed? Don't I get to tell her I did it? Think of what she's going through." Engle ended with a hint of a smile.

"Mr. Engle, I don't want you to say another word."

There was a pause as Moore shifted to a conciliatory tone.

"Mr. Engle, let me try to explain. It's not as simple as you may think or as simple as any of us may want. People plead guilty for many reasons. Some because they *are* guilty. Some may not be guilty, but they choose not to go through a trial. And that's all right. The law allows for both. But the law says no one—no one—no matter what his motive, should be allowed to plead guilty unless he knows what he's doing and why. So the court—that's me this morning—looks closely at any attempt to plead guilty to determine if it is knowing, intelligent and voluntary. If *one* of these is not there, the law will not *allow* me to take a guilty plea from you. Do you understand that?"

"No. In a word, Judge, no. Voluntary or knowing or not, I did it."

"And God may punish you one day for your sin, Mr. Engle. I'm not God. I'm not concerned here, now, with your sins."

Engle cocked his head slightly to the side.

"And if there is no God, Judge?"

"Then our laws are more important than ever, Mr. Engle." Moore made the statement without so much as a pause. He thought he had won the sparring match, at least temporarily. But you would never have known it by looking at the grin developing on Engle's face.

"Now, Mr. Engle, have you examined the papers I gave you at the end of your last appearance here?"

"I have, Judge."

"Then let's go through them, if we may, starting with your right to represent yourself."

Moore had decided to first consider whether Engle could discharge Bennett and represent himself. Thereafter he would decide if Engle, represented or not, could give up his right to a jury trial.

The judge had before him a litany of rights Engle would be giving up by choosing to act as his own attorney.

"Mr. Engle, has anyone attempted to persuade you to represent yourself?"

"No."

"This is your decision alone?"

"It is, yes."

"Have you discussed this with your attorney, Mr. Bennett?"

"Yeah, and he's against it."

"Tell me in your own words why you wish to be your own attorney."

"Because I want to plead guilty and I want to control this thing."

"What do you mean by 'this thing'?"

"The trial here."

"There is an old adage that a person who represents himself has an ass for a client. Do you understand that saying? I don't mean to make light of you in any way, Mr. Engle, but . . . ."

"I understand it. It means I won't know what I'm doing."

"Mr. Engle, have you ever represented yourself in a courtroom before?"

"Yes, I have."

"What was the nature of the proceedings?"

"A traffic ticket."

"A traffic ticket. . . . Well, Mr. Engle, do you understand this is a death penalty trial? Actually, there are two trials we're talking about here. One to decide guilt, one to decide punishment. And you'd have to pick a jury if you want a jury."

"Uh-huh."

"You need to answer yes or no so the reporter can take it down. 'Uh-huh' can't be spelled well by the reporter. Now, what does voir dire mean, Mr. Engle? If I were to say you may conduct your voir dire, would you know what I was talking about?"

"No."

"How about cross-examination? Direct testimony? Rebuttal? *In limine* motion. Sustained, overruled? Any of those terms familiar to you?"

"No, none of them, Judge."

Moore's questioning slowed. The pace had been too fast. On the record, it might appear he hadn't been thoughtful enough in questioning Engle.

"Do you understand there will be no one to help you except an advisory attorney, if you want one, and he can't present the case for you? The prosecution won't help you if you start making a fool of yourself, and I can't help you either."

"I know, but it doesn't make a difference to me, none at all."

The judge continued to methodically hammer at Engle, if not getting him to change his mind, then making for himself a solid record if there were ever an appeal. After thirty minutes of inquiry, Moore had finished his exploration of Engle's knowledge of the law and of his education and work history, which were scant at best. Bennett added nothing to the discussion. This was between the judge and Engle. Bennett was confident Engle could be found to be acting voluntarily and knowingly. Whether he was acting intelligently was a riskier proposition. Bennett would bet money the court would find he was not acting intelligently and would not allow him to represent himself. In Bennett's experience, judges as a lot abhorred having to deal with pro per defendants— people representing themselves—bumbling around in even minor cases. In a death penalty case it would be a nightmare increasing everyone's workload and the possibility of an error that was so prejudicial to the defendant that a new trial might be ordered. Moore would lean heavily toward resolving doubts against allowing self-representation.

"Mr. Engle, the court is convinced your intelligence is adequate and your desire to be your own attorney is voluntary. I am not convinced, however, that you are knowingly and intelligently giving up your constitutional right to counsel. I will let the record speak for itself. You will be at a distinct disadvantage if you represent yourself in a matter this complicated. You haven't the slightest idea of the mechanics of presenting a jury trial. You would be wholly inept. I am therefore denying your request to represent yourself. Mr. Bennett will remain as your attorney. Now, on the question of your entering a plea of guilty while represented by Mr. Bennett. He refuses to allow it. I must agree with that decision. The Penal Code of California section 1016 specifically prohibits a plea of guilty by you, Mr. Engle, unless your attorney agrees to it, and he does not agree to it. Your request to enter a guilty plea is denied. Do you wish to enter a plea at this time?"

"Yes, Judge. Guilty. Like I said."

"I have ruled that is not acceptable. At this time a not-guilty plea will be entered for you and special circumstances will be entered as denied. We need to confirm your preliminary hearing date. Do you want more than the usual thirty days, Mr. Bennett?"

"Thirty days will be fine, your Honor."

"Okay, Mr. Bennett. The preliminary hearing is set for thirty days from today. This record will remain sealed pending further order of the court. Anything else?"

Engle, smiling, shook his head.

Bennett stood.

"Yes, your Honor. On behalf of Mr. Engle, I wish to exercise his right to have a second attorney appointed who would serve as co-counsel for him. We would ask for Alan Larson. He is a class five. As your Honor is aware, under Penal Code section 987.9, the appointment of a second attorney is discretionary with the court. We are also requesting the mandatory appointment of trial experts to assist the defense, both in psychological and in investigative services, as well as an expert to assist in selecting a jury.''

With these first requests for money, the capital case against Robert Dean Engle was born.

Bennett knew it. The judge knew it. It was a giant money machine geared to one thing only: preventing the death of Robert Engle.

In short order, the flow of money would start to feed the case at an amount held strictly confidential. Not even the trial judge would be privy to how, specifically, county funds were being allocated and to whom. A second judge would be appointed to monitor monies given the defense. The reasoning was that to release the costs would improperly make the defendant divulge his trial strategy. Bennett could recall only one San Diego case where the total cost had been released after the defendant had been found guilty, and those figures were available only because the defendant had committed suicide in prison; with his death, there had no longer been a viable argument that confidentiality was somehow needed to protect him. That trial alone had cost the county in the millions. In another case where the death penalty had been asked for but not imposed by the judge, the costs released had been a staggering six million dollars.

In truth, no one really knew how much capital punishment was costing the counties or the state. And Bennett was certain no one wanted to examine the cost. Everyone's interests were best protected by looking the other way. The prosecutors didn't want the public to see what the costs were lest they risk someone's asking whether the punishment was worth the costs, and the defense didn't want the costs known lest they incur the wrath of the public for enriching the coffers of experts whose assistance was being billed at as much as two hundred fifty to three hundred dollars an hour.

"Mr. Larson is hearby appointed. As for your other requests, please make them in writing, Mr. Bennett; you know the routine. Do you wish to state anything for the record, Mr. Engle?"

"You mean you're really going to give me *two* attorneys, Judge? I only want one; I mean, I don't *even* want one."

"I'm not in any position to deny the requests, Mr. Engle. I'll expect all assistance requests to be directed to the court within two weeks, Mr. Bennett, under the confidentiality statutes in the Penal Code."

"Yes, your Honor. May I speak with my client very briefly before he's taken back to the jail?"

"Certainly, Mr. Bennett. In the jury box there. Court is in recess."

With that, Moore left the bench as quickly as he'd ascended to it.

Bennett huddled with Engle as two courtroom deputies stood close by, but far enough away to assure Bennett privacy with his client.

"Mr. Bennett, I don't believe it. I stand here, I say I did it, and the judge says I can't plead guilty and gives me *two* attorneys and all the help I want." Engle was amused by it all, smiling, even chuckling.

Bennett tried again to explain there were good reasons for the law's requirement there be an appearance of justice; that the technical rights were as important as their substance. It didn't phase Engle. If he understood, he didn't care.

After Judge Moore left the bench, his clerk called the next case and took her written notes on the Engle matter to him. She rapped gently on the door to his chambers and entered, as was her custom, without waiting for a response.

"Counsel is ready in the next case, Judge. I brought the notes on Engle."

Moore was looking out the window, its glass thick with dust and dirt. He spoke without looking away.

"You know, Lydia, there's so much lying and maneuvering in that courtroom. And out there a few minutes ago was probably the truth. He said, 'I did it. Let's get this over with.' And I had to reject it."

"Well, Judge, if you ask me, I just think it's like he said. He did it, and the whole system seems cockeyed to me too." She caught herself. "But what do I know? I'm sure there's more to it than that. There's the statute. You just can't second-guess yourself."

"I'm not second-guessing myself, Lydia. Sometimes I'm just not sure if what I'm saying out there and what I believe are the same thing."

"Well, if they were, you wouldn't be a very good judge."

"I guess that makes me a pretty good one, then. I'm going to take a fifteen-minute break before the next case. Tell counsel they can go get a cup of coffee."

"I'd be happy to, Judge." She was almost out the door when he abruptly, almost absentmindedly, resumed the conversation.

"You know, Lydia, I took a big chance out there. That man may not have the technical legal skills to be his own attorney, but he understands what's going on. I'm not sure the law's on my side in denying his right to be his own attorney and throw himself on the mercy of the jury."

"Well, it's out of your hands now, Judge. You have to trust the system's going to do the rest."

"The question, Lydia, is whether the system can deal with him at all. I just hope to God I haven't been the one to push the flusher that's going to send this case down the toilet four years from now."

PART THREE

THE VICTIM

17

⬥

Coffee cups and files so thoroughly littered the circular walnut table that barely a hint of its glossiness showed through between the pages. The prosecution team—Judith, Farrell, Pike and Abrams—had assembled in the turkey-shoot room, nicknamed such because it was used once a week by the trial staff to decide which of the pending trials were so bad, were such gobblers, that they should be disposed of by dismissal or plea bargaining. Now, the day after Engle's not-guilty plea had been entered, decisions had to be made. The course of the trial strategy needed to be set.

"I've been through this with all of you individually," Judith began, trying to sound informal. "We may lose our best evidence when Bennett challenges the search. If that happens, we have a very weak case. I'll put it to you bluntly because I have to. How do you feel about plea-bargaining the case at this point? Do we want to consider telling Engle we'll drop the capital punishment charge in return for a guilty plea to first-degree murder and life without the possibility of parole?"

"You're assuming Bennett will allow a plea bargain.

Would you if you were Bennett?'' Abrams asked.

Pike and Judith answered in unison. ''No.''

''Neither would I,'' Abrams responded. ''Besides, Bennett's already opposed a plea bargain. That tells you something about where he's coming from.''

Farrell had said nothing. When he did speak, what he said was characteristically brief and direct. ''If we can keep the evidence in through the preliminary hearing, we have a slam-dunk case. If we don't, we have a weak one. We've had weak cases before.'' He looked at Judith. ''And we've won them.'' There was an understanding silence between them before he continued. ''It's too early. Let's see if we draw a judge who's bold enough to look Deborah Solomon in the eye and kick the evidence.''

''As I see it, Judith,'' Abrams said, ''aside from the purely tactical considerations, it would be a public relations nightmare to offer a plea bargain so early. Can you imagine, after the media circus this has caused, trying to explain why we are willing to drop the death penalty? I don't think we have any choice. We go forward with it. Maybe later we talk again if we lose the evidence.''

Abrams was right. There was no choice, even if the evidence looked as bleak as it did to all of them. Disaster might loom on the horizon, but the direction was dead ahead.

''Okay, it's decided, then,'' Judith said. ''We proceed on to prelim. I'll start assembling our initial witness list. While we're here, can you give us an update, Pike, on the status of the investigation?''

''Mike and I are trying to reconstruct where Engle was during the week before and after Kelly Solomon disappeared. It's not easy. We can't put him close to the girl. We've started interviewing the city park personnel assigned to the area around the field, and the Cal Trans employees who had been restriping the freeway overpass the day she disappeared. Maybe someone saw something unusual. It's going to take a while. We have a list of about seventy-five people. We're just starting at the top and working down.''

It was inevitable. They would have found her name in the maze of potential witnesses. After every potential item of evidence was collected at the field, they would begin to broaden the scope of the search to include examination of every name on every list of every agency whose employees worked in the area of the murder scene. They would have found Niki Crawford sooner or later. She was number thirty-five on the list of agency employees who might have seen something unusual.

Any discussion with her was probably going to be routine and uneventful. Just like the thirty-four before her. But there was something about her voice when Pike called to arrange an interview. It was halting and noncommittal at first. She had maybe seen a strange car. Then her voice became self-assured. She had no evidence to offer. It would be of no use talking to her, she explained. But Pike finally persuaded her to let him talk with her and show her some photos.

Niki Crawford lived in a small Spanish-style stucco house along one of the canyons in Mission Hills. The brown paint on the front wood beams was beginning to peel, and some of the red tiles on the roof had shifted. Through the white lace window curtains Pike could make out the form of a young woman sitting in an overstuffed chair, reading a book. She saw him and the other man as well, rising and moving toward the door before they could knock or ring the bell. When the door opened, a short, muscular woman stood before them. Her blond hair was drawn into a ponytail and secured by a rubber band at the nape of her neck.

"What can I do for you officers?" Her voice was softer than Pike would have expected.

"Miss Crawford? I'm Detective Pike Martin from the San Diego Police Department. I spoke with you earlier. This is Sergeant Abrams. We're investigating the murder of the little girl I told you about, Kelly Solomon. You may have read about her in the newspaper or heard about the murder on TV. Her body was found in the field off Interstate 8 near the 805 overpass."

"Well, yes. We've all been talking about it. I'm familiar with the area. I'm sorry, but I'm not going to be able to help you out."

"Sergeant Abrams and I have been assigned to investigate the murder, and quite frankly, at this point we don't have a lot of information about how the murder occurred. Any information we can get would be helpful. Mind if we sit down?"

"Okay, I suppose. This won't take too long, will it?"

"No," Pike replied, moving toward the couch. "We just have a few standard questions."

Niki remained standing until both officers were seated next to each other on the couch. Then she walked over to a small dinette table and took a seat on one of the wooden chairs, ignoring the stuffed chair nearest the couch. Even though the dining table was only ten or twelve feet away, she had placed a noticeable distance between herself and the officers.

"The field where the body was found is in your patrol territory," Pike began. "Do you remember seeing anything unusual or suspicious in or near the field during the first part of September? Anything. Even simple things could be very important."

"No," she said curtly.

"Maybe this will help." Pike reached into the breast

pocket of his jacket, got up and handed Niki the three photos he now carried around like someone else would carry children's photos: Kelly Solomon's fourth-grade school photo, Robert Engle's booking photo and a picture of Engle's blue Toyota truck. Niki took the pictures, barely glancing from one to the other.

"I've never seen the girl . . . or the man."

She handed the photos of Kelly and Engle back to Pike, and kept the third.

"You sure you got a good look at these, Miss Crawford?" Pike asked, still standing over her.

His question went unanswered. He tried again.

"How about the truck? Ever see that kind of vehicle parked near the field?"

"I . . . think I remember a truck like this at the field around the time you're talking about. But I don't know if it's the one in the picture here. It's a pretty common kind of vehicle." She handed the photo matter-of-factly to Pike without looking at him.

"When did you see it, Miss Crawford?" he asked.

"I don't know. It must have been about a week before the body was found out there."

"Tell us about it, can you?"

"I was driving past the field after work, on my way west to the shopping center."

"Can you tell me what made you notice it?"

"I really don't know. It was just . . . there."

"On the road or off?"

"I can't recall."

"How about people? Anyone around it?"

"I really don't recall anymore."

"Would you have noticed, do you think?"

"If a guy would have been near it with a kid? Yeah, I'd have noticed."

"Can you tell us anything else about the vehicle?"

"No."

"Can you recall the date or the day?"

"No, I can't."

"Maybe you have some kind of receipt from the shopping center you can look at to help pin down a date?"

"I might. I'll have to look for one. I could have a receipt if I still have a store bag. I might have a canceled check in a week or two. I bought a sweater that evening."

"It was evening?"

"Mmm. Yes. About seven o'clock, I think." Niki began picking at her fingernails. For the first time, she looked up at Pike. "I think I remember now. I was driving past the field and this—this truck, like the one in the photo, was sticking out onto the frontage road. It was parked in the opposite direction of how people park—it was facing the oncoming traffic. Facing me."

Pike sat facing Niki.

"I'll ask you again, Ms. Crawford," Pike said. "Do you remember seeing anyone near the truck or even at the turnout?"

"I didn't see anyone. Just a truck."

"Would you mind looking at these two photos again?" He placed the pictures of Engle and Kelly Solomon on the table in front of him.

"I'm sure I didn't see those people. I really don't have to look at them again."

"Well, can you look around for us and see if you can find a check or receipt with the date?"

"Sure, I'll try."

"How about anything else? Do you remember anything else about the truck, like any of the letters on the truck's license or its color?"

"It was a dark color. That's about all I remember about it."

"Could it have been blue?" Pike asked.

"Maybe. But I'm not sure. It was getting dark."

"Think, if you can for a moment, if you noticed anything else about the truck, its tires, anything," Pike suggested.

"I'm sorry, I can't talk anymore. I've got to be at a training exercise in about twenty minutes."

Pike stood and held out his hand to her.

"Good to meet you, Miss—it is Miss?—Crawford."

"Uh, yes."

Her grasp was weak and he thought he detected a clamminess in her extended hand, which he held longer than he needed, forcing her to pull it from him.

"Can you check on those receipts for us? Maybe this afternoon?"

Niki shrugged. "Sure."

She walked the men to the front door, closing it again before they had stepped off the porch.

It was all wrong. She should have taken her time, searched her memory. Asked about the girl who'd been killed. Been cooperative, for God's sake. That was what anyone would have done. That was what everyone had done so far.

Pike and Abrams stood outside their car.

"I think she's telling the truth, Pike, when she says she saw the truck. But she's not telling us everything. You wanna come back on this one pretty quick?"

"Let's give her a few days to come up with a receipt and think this through. But no more than a few days. My guess is she's not going to volunteer a whole lot and we'll have to abandon the subtle approach."

"You have a better one?"

"Maybe."

Abrams remembered Judith Thornton's words of caution about keeping Pike contained.

"Take it easy, Pike. If she saw something, we don't want to scare her off."

18

In a case of any significance, especially those involving violent crimes, it was the policy of the district attorney's office to explain the criminal justice process to the victims, make them aware of the difficulties which might lie ahead and, where appropriate, consult with them to solicit their views on such matters as plea negotiations. There would be no exception with the Solomons. The subject, however, became far more complicated because they were dealing with the death penalty. Nothing could adequately describe what they were about to experience. They needed to know the complicated process involved and the uphill battle facing them.

Judith had summoned the Solomons to her office, offered them coffee and found a comfortable place next door in the staff lounge where they could talk.

"Engle has pleaded not guilty. That means he has a trial in Superior Court. All of our felonies are tried in the Superior Court. But before he can be made to stand trial, he has a hearing in the Municipal Court. That hearing is called the preliminary hearing. At the preliminary hearing, we have to show there is enough evidence to

163

take him to trial. It's a safety feature in the system to make sure the prosecutor isn't abusing his powers, and it's designed so that an innocent person won't be dragged through the system. That's where we are right now. Engle's preliminary hearing is the next step we face.''

''How complicated is the hearing?'' Deborah Solomon asked.

''It's not a trial. In fact, most of the time the defendant doesn't even offer any evidence. We just have to put forth our basic evidence. And that's usually not too detailed. The court sends the defendant on to Superior Court if it finds a crime has been committed and there's a reasonable suspicion the defendant committed the crime. The court doesn't have to find he did it beyond a reasonable doubt. That reasonable-doubt test comes later at trial.''

''Do we have to testify?'' Deborah Solomon asked.

''Maybe.'' The room fell silent. This was the part Judith was not anxious to discuss.

''This is uncomfortable, but I need to level with you both. The preliminary hearing isn't going to be easy. We have evidence against Engle, strong evidence. But one of the officers who searched Engle's motel room took evidence before there was a search warrant. If the search is challenged and the court concludes it was illegal, the evidence can't be used at trial.''

''What evidence, Mrs. Thornton?'' Deborah Solomon asked.

''Strong evidence. Some writing and . . . a tool.'' Judith stopped there, hoping they would not press her too strongly on why the officer had bungled the search. When they did not, she moved to an even more sensitive subject. ''Because we might not have that strong evidence at trial, we have considered either dismissing the charges until we have more evidence or plea-bargaining to be certain Robert Engle is put away for a long time.''

Deborah Solomon immediately recoiled, putting her coffee mug down hard on the small table near her. ''My God, you can't let that animal out to kill another child, Mrs. Thornton! That's unthinkable. And as for plea-bargaining . . . I don't like it. If you're saying we need to . . .''

Having elicited a response to the idea of plea-bargaining, Judith backed away from the subject.

''We haven't decided anything along those lines, since it's too early. And I'll let you know about any major steps in the prosecution. Nothing will be done along such drastic lines unless we talk with you both first.''

Deborah Solomon was firm. ''We just want to see this man put away so no other family has to go through what we're going through.''

''This is only the start of the beginning. If we get past the preliminary hearing, we have a trial facing us. We're talking six months to a year until a death sentence is imposed. Then there's an automatic appeal to the California Supreme Court. That could take a year to two years. If we get past that step, we're into the federal courts and their own appeal processes.'' Judith added another teaspoon of sugar to her coffee and stirred. ''Including the federal appeal processes, it could take ten or twelve years.''

Deborah shifted uneasily in her chair. ''Twelve years? How could it possibly take so long?''

''The federal courts. That's where the going gets tough. Engle can move through the trial courts by filing what are called writs of habeas corpus with any constitutional challenge he wants to make. Each of these writs moves through the trial court, then to the circuit appeal court, then to the U.S. Supreme Court. And when he's through with that issue he can start over again with another issue. There are no limits, really, to the number of issues he can raise. He can keep doing this until there's no issue left to raise. Each one of the issues could delay a final result for up to six months or a year. We've had the federal appeal court sit on issues raised in capital cases for two years, some for three.''

"How can they do that?''

"Federal judges are pretty powerful people. They answer to no one except the U.S. Supreme Court. Maybe. Each of them does what he wants. And each one of them has his own view of capital punishment.''

"Mrs. Thornton, I'm forty-two years old. In twelve years I'll be fifty-four. If he's found guilty he might outlive me.''

"He might,'' Judith said. There was silence. Then she continued. "I'll be blunt. Don't expect this to be fast. We have three hundred and thirty inmates on death row in California. We've had one execution between 1967 and 1992.'' Again there was silence, before Judith changed the subject. "One thing I'd like to caution you about, and that is talking to reporters. To the extent you feel comfortable with it, by all means go ahead. But you are not obligated to talk to anyone. *Anyone.*''

"I can't talk to reporters without breaking down. I can hardly talk about Kelly without crying. Abe's taken her pictures out of the living room.'' Deborah looked at her husband. "Because I can't look at them and stay calm,'' she added. "Things come up and I see her face. Pleading, crying . . . oh, God, the pain she must have gone through, and to have known that . . . animal was not going to stop . . . that she was going to die . . . How can I not feel this hatred . . . I . . .'' She began to sob.

Judith reached under the table and pulled out a box of tissues, handing it to her.

"You're going to be on an emotional roller coaster. Because, as I've said, even if it's a quick trial and we get a fast conviction, there's the whole appeal process. You're going to be elated one day and despondent and/or frustrated the next."

Abe Solomon had been somber and silent, listening to the two women discuss the future of the case. He was a man of few words. But discussion of the years it might take to see an end to this chapter in his life jarred him from his silence.

"I want to see Robert Dean Engle die in the gas chamber, Mrs. Thornton." He was breathing deeply. "However long it takes, I want to be there when he's going to die. When he knows he's seen his last television show. When he knows he won't see another Saturday morning or another baseball game. I want to see his body when they carry him out of that chamber. Only then will there be some finality to this. Only at that moment will this be over for me. He's destroyed my life. Nothing anyone does is going to get back what I've lost. But I want to see justice done."

"It's not going to happen very quickly, Mr. Solomon. But when it does happen, I promise you that you'll be one of the witnesses."

"When he sits in that chair, Mrs. Thornton, when they strap him in and the cyanide gas surrounds him, when I can see his face with fear on it instead of that smirky smile, that's when maybe I can purge the hatred I feel for him and find it in myself to forgive him. If I can forgive him, maybe I'll find peace with myself. And whether I'm alive or not, I want him to die suffering. The way Kelly suffered."

19

＊━━＊

"Hey! Niki! Over here! You've got to see this! Whoooeee . . . better hold your nose."

She yelled back, "I'm busy, Todd. Make it wait!"

"No, now, you gotta see it now! Come on!"

Frustrated, Niki dropped her equipment and tramped through the dry grass toward the place where the voice was coming from. She'd been temporarily assigned to a special team charged with spraying insecticide along the river. The spraying equipment had been easy to work with, and it looked as if their goal of finishing by the evening break would be accomplished.

"What have you got that's so important?" Niki asked.

Her teammate had his back to her. When he turned, in his hands was a long piece of something she identified immediately as a body part. Her eyes quickly scanned the item. Judging from its size, it was part of an animal. Probably a deer. It wasn't from a human. But the sight of it made Niki reel around and gag, her hand flying to her mouth.

She moved quickly toward her gear, yelling over her

shoulder, "You stupid jerk! Just drop it. Drop it. Spray it . . . don't you know it was alive—it was alive, you shit!"

Later, Todd apologized. Apology accepted. But as he packed his gear for the ride back to their headquarters, he went out of his way to ask the field supervisor, Len Herald, what the hell was happening to Niki. She had, he observed, actually sworn at him. Niki. Little Miss Priss.

In the days following her discussion with Pike and Abrams, Niki Crawford's disposition continued to deteriorate. There were angry outbursts in situations that, just weeks before, would have resulted in laughter. It seemed she'd lost her ability to relate to what was happening around her. She had lost her sense of humor. Gradually, then more quickly, she was losing control of her ability to concentrate on her job. For short periods of time her coworkers would lose track of her, only to find her off in some area staring out into trees or canyons. They could cover for her, mask her isolation, but only for so long.

"Todd, have you seen Niki in the last hour?" The irritation in Len Herald's voice was unmistakable.

"No. In fact, now that I think about it, I haven't seen her at all this morning. Maybe she's out today."

"She's here. I've got her logged in at eight. She was assigned out to the machinery sheds to verify the equipment returns from last night." Len looked at his wristwatch. "It's almost eleven. No one's seen her since."

"I'll take a walk and see if she's still there."

The city park machinery was stored two acres away on flat landfill that had once been the city dump. Nearby, a series of large sheds stored the smaller equipment and tools.

There was no sign of Niki at the big machinery. Todd

walked to one shed, then another, calling out to her. In the third storage shed his shouting was met with the sound of movement.

"Niki?"

Todd walked toward the area from where the sound had come. Niki was there, sitting on the wooden floor, her back up against the corner where the walls met, her knees drawn up under her chin, her arms encircling her legs.

"Niki! What in hell are you doing down here? Len's been looking for you. He's not in a happy frame of mind."

Niki looked up at him. "I just needed to be alone for a while."

"Well, let me give you some friendly advice. You're going to be in deep shit if you don't get back up to work."

"It's okay. Really, Todd. I'll be there. I just need a few more minutes."

Todd thought to leave, but decided to address the problem directly.

"Niki?"

"Yeah."

"Is anything wrong?"

"Why?"

"Why? Well, for one thing, your body's here at work, but your head's off somewhere else."

"It's nothing anyone can help me with."

"Find someone who can help you, then, Niki. Because taking three-hour morning breaks isn't going to look good on your next evaluation. Tell me you'll get some help."

Niki looked up at him and smiled. "I'll get some help, okay? I'll get some help."

"I'll tell Len you're not feeling well. Which, from the

looks of you, you're not. I think you should get in to the nurse. Get some Tylenol or stretch out. But do it officially.''

"I'll be out, Todd.''

Todd was shaking his head as he tracked down the field supervisor.

"I found her, Len. She's down in the toolrooms.''

"What the hell's she been doing there all morning?''

"She's not feeling good. She's working slow, is all.''

"Well, did you tell her to get her body up to the nurse? We got workers' comp to worry about if it's work-related.''

"It's not work-related. She'll be up.''

"Todd, you work with the woman. What's going on? One day she's okay and the next she's off in space. Is she having some kind of personal trouble?''

"I haven't any idea.''

"She's not up for any job-performance evaluation, is she?''

"No, not that she's said, and she started the same time I did,'' Todd said. "I've got three months to go before I even start thinking about that. She's doing so well, I can't imagine any problems she would be having with work.''

"Until now. When you see her, tell her to stop by and see me.''

20

From the moment he saw his ex-student's face, Paul Eberle knew something was wrong. Niki's visits were always cheerful, filled with chatter. Today she'd said hello, then taken a seat in the small chair opposite his desk reserved for students he was counseling.

He continued reading the morning paper, wondering if she was going to tell him why she seemed so down. Finally he spoke.

"Can I help?" he asked.

"I can't talk about it."

"Okay."

Eberle had been a police officer with the San Diego Police Department for sixteen years before his retirement in 1965. He hadn't needed to retire. He'd merely realized that was not what he wanted to do for the remainder of his life. He had turned to teaching police science and political science first at the junior college, then at San Diego State University.

Niki had been a student in his political science courses. She was a good student. But there was something else. Maybe a sense of dedication. A certain naïveté. The way he liked to remember himself before he had joined the police department. She'd helped him write several magazine articles, and they'd maintained a friendship even after she'd graduated. Niki would periodically drop in to visit if her duties brought her near the campus.

"Paul?"

"Umm."

"I saw something. I saw a man."

"And what's so important about this man?"

"I want to show you sometime, can I? It's not far from here."

"Sure, I'll go with you. What do you want to show me?"

Up to this point he'd continued his reading. But he stopped when she didn't respond. Glancing up, he was immediately worried by the blank look on her face. He noticed for the first time her hollow cheeks and the dark circles under her eyes.

"How *have* you been, Niki? You're looking a little tired."

"I've been okay, I guess. Just—having a little trouble sleeping, you know. . . . Actually, Paul, I guess I don't sleep at all. I go to bed and I wake up in a cold sweat. I get up early and I stay up late."

"It's because of this man you saw?"

"Yeah. It's like I just . . . just . . . can't cope with this one thing and it's destroying my life. Everything around me is falling apart because of it. Just falling apart."

"What did this guy do, Niki? He didn't hurt you, did he?" Eberle asked, suddenly alarmed for her.

"No. No, not me. I saw him with this kid, a little girl. And I knew something was wrong. I should have done something. I didn't. And it's all gone from bad to worse. I thought maybe it was anxiety. Then a couple of police officers came over to talk to me about the girl and . . . things started, all over again. I'm having these dreams about the man and the girl, and I'm seeing something a little different every time—a little more detail. There's something else my mind's trying to remember, but I don't want to remember it.''

''It sounds to me like whatever you saw, you need to get it all out, Niki—into the open. That'll take the stress off you.''

''I'm sorry. I mean . . . I don't know. Everything's just like . . . falling apart on me. I've got four days to get my act together. If I screw up again, it's going to be over for me at work.''

''Niki—what the hell is going on?''

''I can't concentrate on what I'm supposed to be doing, Paul. There are things I've got to do tomorrow, but I can't even remember what they are. I get top-priority-type things and I totally forget them. It's got me so uptight, nothing's fitting together. I can barely drive from point A to point B without getting like I want to just scream. But I can't.''

''What can I do to help you?''

She was looking past him.

''I'm supposed to check out the apparatus, you know. Troubleshoot. And my mind gets sidetracked into something completely different. The next thing I know, this friend of mine, Todd—I work with Todd—he comes up and touches my shoulder and I just, you know, just . . . explode. You see, I don't remember, just that things are not fitting together. I'm trying, but nothing's helping. . . . Can you help me, Paul?''

''How? What can I do? Name it.''

''Come with me. I need to show you something.''

''I'm free this afternoon. Can you stick around?''

''I'll stick around, sure. I need to show it to you.''

Two hours later, after his last class of the day, Eberle found Niki still sitting in his office. She was seated in the same chair, facing in the same direction.

It took only five minutes to reach the frontage road. Niki indicated the Texas Drive off-ramp and directed Eberle to the turnout, where she immediately pointed out across the field.

"This is where I saw them. Here."

"Saw who?"

"It's over there. Come with me."

He followed her from the frontage road toward the river. Along the way, she bent down and picked up a long stick. When they reached the clearing, she stopped and began tapping the ground with the stick.

"Here. It was right here."

She started walking in a circle, continuing to tap. "The girl. It was right here."

"Niki, did you see something happen after you saw them walking?"

"Paul, I keep dreaming about it, and each time I wake up I see a little bit more. It scares m-me, it really does. I can't stop it . . . it gets so far, you know, and all of a sudden I wake up. There's something in there I can't remember, and it's coming back in bits and pieces. And, Paul, I'm not sure I want it to."

"Niki, you've got to talk to someone—the police— about this. Do you want me to call for you? I can, you know. My contacts are still very good. I'll go with you if you want."

She stiffened. "No, God, Paul. Promise me no."

"How can I promise, Niki? Look, if you've been a witness to a crime, you have a moral obligation to help the police catch the person who committed it. You need to let the criminal justice system take over and get this off your shoulders. You've got to think about this. Think about it and call me tonight, please? Promise me you'll call me tonight.''

"Okay, Paul, I promise."

Niki was silent as they drove back to the college; she resisted all attempts by Eberle to get her to talk about what she had seen. By the time she dropped Eberle at his car, he had remembered the reason for the field's recent notoriety. Could the little girl who had been kidnapped be whom Niki had seen? She needed to talk with the police, and while he'd hadn't promised that he wouldn't make her go to them, he also hadn't promised he would ignore what she'd told him.

Eberle spent the evening waiting impatiently for Niki's telephone call. By 10 P.M. she hadn't tried to reach him, so he called her. There was no answer. He'd give her until tomorrow, and if she didn't contact him, he would have to consider some other course of action.

21

Within ten minutes of his call to headquarters, Paul Eberle had made contact with Pike Martin.

"Homicide? Who's this? Hello, Detective Martin. My name's Paul Eberle. I need to talk with you for a minute. I've got this kid—an ex-student of mine. She came to see me two days ago and asked me to go out to Mission Valley with her. I think she saw something related to the murder of that little girl over there."

"Kelly Solomon?"

"Yes. The real recent one. I think she may have seen the man who did it."

"Name, Paul. Can you give me her name?"

"Crawford. Niki Crawford."

"Niki Crawford . . . We were just out to talk to her a couple of days ago. I *knew* she wasn't telling us the truth. Did she tell you anything specific?"

"Nothing. I can tell you she's having serious stress problems with this. In my opinion, she needs some psychological counseling. Maybe I can talk to her again and try to persuade her to come in."

"Well, I've already made contact with her. Let me

try once more. We told her we would be coming back.''

"Okay. But like I said, she's very disturbed about this. Call me if you need me to go there with you. I've known Niki a long time—long enough to know this has her at the edge.''

Pike's voice softened. "Tell you what. If we need you, we'll call right away.''

When he hung up, Pike telephoned Abrams to meet him at his car in ten minutes. They were going to visit Niki Crawford.

Pike's suspicions had been confirmed. Niki Crawford had lied to him. Now he needed to deal with it, not understand it. He didn't care to understand it. He had no time for that. He needed to know what she knew. And if her friend Eberle was correct and she was emotionally disturbed, that could cause her to fold up, but it could also cause her to spill her guts.

22

"Miss Crawford." Pike held his badge inches from her face. "We spoke with you a couple of days ago. I'd like to show you these photos again. Can you look at them, please, and tell us if you've ever seen these people?"

Niki ignored the photos in Pike's extended hand.

"Look—Officer Martin, right? I've been out training all day. I'm filthy dirty and I have no intention of stopping right now and looking at anything, because I'm going directly into the shower."

"We'll wait," he said, pushing past her.

"Suit yourselves," was all she could think to respond. She wanted to shriek, to demand they leave. They had *no right* to be there unless she allowed them to be. *No right.* And all she could say was, "Suit yourselves?"

Pike, then Abrams, walked over to the sofa as Niki disappeared into the bathroom. They could hear the shower door slide and the shower start.

Thirty minutes later, the shower was still running.

Pike rose from the sofa, where he had been sitting, moved to the bathroom door and pounded on it. "Miss Crawford? Miss Crawford!" The pitch of his voice was rising. "If you don't get out here pretty quick, I'm going to have to place you under arrest."

Abrams raced to his side.

"Jeeez, what in hell are you talking about, Pike? We don't have the authority to arrest anyone here!"

"Shhh—let me handle her. Trust me on this one."

"Pike, you're stepping out of bounds on this."

"We're going to need her, Mike. Give me a minute. Just a minute, that's all."

"Okay, but just a minute, and goddammit, Pike, you keep it under control."

Pike pounded on the door again.

"We want to talk with you, remember?" The water stopped and Pike heard the shower door slide again. Several minutes later, Niki emerged, clean and dressed in Levi's and a T-shirt. She walked past Pike into the day-room.

"Wait a minute," Pike said, coming up behind her. "We need to talk with you."

"I'm sorry. I'm not going to talk about this any-more."

"I'm afraid you are. You *have* to talk to us," Pike said. "So I'm going to ask you one more time to look at these photos." He paused, frustrated and beginning to blink. "I can't understand why you won't for God's sake just take a good, honest look at them. You know this doesn't make any sense."

Niki headed for the outside door, only to have Pike block her path. Exhibiting no sign of the rising anger and frustration she was feeling, she turned and took a chair in a corner of the dayroom.

"I don't want to speak with you. And I don't want to look at your photos."

"Goddammit. Like it or not, you're going to talk. If not now, then in court. You'll get a subpoena and *then* if you don't wanna talk, you're going to find your ass in a shitty, stinking jail cell for a while with some pukey whore breathing in your face." The last part was loud, an invitation to a shouting match. Pike's ire surprised even Abrams. But by all appearances, Niki was unshaken.

"Go ahead. Subpoena me, you blue fart. . . . I'm not going to talk to you." *Oh, Lord, forgive me, what language,* she thought. *I need to control myself. Control.*

At this point Abrams intervened. "Miss Crawford, I'm really sorry Detective Martin is so upset." It occurred to him this had turned into a Mutt and Jeff routine, with Pike the mean officer and him the nice guy working off each other to gain the subject's trust. Sometimes it was an effective interrogation technique. But here it was unintended and useless. Abrams was genuinely embarrassed. He tried a more conciliatory tone.

"A kid's been murdered. Butchered. You're a public servant with a heavy responsibility to the public. If you have *any* information that can help catch the person or persons who did it, you have to tell us. You need to help us. If you have information and won't tell us, you're helping the guy who did it. So if you know something, help us."

"I just don't want to say anything else, okay? Okay? I'd just like you both to get out of here. Especially *him.*"

Pike stared hotly at her as he and Abrams headed toward the door. "It's people like you who are keeping maniacs like Engle on the street. If you don't help us, you're as responsible for that girl's death as whoever dumped her out in that field like a piece of garbage."

From the dayroom window Niki Crawford, shaking, watched the officers get into their unmarked car.

How could she tell them she had seen the little girl with that man out at the field? How could she tell them something she was trying so desperately to forget? Their parting accusations, uttered in reckless abandonment of protocol, had struck her subconscious, releasing the overwhelming guilt she had been trying so hard to keep contained.

23

It was a big break. But it had taken them nowhere except to a new level of frustration. Pike typed his report on the contacts with Niki Crawford and Paul Eberle and hand-delivered it to Judith. Like most police reports, it was terse, factual, containing little in the way of the writer's personal impressions. Yet between the lines in this one, Judith sensed there lay another story and she wanted Pike to fill in the gaps.

"I don't know, Judith. I've been in this business for over twenty years. And most witnesses I can get a read on. You know, you see people standing alone on a corner or talking—interacting—and you can tell something about what's going on inside them. They're sad, or happy, whatever. Her, though, I can't read. I can't tell what's the hell's going on inside her. I only know she admits to seeing a truck like Engle's at the field near the time when Kelly Solomon was murdered. And based on what she told this teacher friend of hers, she saw a man and a little girl and a body. But she stops right there."

"Are you sure she really does have information about the case?"

"I'm sure. I'm just not sure why she's not talking."

"You run a background check on her?"

"A pretty thorough one. There's nothing helpful. She's not related to anyone involved. Never crossed paths with anyone involved. Her mother died when she was a year old, and her father dumped her in a Catholic boarding school when she was nine. She stayed there until she graduated from high school. A tough background, but she did real well—good grades; a shy kid who never challenged authority, never stepped out of line, never got into any trouble. Got a job with the city right out of college and was a superstar employee until several weeks ago, when her work started to get shaky."

"She sounds like a person who would *want* to help us catch this child's murderer. Let's bring her in, Pike. We've only got two weeks to the preliminary hearing. I need to talk with her and see what we've got. If our judge rules the search isn't any good and we lose the pliers and the diary, she may be our only way of linking Engle up to the scene of the crime. And we've *got* to link him up."

"I'll try, Judith, but she's not being cooperative. Don't be surprised if she won't talk at all."

"What do you mean, won't talk at all? Why wouldn't she?"

"Well, she took that thirty-minute shower while we waited to talk with her."

"If you can't persuade her to come in, Pike, then see if this teacher friend of hers, Paul Eberle, can help. Just don't do anything to scare her off, got it? She's under stress . . . a hell of a lot of it. Because, Pike . . . that thirty-minute shower? It was the only place she could go that you couldn't follow her to. I want you to find out what, precisely, Niki Crawford was like before Kelly Solomon was murdered, and what, precisely, she's like now.''

24

San Diego State University sits in the center of East San Diego's residential community, maintaining a peaceful, if somewhat nervous, relationship with the mostly middle-aged, middle-income residents surrounding the campus.

It took Pike ten minutes to park in one of the college's outlying lots and walk the length of the grassy, tree-lined knolls and pedestrian walkways to the faculty offices in the political science building.

Paul Eberle had eagerly accepted Pike's invitation to discuss Niki Crawford. Pike found Eberle sitting on one of the benches in the grassy area just outside the political science building. Although they had met only through a telephone conversation, there was the immediate recognition common to individuals seeking each other out by rendezvous. Following a brief introduction, Pike went directly to the point of their meeting.

"We need some help in dealing with Niki Crawford. We suspect that she knows more about Kelly Solomon's death than she's willing to tell us."

186

"And it's driving her crazy," Eberle added. "I think I told you she took me out to that field near 805 and 8 and acted in what I can only say is disassociative behavior. She said she saw a man and a girl and a body."

"I don't mean to be too personal, but do you mind if I ask you a few questions about Niki?"

"No, go right ahead."

"How long have you known her?"

"Maybe four years. I met her here at the college. She was one of my students, one of my best students. We've kept in touch after her graduation. She comes over once in a while to talk about what's going on in her life, in her career."

"How many classes of yours was she in?"

"If I recall correctly, she was in my general government class and a criminal procedure class. I sent her off to one of the city's college-intern programs and she did so well that after she graduated they offered her a job in the Parks and Recreation Department. That's the job she has now."

"What kind of student was she?"

"Excellent. Smart girl, really bright. She graduated with honors in political science."

"In the years you've known and worked with Niki Crawford, Paul, did she ever demonstrate any signs of being mentally unbalanced?"

Eberle laughed. "Niki? Unbalanced? Oh, my God, no way. She's as buttoned-down as anyone I've worked with here—or anywhere. But I'll tell you, she's not the same girl anymore. She's confused. Depressed. And absolutely preoccupied with whatever she saw at that field."

"Have you seen her since she went to the field with you?"

''Yes. In fact, the day before yesterday she was in to see me. She mentioned you two had had some words or something.''

Pike blushed, hoping she hadn't been too specific.

''Yeah, we . . . I tried to persuade her to open up a little.''

''From what she implied, she didn't.''

''No, she sure didn't. I'm afraid I got a little forceful with her.''

''She didn't mention that.''

''Well, when she came to see you, did she seem more . . . in control?''

''Not really. If anything, I was more concerned about her when she left than I was before. She'd had a fender bender on the freeway that morning.''

''Fender benders aren't that unusual.''

''Two in two weeks? I think that's unusual.''

''Do you know her to be accident-prone?''

''No, not in the least.''

As Pike scribbled notes in a small black notebook he had taken from his coat pocket, Eberle eased into an idea he had been mulling over for the past week.

''Pike?''

''Uh-huh.''

''Did you serve in any war?''

Pike looked up, surprised the topic had turned so abruptly to warfare.

''Just Korea.''

''You see any combat there?''

''Nothing heavy. Why?''

''I was in Vietnam twenty years ago. I'm seeing the same things in Niki that I saw in one of my good friends who was a medical corpsman.''

''What kind of things?''

"Heavy depression. Guilt that he survived and friends didn't. Sleep disorders—really bad ones. He'd be up all night and sleep during the day. He became accident-prone, then tried to commit suicide before he got the psychiatric help he needed. I understand it's a syndrome."

"Are you thinking that whatever Niki saw has done the same thing to her?"

"It's just very similar conduct. All I know is she's not the same girl she was two months ago. She needs help."

"She won't take it from me. There's no cooperation from her at all."

"She'll listen to you, Pike."

"You don't understand, Paul. It's not just her. I was rough on her. Really rough. If you're right and she's suffering from some kind of bad emotional reaction to something she saw . . . I might have done more harm than good. I laid one hell of a guilt trip on her."

"Maybe I can do something more to help."

"I've been thinking that maybe if we can persuade her to go out to the field again, she might say more about what she saw."

"You mean, just try to get her to talk about it?"

"Yeah."

"Do you want to talk to her first?"

Pike shook his head. "Noooo . . . I think I'm going to lie low on this angle for now. Maybe she'll go there with you."

"I'll try. And I'll give you a call if I can persuade her to come in and talk with you."

Following his conversation with Paul Eberle, Pike arranged to meet with Niki's coworkers at the Parks Department, Todd and Len Herald. They confirmed Paul

Eberle's observations. Niki Crawford was not the same person she had been two months earlier. Something major, something extraordinary, they opined, must have happened to her.

25

Niki hadn't been in the house long when the phone rang. It was Paul Eberle.

"Niki, I've been thinking. I'd like you to come with me back out to the field this afternoon. Think you can do that?"

"I don't think so, no. I mean, I don't really want to go."

"Please, I'd like you to come with me. What do you say? Niki, hey, you still there?"

"Yeah."

"Whatever it is you can't remember will come back to you, maybe, and you can deal with it. Look, I'll pick you up at two-thirty. Okay?"

"I hope so, Paul. I really want to remember . . . I want it to go away, but I don't think this is going to help with anything."

As the car neared the turnout, Eberle noticed Niki's hands clench into fists and periodically loosen, only to grasp the edge of the car's bench seat.

"Hold on there, kiddo. We're going to be there just

long enough for you to show me again where you saw the man and the little girl. . . . You doing okay?''

''I . . . I don't think so.''

''You need to try. If you want those dreams to stop, you've got to try.''

But when the car pulled into the turnout, Niki sat, grinding her teeth, moving, finally, when Eberle exited and opened her door.

''How important is it I do this?'' she asked.

''For you, very. For the police, very.''

Slowly, the two walked the width of the field. At last Eberle suggested they follow the trail to the water.

Niki followed him and stopped short of the clearing.

The wind had suddenly picked up. She could hear it rustling the leaves of the eucalyptus trees. The horrid smells of the night she had found Kelly's body returned.

''Now, can you tell me, Niki, in which direction it was you saw the man walking? Niki? Hey! Where are you going?''

Niki had begun walking, then sprinting, back to the car.

''Hey! Niki! What's the matter? Where the hell are you going?''

In the car, she sat, her face in her hands. Shaking her head.

''No, I can't, I just can't.'' No amount of persuasion helped.

Back in his office, Eberle telephoned Pike to tell him the attempt to jar Niki's memory had been a failure.

On Eberle's chair the next morning was a telephone message. It read, ''Niki Crawford called at nine. Please call ASAP.'' There was a telephone number.

''Niki?''

''Paul, I tried to call this morning.''

''How're you feeling today?''

"Real confused."

"Do you think it might be easier if you told it to the police?"

"No way."

"Is there anything that's going to do it?"

"I don't think there's anything I *can* do. When I woke up last night it was unreal."

"More nightmares?"

"Oh, yeah, it's just . . ."

"Niki, tell me about the dreams."

"It's like watching a movie. I wake up in a cold sweat, shaking all over." Her statement dissolved into a bloodcurdling laugh.

Oh, Jesus, Eberle was thinking, *she's going off the deep end.*

"Niki, get hold of yourself here. You've got to vent all this . . . take that first step."

"My foot was in the door yesterday and I backed out."

"No, Niki, your foot's in the door right now."

He could hear her breathing.

"Niki . . . hello . . . you with me? Niki, come on, talk to me." He whistled into the phone. "Niki, come on. There's no sense punishing yourself."

"I'm here."

"You were silent for quite a while."

"I was?"

"Stick with me here. Can you work through this with me? We've been through it to a point; why can't we do it now?"

"I . . . I just can't. I don't think anyone can know how much—"

"How much what?" Eberle interrupted.

"How much I want to say it but can't."

"But listen, Niki, you can tell me what it was you

saw. I think you want to tell someone. Why are you punishing yourself? Because, you know, it sure seems like that's just what you're doing.''

"Tell me something, Paul. Can a good person commit a mortal sin?''

"Can a what? What's a mortal sin?''

"A sin that destroys your soul.''

"Good people don't commit mortal sin, Niki. But even good people make mistakes.'' Immediately after he had said it, he regretted his use of the word "mistakes.''

"But how do you know if what you've done is a mistake or a mortal sin . . . or a . . . crime?''

"You don't think you've committed any kind of crime, do you? Well, you haven't.''

"Not a crime, no. It was the choice—my choice—that was wrong. That man's got to be sick, crazy—I'm not. I knew right from wrong.''

"Just a minute. If you're going to talk theology, whatever happened could just as well be God's will, and let it go at that.''

"If this was God's will, then no one's responsible for anything.''

"Goddammit! Niki, I don't think this debate gets us anywhere. Come on back to the real world and take off the hair shirt. You saw something. Maybe there's something you should have done. But you can't pretend it never happened.''

"I just don't want to go through it again.''

"But you'll continue to go through it until you get rid of it. Would you like to try talking to a doctor instead of me?''

"It's not gonna make any difference.''

There was a long sigh from Niki's end. Then complete silence. Several minutes passed before Eberle spoke.

"Still with me?''

"What?"

"Will you talk to me?"

"Will I what?"

"Did you hear me ask you the question?"

"What question?"

"Just talk to me, okay? You keep putting me on hold."

Eberle looked at his wall clock. It was 9:32. He couldn't let her hang up. Not in her state of mind. Then it was 9:40.

"What's going on, Niki? Your mind's wandering or something. Do you have any idea how long it's been?"

"Huh?"

"Well, it's been at least seven minutes since I started looking at this clock. I don't know how long it was before that. Maybe a couple more minutes. I want to help you, but you're not letting me."

"I'm just shaky."

"Okay. Can you talk about it tonight?"

"I don't think so."

"What do you want to do?"

Her voice dropped to a whisper. "I feel like I got a time bomb inside me that's ready to blow."

"Niki, will you do me a favor and go talk to the D.A. who's handling the trial? She'll understand, I promise. No pressure."

"Will the police be there?"

"Maybe the investigators."

"I don't know. I'll think about it."

26

Pike's written report succinctly summarized his findings concerning Niki Crawford's changed personality and Paul Eberle's failed attempts to draw her out of her growing depression. Judith set the report on her desk and clasped her hands on it. Post-traumatic stress disorder. Internalized guilt. Niki's erratic behavior was being caused by what she had seen and, realistic or not, perhaps by what she felt she might have done. It all made sense. One day there's a fine young woman doing well at work and in her personal relationships. She experiences something traumatic, something grossly out of the ordinary, something grotesque done by one human being against another human being, maybe against her; and that all changes. She becomes withdrawn, depressed, erratic, even suicidal. One witness to a shotgun murder Judith had prosecuted had been driving on a San Diego street, blacked out and found himself driving east on Interstate 8, headed for Yuma, Arizona.

Because Judith had dealt with the syndrome before, particularly with victims who had suffered violent crimes, she knew that if Niki's problem was not confronted and dealt with, her value as a witness would be marginal and unpredictable; not to mention the continued devastating damage to the woman herself.

The problem was that Niki had been resisting all offers of help. The most that could be done if she failed to cooperate would be to follow her testimony with that of an expert witness who could explain Niki's behavior and what it was she was going through. This would especially be necessary if Niki's testimony were erratic or bizarre in any way. It might happen. Judith had seen both victims and witnesses fall out of the witness stand into fetal positions when required to recite and relive the events of particularly horrible traumas. The standard procedure was to follow up their testimony with an expert to explain what the jury had seen and why the witnesses had reacted the way they did. The problem with Niki was going to be finding the reason for her behavior and getting her to talk about it. Why would simply seeing Engle and Kelly Solomon walking across the field cause such extreme reactions, such a deep guilt trip? There had to be something more than that. Niki had seen something more. Maybe the assault itself. She'd seen the body. That was what she'd told Paul Eberle. But when had she seen the body? And what, if anything, had she seen with it?

27

Niki stood at the edge of the canyon and looked at her wristwatch. Fifteen minutes until lunch. Her park crew had been clearing the firebreak in Tecolote Canyon Regional Park. They'd brought in the large equipment and the job could likely be completed by the end of the day. Niki was tired. She needed a vacation. The snow was pretty good up at Big Bear right now. Maybe, she thought, if she could just get away for a few days, she could put her life back together.

No sooner had the thought crossed her mind than, from somewhere behind her, a low, grinding sound began to rise. The bobcat tractor was sliding sideways off the hill where she'd parked it minutes before.

Had she set the brake?

It was too late. The vehicle was on its way down.

She ran toward the four thousand pounds of metal sliding toward her, not heeding the frantic shouts to stop. Even as she ran, she realized there was nothing she could do. She revised her direction, but she knew it was too late. A prong of the shovel struck her leg from the side. It was strange, she thought even as she tumbled;

the pain was happening around her shoulders and head, not her leg. She came to rest near one of the large sycamore trees, sat upright and looked around. The men were running toward her. Why? She was okay.

Then she looked at her left leg.

Her foot was a mass of red and white. That was the last thing she remembered before passing out.

As the paramedics lifted her into their ambulance, the police officers recorded the observations of those nearest the event.

One incredulous voice rose above the others. "Man, it was like crazy . . . I swear, she ran right at it—right at it!"

28

Judith was in her office with Pike as soon as she had gotten the word from the court.

"Hern's the prelim judge. He'll call it the way he sees it. And if he thinks the search is illegal, that's the way he'll rule. We haven't much if that's his call."

"We have Niki Crawford," Pike said.

"I don't see that yet, Pike. I've taken a look at your report on her. I'm not convinced we should use her until we check her out. That last attempt to get her back to the scene concerns me immensely. She can't confide in this friend of hers, Paul Eberle, and then she's falling apart on the telephone? That's all we need—to call her to the stand and have her space out on the record, in front of the judge. Even if she comes to her senses later and appears lucid, her prelim testimony would be used on cross-examination at trial and Harley Bennett will rip her apart."

"And what if we don't use her at all?" Pike asked.

"We got the same nothing, but without complications."

"Is there any chance the defense will call her at the prelim?"

"It's a cinch Bennett *won't* call her. It could backfire terribly. She might be great at the prelim, nail Engle to the floor and disappear before trial. Then *he's* stuck with terrific evidence against his client at trial. It's a big gamble he would never take."

"What's our risk if we put her on?"

"Our risk is about the same either way. Close. It's in Hern's hands, and a lot will depend on how the evidence fits together. As I said, if Hern doesn't think there's enough credible evidence, he'll dismiss the case."

"And if he does . . ."

"Right."

"Engle could walk. He'd probably be released. We can recharge him right away if we get additional evidence somewhere. But by that time . . ."

"He'll be gone?"

"Like a cheetah."

The buzzer on Judith's phone line sounded. She listened, emotionless, to the voice of her investigator, caught her breath, then said, "Thank you. Just keep me posted." When she hung up she stared blankly at Pike.

"That was Mike. Niki Crawford's not a factor in the prelim anymore. She's had an accident. She's in Sharp Hospital with a bad foot injury. She'll be okay. But she won't be in any shape to testify in the very near future."

The two sat, silent. Judith finally spoke.

"Life just got simplified. We haven't any choices anymore. We're back to Plan A. We put on what we have and let the judge decide. But if he kicks out that diary and the pliers, you'd better have someone available to tail Engle when the whole case caves in. As best you can, keep track of where Niki Crawford is and how she's doing."

29

In his small cell that smelled of urine and the vomit of the new inmate in the next cell, Bobby Engle paced. He had been up late. Writing . . . writing . . . pacing the square of concrete. He nibbled periodically at the two-inch stub of a pencil he was allowed to use. The pencil was short to prevent his trying to use it as a weapon against himself or someone else. It would do for now. He had read Bennett's proposed argument on why the pliers and his diary must be excluded. He had read with delight the flowery, self-righteous prose Bennett had used to castigate the dim-witted officers who had pushed him so callously to the asphalt. And then there was the stealing of his beloved alligator. He underlined and edited, and finally wrote the words "This is going to be fun" at the bottom of the last of the thirteen pages of case law.

30

Most of the time the process of the law, the nuts and bolts of putting on the preliminary hearing, is pretty routine. Cut-and-dried. The witness list is in the file. The technicians, experts, get fitted in wherever you choose, whenever they're available. They follow a set pattern of questioning to establish the various scientific conclusions—time of death, cause of death, percent of alcohol in the blood. So methodical is the testimony that most times the defense attorneys—at least the good ones—stipulate to the conclusions for purposes of the preliminary hearing. Every once in a while an aggressive, or naive, attorney will choose to challenge and drag out the expert testimony as long as possible, but unless there is a genuine problem with the expert evidence, such antics usually serve no more than to irritate the preliminary-hearing judge—particularly those judges who believe the preliminary hearing should be kept to its basic function: to decide if a crime has been committed and whether the evidence presented creates a reasonable suspicion the defendant is guilty. This burden is far less onerous than the reasonable-doubt standard the prosecutor must meet in any trial. Yet, despite the perfunctory nature of most preliminary hearings, it could also be a stopping point, the end of the case. And that was a distinct possibility today.

"Come to order, please. Court is in session, the Honorable Charles Hern presiding."

The bailiff's voice was strong, bringing the din of cameramen and newspaper reporters to an immediate halt. Hern carried nothing to the bench with him. He had read the entire file the previous afternoon and, as with most preliminary hearings, the fireworks, if any, would probably take place at the end of the proceeding, when defense counsel would argue there was not sufficient evidence to make the defendant stand trial.

"Counsel, is there anything we need to discuss prior to commencing these proceedings?"

Bennett and Judith answered in unison, "No, your Honor." Then Bennett added, "I just want to state for the record, your Honor, that Alan Larson has joined the defense team as additional trial counsel and is present at counsel table." A thin, woolly-haired, fortyish, wiry man with a scruffy mustache stood next to Bennett.

"Good morning, Mr. Larson."

"Good morning, your Honor."

"Mr. Bennett and Mr. Larson, a few rules before we begin here. I am sure they're familiar to you. Only one of you will question any given witness. Only one of you will argue any motions to be made."

"Yes, Judge," Bennett replied. "I've spoken to Mr. Larson concerning the court's protocol, and I will be handling all questioning and argument during the preliminary hearing. I wish to indicate to opposing counsel and the court that at the conclusion of the hearing we will be bringing a suppression motion pursuant to Penal Code section 1538.5 to exclude all evidence found in

Mr. Engle's Riverside motel room on the ground there is no warrant. We have filed points and authorities on the issue.''

''I have reviewed the written argument you've submitted, Mr. Bennett. It was received and file-stamped three days ago, and yesterday we did receive the People's written response. I must say the arguments you both make are well presented. I will, of course, need to listen to the witnesses. If there's nothing more, the People may call their first witness.''

''Your Honor.'' Bennett suddenly remembered a standard but practical step in the proceedings. ''We would like all witnesses excluded from the courtroom.''

''The People designate Pike Martin as the investigative officer, your Honor,'' Judith said. ''And Deborah Solomon is our first witness.''

''Yes, of course. All witnesses in the courtroom, with the exception of Detective Martin and Mrs. Solomon, please wait outside until you are called in by my bailiff. While you are outside, you are admonished not to discuss your testimony or the case with *anyone*. The point is to keep you from fashioning your testimony around what you are hearing. The one exception is Officer Martin. As the People's investigator on the case, he gets to hear all of you.''

With that, the bailiff led the ten prosecution witnesses out the door.

''The People call as their first witness Deborah Solomon.''

One after the other, the witnesses established the chronology of events the day Kelly Solomon had disappeared. The child's mother. The police officer who had taken the report of the disappearance from the child's mother. Then Officer Chin, who had found the body. The medical examiner, who would determine the probable cause of death and testify to the evidence of torture. These witnesses went unchallenged by Bennett. As was predictable, he stipulated to the medical testimony for purposes of the hearing. Bennett had obviously chosen to zero in on the major weakness, so he wasn't going to fool around and nibble at loose ends or waste his energy or strategy battling over the existence or nonexistence of torture. No, he was indeed going for the jugular—the weak spot they all knew existed. Only two witnesses could in any way tie Engle to the dead girl.

"The People call Tara Markham." The little girl, dressed for Sunday school in black patent-leather shoes and a rayon dress, came in, and the clerk directed her to the witness chair.

Child witnesses could be squirrelly. Most couldn't remember details of events from one day to the next, let alone details of what had occurred months earlier. You could ask a child a question one day and get one answer, and the next day get a different answer to the same question. At eight, Tara was considered an "older, safer" child. But she was a child nonetheless. Judith would keep the questions simple, direct, short. Aggressive defense counsel would keep the questioning complicated, obscure and lengthy.

"Tara, can you spell your full name for our records?"

"Yes. T-A-R-A M-A-R-K . . . um . . . H-A-M."

"How old are you, Tara?"

"Eight."

"Do you know what it means to tell the truth?"

"Yes. You don't lie."

"Okay. Your Honor, would Mr. Bennett like to ask questions about her ability to tell the truth?"

"Mr. Bennett?"

"No, your Honor. I have no questions."

Judith continued. "Now, Tara, I'd like to ask you

about Kelly Solomon. Did you know her?''

"Yes. . . .''

"Can you tell us a little bit about the last time you saw her? Do you remember where that was?''

"Yes. At the roller coaster at Mission Beach.''

"Did something strange happen when you were there with her?''

"Yes. A man came up to us.''

"What did he do or say?''

"He wanted to take our picture for a magazine.''

"Did he talk to Kelly?''

"Yes. He liked her a lot.''

"Did Kelly leave you after this man approached you?''

"Yes, she left. I stayed at the park.''

"Did the man leave?''

"He left when a woman came up to us after he took our picture.''

"Do you see the man who did that in the courtroom today?''

"I'm not positive, but I'm pretty sure—I think he's sitting over there.'' She pointed toward the defense table.

"Your Honor, can the record reflect the witness is pointing toward the defense table?''

"Yes, it may.''

"Okay. Tara, can you tell us what he is wearing?''

"Uh, yes. I think it's the guy in the yellow shirt there in the middle.''

The courtroom erupted in laughter.

Bennett rose. "Your Honor, can we have the record reflect the witness has identified Mr. Engle's co-counsel, Mr. Larson?''

Hern banged his gavel to silence the audience. "Come to order, please. Yes, yes, the record will so reflect.''

Oh, shit, Judith thought to herself. Luckily, there was no jury to impress. She maintained a calm demeanor, walking behind Pike and putting her hands on his shoulders.

"Tara, do you remember looking at some pictures that this man brought to you at your home?"

"Yes."

"Your Honor, we've marked this group of photos— may I approach the witness?" Judith asked.

"Yes, you may, Mrs. Thornton."

She laid the photos out in a row on the wide wooden rail in front of the child.

"Tara, are these the photos you were shown?"

"I think so."

"Did you identify anyone in these pictures as the man who took your photo?"

"I think I did."

"No further questions, your Honor." She would let Pike testify as to which photos the girl had identified. That was safe. Why risk another misidentification here?

Bennett rose, unsure about how much to ask on cross-examination. He approached the Markham girl slowly.

"Tara, can you look at those photos and tell us who it was you identified at your house when Mr. Martin brought them to you?"

"No, uh-uh."

Bennett took a moment to think. He knew Pike Martin would clean up the photo ID. He himself could drill her on the misidentification in court—play it up for the press and get another laugh, perhaps. But it wasn't necessary. She was a useless witness here and would never withstand being called to testify at trial. Even if she identified Engle at trial, she would be impeached by her disastrous identification at the prelim. Her only contribution now to the prosecution was the photo ID, and it was next to useless.

"No further questions, your Honor."

"Mrs. Thornton."

"Your Honor, the People call Leland Henrickson."

Under careful questioning, Henrickson slowly, methodically, detailed the steps that had gone into the reconstruction of the fingerprint that he had then identified as probably belonging to Engle.

It didn't take Bennett long to put Henrickson's testimony, and the fingerprint, in perspective.

"Mr. Henrickson, I'd like to ask whether it is *possible* the fingerprint found on the beer can out at the scene is *not* that of Mr. Engle. *Possible.*"

"It certainly is . . . possible."

"No further questions."

"Mrs. Thornton?" Hern was moving the prelim quickly. He glanced at the courtroom clock. It read the hour of ten. The time he usually took his morning break. "How's our reporter doing? Would you like a break?" Hern was one of those judges who believed the reporter, whose job of recording testimony carried perhaps the most sustained pressure in the courtroom, needed a break every twenty minutes.

"No, your Honor," the reporter snapped back. "I'm doing just fine, Judge."

"Okay. Ms. Prosecutor?"

"Pike Martin."

Pike took the stand and explained, as best he could, the finding of Tara's picture in Engle's apartment and Tara's subsequent identification and misidentification of Engle. Bennett asked no questions on cross-examination.

After the lunch recess, the nuts and bolts of the case started.

"The people call Officer Thomas Axelrod."

Bennett leaned over his counsel table. Axelrod. Riverside police officer. Discoverer of diary and pliers. Hero. Asshole. By the time Bennett was through cross-examining him, it was clear there was no warrant. No legal search. At the end of Axelrod's testimony, Judith was left with the dizzying realization the future of the case was now in the lap of the judge.

It took all afternoon to set out the events surrounding Engle's arrest. Finally, the last witness had been called.

"The People rest, your Honor. We have no further witnesses," Judith announced in a strong, clear voice.

Bennett stood.

"Your Honor, at this time the defense moves under Penal Code section 1538.5 to suppress all evidence taken from Mr. Engle's motel room the night of his arrest. You have our points and authorities on the issue raised."

Hern looked from Bennett to Judith Thornton.

"Is there any other evidence the People wish to introduce at this time?" he asked.

"No, your Honor."

"I've read the authorities you've given me, Counsel. On the suppression issue, it is painfully clear to the court that a search warrant was necessary. It is incredible to me that in this day and age, given the care taken in sensitive cases such as this, the law can be so blatantly disregarded by law enforcement. But it does happen. And when it does, the court has no choice but to conclude the items must be excluded. The evidence taken from the defendant's motel room was illegally seized and is therefore excluded."

"Thank you. Your Honor, of course it is Mr. Engle's position that there is now insufficient evidence to bind him over for trial. I would most strongly urge that *all* the prosecution has presented is half a photograph not even containing the likeness of Kelly Solomon, a fingerprint from a beer can . . . that's it. There's nothing else. Absolutely nothing else. I know, Judge—we all know—that the facts of this case cry out for justice. Someone has done the most heinous, heart-wrenching of acts—brutally murdered an innocent little girl. Someone must be accountable for it. Someone must be brought to justice. But, I beseech you, not on the evidence you have before you. If our system means anything, it means the People *must* meet their burden of proof, and if they have not, we must be courageous enough to say so.''

Bennett sat down.

Judith rose, not waiting for the invitation to speak.

''Your Honor, I need not stress that the burden of the People is to show a crime has been committed and there is a reasonable suspicion the defendant is the perpetrator.''

''I know, but, Mrs. Thornton . . .''

This was trouble. She knew it. Hern had used the ''but'' word. He was unsure.

''Where is the *link,* any link, between Mr. Engle and the child's death?''

''It is a linking of circumstantial evidence, your Honor. His fingerprint was on a can at the scene. There is a probability, a high one despite Tara's testimony here, that he was with Tara and Kelly the morning of the kidnapping.''

''But where is the *link* to the murder? *The link?*''

''It is in the evidence I've just outlined, your Honor.''

Hern's questioning ceased. He looked around the courtroom—at the reporters, Deborah Solomon. He was about to speak, then caught himself.

''Court will be in recess until tomorrow morning at nine.''

Pike turned to Judith. ''Well?''

''Brace yourself. It's going to be more than close.''

Hern sequestered himself in his chambers, winnowing through the notes he had taken during Engle's preliminary hearing. There was no doubt the evidence presented to him was too weak to withstand the rigors of trial and the standard of reasonable doubt necessary there. But here, in the admissible evidence, was there a reasonable suspicion Engle had *actually* killed the child? It was a judgment call.

The next morning Judith arrived in court prepared for the worst, carrying the sinking feeling that defeat might actually set upon them. Well, if it did, there would be hell to pay. But not for them. For the court. And all the attorneys knew it. As they arrived at the courtroom, they declined comment to the press—the reporters and television anchors—assembled in the hallway. They did not wait long before Hern took the stand.

"Come to order, please," said the bailiff.

"Counsel, I've examined the evidence presented. It's clear the crime of murder has been committed. And there is a reasonable suspicion the defendant committed the crime." Hern simply repeated the test into the record. That was all the law required the court to say in order to send Engle on his way to trial in the Superior Court.

Judith visibly relaxed as Hern continued.

"Mr. Engle, you will continue to be held without bail. Your arraignment before the Superior Court, at which time you will enter your plea of guilty or not guilty in that court, is set for fifteen days from today. Thank you, Counsel. Court is adjourned."

"Your Honor, if you please." Bennett stood, frowning and clearly disappointed, the inflection in his voice rising and falling. "Can you state for the record the evidence upon which you have based your decision? I just don't see . . ."

"The record can speak for itself, Mr. Bennett."

"Thank you, your Honor."

Outside the courtroom, Farrell paused long enough to tell the assembled press how gratified the prosecution was with the court's ultimate decision to bind Engle over for trial, and to emphasize his faith in a speedy and successful culmination of the case.

The morning after the preliminary hearing, the prosecution team was back in the turkey-shoot room. Pike was sweating when he came in. Abrams was glum. They knew Hern had compromised. He'd kicked the evidence but sent Engle on to Superior Court for the trial. And he had done so on the simplest of evidence. Engle could challenge Hern's order once he got to Superior Court. He could bring a Penal Code section 995 motion and have the Superior Court review the evidence presented at the preliminary hearing to see if there was enough of it for Hern to have done what he did. But that was a long shot at best. The Superior Court would probably find the evidence to be skimpy but adequate and send the case on for trial.

"Well, we're back to where we were two weeks ago," Judith began. "We have no evidence directly tying Engle to the Solomon girl. We're running a terrible risk here now. If we go forward with what we have, we've lost the case. Let's talk for a moment about Niki Crawford."

"She's of no use to us," Pike said, blinking at Judith. "We can keep trying, but she's a loose cannon. If she saw something, she'll need a hell of a lot of psychological help before she can help us."

"Well, we still have our alternatives. I don't want to be the one to bring this up, but you know as well as I that if we go on to trial and we lose, it's all over. Once the first witness is called, double jeopardy attaches, and whatever happens—short of a reversal on an appeal— we can't retry the man. Do we want to go with what we have?''

''Or do we what?'' Pike asked.

''Or do we dismiss the charges and wait . . . tail him until we develop more evidence?''

''You mean, Judith, tail him until he tries to kill some other kid? And just hope we catch him in time?''

Judith remained calm in the face of a clearly rising temperature in the room. ''This is only for purposes of discussion. It's been done before, Pike. What was it we waited in the Stoddard case? It was two years before we had enough to charge him.''

''Yeah, but Stoddard had lived in San Diego for twenty-five years before he killed the Michelson kid. If we let Engle out the door, he's not sticking around. We don't have the resources to tail him day and night for an indeterminate period of time.''

''And what about the victim's family?'' Abrams added. ''How in God's name do we explain to them, let alone to the press, why we let the guy loose again?''

''Okay. How about plea-bargaining the death sentence now?'' Judith was still the picture of calm, but her jaw was set tight. She was not enjoying the hypothetical offers she was presenting to the team. She turned to Farrell. He put his coffee cup on the table, stretched his body into a straight sitting position and leaned forward.

''We can't dismiss the charges. Parker will never agree to it. And Pike's right; the risk is too great that we'll lose him before we can develop anything else. The plea bargain's a rougher question. Parker's going to have to make the final decision on that call. My feeling is that we broach the subject with Bennett. I for one would rather see Engle in prison for life than run the risk of losing him completely. If all else fails, we put it in the hands of the jury. Let them decide. And we all live with the decision.''

31

Bennett and Larson were in a jubilant mood. The disappointment of the preliminary hearing had worn off. They hadn't prevented a bind-over to Superior Court, but they had succeeded in knocking out the evidence that would have made the case easy for the prosecution. There was nothing now standing in the way of a go-for-the-throat defense.

"We have them where we want them, Bobby," Larson gloated. "I think we can get them to drop the death sentence. We might be able to do even better. Maybe they'll even bite a first-degree murder with the possibility of parole."

"I don't think so." Bobby was nonchalant and smiling. "I think we have a good case myself."

"Wait a minute, Bobby," Bennett said. "If we go to trial, we run a risk the jury's going to bring in a guilty verdict with capital punishment. If the jury's generous, it'll bring in guilt without the death penalty and you'll get a life sentence. Why not go for a sure thing?"

Bennett put his hand on Engle's shoulder. "Bobby,

you wanted to plead guilty not a month ago. What's changed?''

"The case, Mr. Bennett. I've spent hours looking at the police records and reading your legal arguments. They don't have anything against me. The reports on the woman who was out at the field, the loony one—she's not going to testify against me. No way.''

"What makes you so sure, Bobby?" Bennett asked.

"I know she won't.''

Bennett and Larson exchanged glances. They had the same thought. Niki Crawford was a potential witness to something, and Bobby knew what that something was. So far, Niki Crawford was a mystery woman discussed in police reports, but she had supplied nothing which could damage them. Her status, however, could change, and judging from Bobby's comments, there was reason to suspect that grounds for a charge existed.

"Be sure you check out the Crawford woman," Bennett said, almost as an aside to Larson before turning back to the problem at hand.

"I won't plead guilty, Mr. Bennett. I want out of here. And we have the kind of case where that can happen. Besides, what have I got to lose? The worst that can happen is I can be found guilty and put to death. And how long would that take?''

"There are three hundred thirty men on death row in California," Larson said, suddenly understanding the thrust of Engle's questions. "Only one person has been executed in this state in twenty-five years. I can pretty much guarantee that it's going to be a good ten years, Bobby, before you have to worry seriously about the gas chamber.''

"See, Mr. Bennett? Like I said, what do I have to lose? And if we beat the rap completely . . . I'm out of this shit hole. I want my shot at getting out of here. I won't plead guilty. And besides . . . I'm going to enjoy it.''

Bennett reflected, shaking his head gently, looking into the intent eyes of Larson and Engle. Larson was rubbing his fingers together. He wanted a trial so badly he could not contain himself. "Let's give it a chance, Harley. Bobby's right. We have nothing to lose.''

"Okay, okay. We tell the prosecutor no deals. But before we do that, I want a breakdown on Niki Crawford to be sure there's nothing that's going to burst your bubble in the middle of trial.''

"One thing more,'' Larson said, directing his comments to Bennett. "We need some positive press, as much as we can get. Several reporters are doing series articles. We need to talk with them, establish a relationship if we can. I want them to disseminate a picture of Bobby that's as sympathetic as possible.''

"That's your forte, Alan. I leave that to you. Just . . . let's consult before any in-depth interviews.''

32

Bennett's choice of Alan Larson as second attorney for the defense was no accident. Larson had handled capital cases at trial and on appeal, and he knew how to create issues at the trial level that could be raised on appeal.

At forty-seven, the wiry man with the unruly woolly hair, steel-blue eyes and sharply chiseled nose was known throughout the state for his scathing contempt of the death penalty. His specialty was mitigation—exploring the factors in a defendant's background that might explain his despicable actions—drug abuse, mental illness, physical abuse—factors which might somehow garner mercy from the jury; mercy which would convert the will to kill the bastard to the desire to grant life without parole.

Larson's past was not beyond reproach. A transplant from Alabama, he'd left that state three years earlier under a cloud. Having established the state's first capital appeals program, his success-at-any-cost, break-the-rules-if-you-must attitude had quickly got him into hot water. There had been allegations of jury tampering and irregular reimbursement of funds. In the end, he had resigned his position, only to have the agency chief reject the resignation and fire him. Still, he had his followers and they extolled his virtues.

Larson brought balance to the defense. He did the things Bennett would not do but realized had to be done: tactical choices that pushed at the edges of ethical limitations.

Bennett and Larson had agreed to meet with reporter Jon Kolker. His reputation was impeccable. They felt they could be candid with him. They could trust him. They might even coax a favorable story out of him.

As they drove over the arching Coronado Bay Bridge to meet him for lunch, Navy battleships and sailboats crisscrossed wakes beneath them. It was a patent San Diego day, the kind memorialized in photos by the Chamber of Commerce. There was a crisp, cold bite in the air and a clear blue sky, a combination that said without anyone's looking at the calendar that the football season had begun. The red-roofed turrets of the Hotel del Coronado loomed upward on the horizon, its century-old Victorian gingerbread architecture towering over the buildings surrounding it.

Briefly Bennett and Larson reviewed the topics they did not want to discuss: the feelings of Kelly's parents, the facts of the case and, of course, Bobby's relishing the prospect of a trial.

After parking their car on one of the residential side streets adjacent to the hotel, Bennett stood on the sidewalk and waited while Larson rummaged through the mound of files in the backseat of the car, looking for his briefcase. Joggers were plentiful today, sweatbands coiled around their heads, elastic running suits clinging, wet with perspiration, to their bodies. In the distance he could see a few men standing at the shoreline, fishing poles poised hopefully but their owners undoubtedly reconciled to rest, not necessarily to success. San Diego moved in recreational circles. It jogged, sailed around the bays, biked along the roadways and in its spare time went to the museums of Balboa Park, the zoo and Sea World. Visually, it was clean, bright, even breathtaking, like some sprawling, immaculately manicured woman you realize might have no soul, no spirit, behind the looks.

There was no doubt in Bennett's mind: he loved the city. But it was such an enigma to him. Even in the height of the turmoil of the sixties and seventies, when colleges across the country found themselves the center of social reform and turmoil, this city, with its two major college campuses, remained unexcited and calm, distanced in all its beauty from the woes of society. The population was here to play and relax, not to change the world. Its world was, after all, pretty nice. No, Bennett had decided long ago that there might never be a major social upheaval here. The soul of San Diego was really too shallow to muster the degree of outrage that insurrection and disobedience required.

He took a deep breath of the sea air. It was such a beautiful day. Larson made his way to Bennett's side.

"Ready?" Larson asked, checking his briefcase for a notepad.

"Ready. Kolker said he'd meet us in the patio lounge out by the tennis courts."

Kolker was already seated and waiting for them. In the first minutes of discussion it became clear that his primary interest was in their role as attorneys and their views of capital punishment.

"How do you guys sleep at night, knowing you're defending the likes of Engle? I couldn't do it."

He was baiting them. But it was okay.

"Well, we're not the consciences of the community.

We leave that job to the jury, and to you newspaper reporters,'' Bennett responded.

"Yeah, but how can you divorce yourselves from your feelings like that? How can you do any kind of justice to the justice system that way?''

"Define what you mean by 'system.' It's a system of law, not justice.''

"Well, with all due respect, that sounds—well—'silly' is the word that comes to mind, Harley.''

"No, wait, now. The word 'justice' . . . is premised on feelings. That statue of Justice is blinded for a reason. We can't let our emotions and gut feelings control how we deal with our criminal system. If we do, why not just turn Engle over to any group of angry people and let them decide his guilt and punishment?''

"And you stand in the way of that,'' Kolker said, more as a statement than a question.

"I stand in the way of that. The rule of law stands in the way of that. We're his experts who are trained in the rules of law. We're the ones who assure emotions aren't used to decide if he's guilty and, if he is, what we do with him. The system's ability to deal with the Engles of the world is less important than a retreat from the law.''

"How do you tell that to Deborah and Abe Solomon?'' Kolker asked.

"I don't. They wouldn't understand. They might have at one time. Not now. You explain it. At least you should. Sometimes I think that's an impossible thing to do. But that's why Alan and I are here this afternoon. It needs to be explained.''

"Rule of law? If the rule of law is supposed to govern capital cases, how do you both explain your creation of such havoc in the courtroom? I hear, Alan, you've pulled some pretty interesting stunts during trial.''

Larson joined the fray. "You've been doing your homework, Jon. Did you have any particular stunt in mind?"

"As a matter of fact, yeah, I did. The one where you jumped over the banister in the courtroom in front of the jury—and the judge. I hear that one got you a five-hundred-dollar fine."

Larson feigned a heavy sigh. "Yes . . . but I brought in a not-guilty on that one."

Kolker grimaced, inviting a reaction.

"You're frowning, Jon. You still think there's ethics involved in capital cases. There aren't. There are only dollars and cents and control of the courtroom. It's a war now."

"Why, Alan? I don't understand why."

"Time, Jon, time. That is what we buy. Every stay of execution, every writ of habeas corpus that issues, every evidentiary hearing for every jailhouse snitch who turns state's evidence, keeps someone off death row or post-pones the gas chamber."

"That's anarchy."

"The act of death is anarchy, Jon. Using a needle for a lethal injection or gas, seeing a human life dissolve right there in front of you—that's anarchy. And that's what this is all about." He leaned forward, inviting a response from Kolker.

So that was what it was all about. There were no rules, there was no law, when it came to preventing a death sentence. And to those who hemmed and hawed and bemoaned the war, Larson would say, "Just try to stop me." He would irritate the judge until he made a mistake and his client got a reversal. He wouldn't mind. He'd driven the best of them up the walls—successfully, one might add.

"I think I understand where you're coming from,

Alan. But let me be sure," Kolker interjected. "Your goal in the courtroom is to create mistakes. I'm sorry, I can't help smiling. I'm somewhat incredulous. It all runs so counter to everything I know about trials."

"It's not new. The attorneys in the system know it's there. The prosecution prepares for it."

"Yeah, but your outlook on the system is new to me."

"That may be, Jon. I guess now that I think about it, you wouldn't have found me out there ten years ago. I guess you could call me a new warrior. We thought we could change the public's mind, persuade it the death penalty is barbaric. All we got was more humane ways to commit the ultimate act of death . . . lethal injection rather than the guillotine. But the end result is still death and that's what's barbaric. The guy still dies."

"You frighten me, Alan, you really do. But I'm not sure why. I'd rather fight this out on the straight ethical question. For or against the death penalty. Not the guerrilla warfare you're talking about."

"That's my point, though, Jon. Don't you see? The ethical battle is over. We've fought for twenty years on that battleground. And we've lost. Eighty percent of the people in California still favor the death penalty. We— I fight the battle on my own terms now. From the first jury-panel call to the moment they might strap that man into the gas-chamber chair, I will do everything and anything I can to prevent that punishment from being imposed. That's my whole reason for existing, for being an attorney. There is no challenge too late, too procedurally incorrect."

"You mean there is no rule of law," Kolker added.

"There is no rule of law."

"Harley, do you subscribe to Alan's approach?"

"I think that . . . it is a valid approach. It has a place

in the presentation of a case. I suppose I'm somewhere in the middle. Those who oppose the death penalty as personally as Alan and those who favor its application will always be at odds. They will never understand one another. It's easy to say the law should change without guerrilla warfare, but I would remind you that our country was founded on civil disobedience. In the end, the public will prevail. Laws will change, maybe to keep my friend here from jumping over banisters.'' Bennett grinned at Larson.

"Do you think there's a chance your client will actually walk on this?" Kolker asked.

Larson replied. "He is going to walk, Jon. Just keep watching."

"I will, Alan. I promise I will."

PART FOUR

THE NEW WARRIOR

33

The law of California requires all police reports be made available to defense counsel as soon as they are prepared. Alan Larson had read the police reports detailing Niki Crawford's mysterious and tenuous connection to the Solomon murder case, and he could read between the lines as well as the next person. Niki knew far more than she was telling. He'd pieced together the prosecution's evidence. It could all be dealt with. But Niki Crawford was the potential surprise witness capable of doing real damage to the defense case. He didn't like surprises. And so the gamble he was about to take was worth the risk of approbation he might garner if he were caught.

It wasn't a matter of conscience, or even of ethics. It was information-gathering, pure and simple. He didn't intend to hurt anyone. That thought hadn't ever entered his mind. No, it was just that he didn't care if he hurt anyone. He needed to assess Niki Crawford up close. Maybe even learn the truth from the woman, who was so unwilling to divulge it.

Niki was easy to find. Her address and phone number had been prominently displayed on the police reports detailing Pike's interviews with her. Given her obvious desire to avoid all discussion concerning the death of Kelly Solomon, Larson decided to drop in on her unexpectedly and utilize a somewhat different approach than had the police officers. He didn't want an outright confrontation with her. That was a waste of energy, and in his experience, it was always unproductive. But he was not above some harmless chicanery.

In his beige twill pants and blue knit shirt, Larson approached Niki's house, still formulating exactly what he wanted to say to her. By the time she answered the door, he had decided on his course of action.

"Miss Crawford?"

"Yes . . ."

"My name is Jeff Solomon. Please, is there some way I can talk to you for just a minute? My little girl's the one who was murdered at the park turnout where you work."

Niki stepped backward. She'd been caught off guard, just as Larson had hoped she would be.

"I'm so sorry to bother you like this, but my little girl . . . she . . . someone has killed her. I need to talk with someone, anyone, who has any information about it . . . please. The police say you saw the person who did it. . . ." He was hoping his blue eyes were sufficiently pleading.

"Why . . . I . . ."

"Can I come in?"

Larson took a step forward.

"Well, I guess so."

He pushed gently on the door separating them and waited a moment for her to adjust her position sideways to accommodate his entrance.

Larson, his shoulders slumped forward in mock despair, glanced forlornly around the room, walked to the sofa and sat down, without specifically being invited to do so.

For an awkward moment Niki was not quite sure how she should react, what she should say. Lacking words, she went to the sofa and sat next to him. Larson watched her carefully, noticing the slight limp remaining from her accident.

"I was so sorry to hear about your little girl's death, Mr. Solomon. I . . . can't imagine anything more horrible than . . . that. But I don't know how I can possibly help you."

He had a choice here. He could pander to sheer emotion or get right to the point.

"The police reports all say you are a witness to the . . . to Kelly's . . . death." He could have phrased it differently. He could have said it had been reported she might be a witness. Larson chose instead to catch her off guard again in the hope this form of confrontation might shake loose an admission. It didn't.

"Oh, I wouldn't say that . . . no, I wouldn't . . . I . . ."

"It's not for me that I'm asking, Miss Crawford. It's . . ." He was trying to think quickly. "It's for my wife. You see, she's hurting so badly. Anything you tell us would be confidential. . . . Did you see who it was that . . . k-k-killed her?" The stutter was effective, he thought.

She caught her breath and shook her head. Her physical reactions intrigued him.

"No, really, I didn't. I mean, I didn't see anything. I don't know why the police even wanted to talk to me in the first place. If I had seen anyone do something like . . . what happened to your child, I would have . . . told . . . someone."

Niki's right leg began shaking, her knee bouncing up and down.

He watched her knee. He'd hit on something here. What was it she had said? *If she had seen what happened.*

"Did you see . . . her body?"

"Uh . . . what . . . the body? No, I didn't . . . I couldn't have. I didn't see anything."

She was trying to convince herself. Now maybe an emotional plea.

"Couldn't you have? Please. Just think back. We need to know . . . any little detail. You know how it is . . . I lost my little girl. We keep trying to piece her last hours together . . . we have to know what they were like for her. Can't you remember?"

"I didn't see anything."

There was a belligerent tone rising. He'd pushed a button.

Larson could see Niki's leg still moving rapidly up and down, her knee still bouncing.

"Can you tell me if you saw anything like a man with a little girl, anything that looked different or funny?"

"I'm sorry, I didn't. Please . . . this is very hard for me. I do know how you're feeling . . . I do, really . . . I do."

Niki, who had been sitting rigidly, began rocking back and forth. Larson had seen fetal rocking hundreds of times in defendants, victims of violent crimes and witnesses. She was reverting, using the most primitive and basic of defense mechanisms to avoid the pain involved in confronting the truth. An even more direct approach might be useful now.

"What did you see out there?" As soon as he had asked the question, he knew he'd lost his cover.

The question had jarred her. It was too clinical. Too detached. As that thought sank in she realized the first name this man had given her was Jeff. She searched her memory. Jeff wasn't the name of the girl's father. She was sure of that.

She stopped rocking and looked at him. "What did you say your name was?"

Larson didn't answer.

"Who are you?" she asked, almost under her breath.

"Please . . . forgive me, Miss Crawford. My name is Alan Larson. I'm one of the defense attorneys who's been appointed to help the man accused of killing Kelly Solomon. I needed to talk to you and . . . I was afraid you might not want to talk with me. It's just very important you tell me what you saw."

She stood, silently staring at Larson, the anger slowly rising in her. Larson stood too. Taking one of his business cards from his pocket, he extended it to her. When she did not reach for it, he laid it on the cocktail table in front of the sofa.

"Maybe we can still talk, Miss Crawford. I'm authorized to compensate you for your . . . cooperation." Most of the time the payment-for-information pitch didn't work. But it was always worth a try.

"Get out." She was monotone.

"I'm sorry I had to do this. Please, if you want to talk, call me. Any time of the day or night." Halfway to the door, he turned. "And the compensation offer still stands."

A low growl was emitting from her throat as he made his way to the door.

When he had gone, Niki sat down again, confused, shaking with anger. She wanted to be anywhere else.

As for Larson, he had gotten exactly what he had come for. He knew he wouldn't get specifics from her. But what he did get was invaluable. She had seen something. And whatever it was, it had so traumatized her that she was suppressing it. Moreover, and this pleased him the most, she was fragile. By the time the prosecution called her to the stand, he would know exactly what buttons to push to utterly destroy her. Guilt. Blood. Bodies. In that order. He had gone to Niki Crawford hoping to find out what she'd seen. He had left with something far better—the knowledge that he could neutralize her.

Larson ran the last hundred feet back to his car. He had struck pay dirt.

34

It had snowed all week, but Highway 330 to Big Bear
had been plowed, leaving sharply carved piles of white
ice lining the road. Niki Crawford pushed the buttons
that lowered the front windows of her car.

At Running Springs, four miles short of her destina-
tion, Niki pulled her car into the parking lot of a small
coffee shop. Although a tiny bell rang as she pushed the
door open, she stood for a minute at the cash register,
waiting for someone to seat her.

"Just take a spot. I'll be right there," a woman called
out from somewhere behind the kitchen door.

Alone in the restaurant, Niki sat at one of the red
leather booths next to a window. It didn't take long for
her to choose something from the single-page typewrit-
ten menu tucked behind the sugar dispenser.

"Well, what can I get you this morning, dear? How
about a cup of coffee?"

The waitress had begun the questions as she came
through the swinging kitchen door.

"Coffee, yes, please. And two eggs, scrambled. With
wheat toast, no butter."

"It'll just take a minute. Are you here to ski?"

"Uh, no, uh . . . need a couple of days to myself."

"Well, that's as good a reason as any for coming up here. I came up to sort things out fifteen years ago when my husband died, and I just stayed. I sold everything down in Colton. Are you staying here in Running Springs?"

"No, I rented a little cabin in Big Bear City, out on Fox Farm Road. Near the Trout Farm. I've stayed there before. It's walking distance to the shopping area."

"I know that area. But I'd be real careful if I were you. There's been four attacks on women out near there this last week. Some guy strong-arming folks. He follows them. Just be careful, is all. I'll get your breakfast."

As Niki ate, the woman disappeared again into the back of the restaurant. "Just leave your money at the register," she called out.

When Niki had finished eating and was back at her car, she stood looking up at the towering pines blanketed with patches of white. It was good to be outside again. She could stay here forever. Forget that little girl. Start all over. It would be easy.

Her intended two-day stay stretched to four, and she had told the real-estate rental office to reserve the cabin for a week longer. This morning the Snow Summit ski resort was not crowded—the way she liked it. Before her accident she had tried to come up here twice a year to ski for a few days. She was a passable skier, just good enough to make it more fun than work.

She sat outside on the wooden deck, sipping coffee. One at a time and in small groups, skiers raced past her in their neon-colored nylon outfits. Slowly a discomfort began to grow within her. Its source was hard to identify. It wasn't their smiles or her envy of the freedom with which their bodies moved. She struggled to isolate the feeling.

The ski poles they were carrying were irritating her.

The sudden realization generated a dread from deep inside her. A fear which rose and seized her, momentarily quickening her pulse, taking her to the brink of panic and releasing her, confused and agitated. And with it had come a flicker of knowledge, startlingly swift in its emergence. Had she sat for a moment more, maybe it would have come all the way back to her. But she left. Whatever door had begun to open, she slammed shut.

For the next week Niki divided her time between reading and taking walks. Her foot had given her no trouble the entire time, and the exercise felt good.

That evening she walked to the grocery store. By the time she started back with a bag of groceries, the sun had begun to go down. It would take her at least twenty-five minutes to walk the stretch of highway past the lake, then north a quarter mile through the steep, winding streets which led to the cabin.

As she turned off the highway and away from the security of traffic, daylight had disappeared, replaced by silver moonlight reflecting off the white snow. Crystal-clear. Clean. Silence. Light and dark were folded one into the other, each at peace. A benediction. She could hear only her own footsteps and the periodic sloshing of snow falling from the trees.

Then there was, she thought, another sound, coming from behind her. The crush of ice. Beneath footsteps?

She turned.

There was nothing but cold wind stinging her face. The waitress's warning returned. *Someone was stalking people in the area.*

Niki tightened her hold on the grocery bag and quickened her pace. Her legs began to ache as she gauged the distance remaining before she reached the safety of her cabin. Faster. Faster. Until she stumbled and fell forward, to the sound of smashing glass. A jar of mayonnaise lay in pieces.

Niki twisted her body, fully expecting to see a figure hovering above her. But there was no one. She turned onto her knees and pulled herself up.

She was hearing things. The plop of snow hitting the ground startled her.

The cabin was a block away. By the time she had reached it, her knees were hurting, and she realized for the first time that they were badly scraped. But she couldn't examine the damage. The feeling that someone, something, was right behind her, right on top of her, was overwhelming.

There was no time to fumble for a key. She couldn't remember if she'd locked the door. Niki threw herself at the door, pushing hard against it at the same time.

Dear God, be open! she thought.

It flew open. Niki slammed it shut, turned the double-bolt lock and leaned against it, breathing in deep, loud gasps. Her hand rubbed the wall for the light switch.

Then she thought she saw something to her right.

She struggled to silence her breathing. There it was again. *My God, he's in here with me! He's here! I've locked myself in with him.* In the darkness her hand swept along the wall for the light switch.

A scream pierced the air. As the room filled with light, Niki's eyes fixed on the movement next to her. In the mirror, on the side wall where her pursuer should have been, was Niki's face—staring back, twisted in terror. She slumped against the wall and slid to the floor, sobbing.

35

Judith was at home, working late into the night. She looked at the clock on her desk. Midnight. She was preparing for a trial that had no evidence strong enough to give her the kind of confidence she insisted on, and the one witness who was a long shot, probably the most crucial witness, had disappeared.

Since she'd heard of Niki's accident, it had been Judith's worst fear that the woman would leave town and not return. Both Pike and Abrams had spent the better part of the past three days talking to Niki's friends and former coworkers. No one had heard from her. No one knew where she was.

The sudden scuffling of footsteps outside her bedroom startled her.

"Elizabeth, honey, what's wrong?"

The child was standing in the doorway, her arms encircling three of the stuffed animals she slept with: Shamu, the whale; Sharkey, the shark; Cheetah, the cheetah.

"I had a bad dream, Mommy. There was an evil devil with shiny red eyes chasing me. He was going to eat me—then he turned into a black horse and rode away.''

''Okay, young lady, let's get you back to bed.''

Judith scooped her and the animals up into her arms and headed for Elizabeth's bedroom.

''I'm scared, though. He's in there.'' She was crying.

''Honey, there's no devil. You just had a bad dream.''

''But, Mommy, he said he's coming back.''

''Oh, yeah? We'll take care of that. Let's take a look.''

The bedroom was all white-and-violet ruffles; the bedspread, curtain valance and the skirt around the dressing room table were perfectly coordinated.

Judith turned on the overhead light. ''See, honey, nothing here. Now watch.''

She turned off the light, paused and turned it back on. ''No goblins in here. . . .''

''Devil, Mommy. It was the devil, not a plain old goblin.''

''No devil either, Elizabeth. Anywhere. Now, into bed.''

The little girl hopped into bed and carefully lined up the three animals on her pillow.

''Mommy, are there real devils?''

''You mean the kind with long red, pointed tails and pitchforks?''

''No, I mean the kind like on the office building downtown, with ugly faces sticking their tongues out at you.''

Judith's index finger tapped the point of Elizabeth's nose. ''No, that's sculpture. Now go to sleep.''

''Rachel my friend, says the devil was an angel once. Is that true, Mommy?''

''I think I remember reading something like that somewhere.''

''She says God is stronger than the devil too, and even

if the devil wants to kill something, God can make him stop. Can He?''

Judith sat at the edge of her daughter's bed.

"God can stop him, yes, but sometimes He doesn't.''

"Why? If He was a good God, he would.''

"Maybe God lets bad things happen so we know what good things should be like. He kind of teaches us by showing us bad things.''

From the look on Elizabeth's face, Judith knew she'd confused her.

"It's like Rachel, your friend, is kind to you. Eric Mills, he teases you. Well, having Eric to deal with makes Rachel seem really nice and gives you a kind of lesson that it's better to be like her. See?''

She'd lost her. It was understandable, since what she had said was either quite profound or downright silly.

"But, Mommy, would God save me?''

The whole topic suddenly became focused.

"Yes, of course He would, honey. You say just a little bit of a prayer and He'll hear you. He can hear every prayer. He'll take that old devil and squish him clean away.''

"And kill him?''

"And kill him.''

That was all Elizabeth wanted to hear. All Judith needed to say was yes, God could and would protect her. She smiled as she drew the covers up to Elizabeth's chin and waited until she could hear her breathing heavily.

As she was about to leave the room, a fear crept over her. Judith checked the window to be sure it was locked.

36

Judith had been sitting in the coffee shop of the Westgate Hotel, near the courthouse, for thirty minutes. The
term "coffee shop" was a misnomer. The Westgate was
every inch a four-star hotel. Its mint-green-and-gold an-
tique decor and crystal chandelier automatically lowered
voices within its tapestry-covered walls. The hotel coffee
shop on the first floor was the less formal of the two
public dining rooms. If one sought live harp music with
lunch, one ate at the Fountainbleau Room on the third
floor. For a faster lunch, the first floor offered an abbre-
viated menu, white linen tablecloths and smaller chan-
deliers.

She looked up from her Cobb salad, one of those con-
coctions of chopped eggs, bacon, turkey, ham and
cheeses neatly arranged in rows over iceberg lettuce.

"Melanie! It's so good to see you."

"Sorry I'm late. Partnership meeting. We're getting
ready to do our summer hiring."

The waiter pulled the chair out for Melanie and placed
the linen napkin on her lap in one continuous choreo-
graphic movement. She took the menu. Her manicured

red nails rested momentarily on it, but she didn't look at it.

"The Cobb for me too, please. Dressing on the side."

Melanie Akerman had graduated from law school with Judith. The only two women in their graduating class, they'd crammed for finals together and served as coeditors on the law review. Both had graduated magna cum laude. Melanie, however, had chosen to pursue a career in civil law, while Judith had opted for government employment.

Perhaps it was the ego bruising Melanie had taken in trying to establish a law career in private civil practice that had made her a militant advocate of woman's rights. She had helped establish the first women's bar association and then served as its first president. She'd been the first woman to march into the males-only Chamber Club Restaurant and demand to be served. She had also been the first woman from any of the local law schools to be hired by Magee, Pinsky, Tuck and McTear, San Diego's largest civil law firm. Up to that time, the most prestigious firms hired from the major law schools outside the city. A year ago Melanie had become a partner at Magee. Despite their disparate careers, she and Judith saw each other for lunch every few months.

Melanie settled into the high-backed chair, relaxed.

"Well, how's it going? I'm reading all about that Engle case. It sounds incredible."

Judith's eyes followed the diamond tennis bracelet on Melanie's waving hand.

"It's challenging. Between trial and home . . ."

The Cobb slipped silently onto the table before Melanie.

"Your mom's doing well?"

"No, not really. She's hanging in there, but it's just a matter of time. She's losing weight now so fast."

"I'm sorry. I don't envy you. How's Elizabeth taking it? She's close to your mom."

"Oh, she's fine. She's always fine. You're looking well."

"Too much work. Too many meetings, but I still love it. Tom's still happy at the city attorney's office. I just wish I saw a little more of him at home. Next year I'd like to start thinking about having a kid."

"The same Melanie. You're still trying to complicate your life. I'm trying to simplify mine."

"Never simplify. Simplify and you die! You end up on the slow track with no options."

"I'm optioned out. I used to think choices were all I wanted." Judith laughed. "Remember how offended we'd get when we thought some option was closed?"

"Well, I guess I should apologize, then, beforehand, but I wanted to have lunch today to talk about an option of sorts." Melanie glanced around quickly to ensure what she was about to say remained private, and leaned forward. "What if you were offered something outside the criminal system? Would you consider taking it?"

"What?"

"What if you were offered a position in a civil firm?"

"Don't beat around the bush, Melanie. What are you talking about?"

"I'm talking about my firm. We're trying to set up a new litigation department to handle administrative cases, especially medical licensing matters. Think you might be interested?" Hearing no immediate response, she added, "How's one hundred fifty thou a year sound?"

"This really has hit me out of the blue, you know! I'd have to think about Elizabeth. She's the priority. I'd like to spend *more* time with her, not *less*."

"Afraid she won't remember you?"

"It's not *whether* she'll remember me. She will. It's

how she's going to remember me. What am I now? Pushing into my forties. And do you know what my very best memory is of my mother? It's a simple little thing. Her sitting on our back porch at the first house we lived in, a little, nondescript two-bedroom house. She's just sitting on the top step watching me play. And every once in a while she'd call me over to have a slice of an apple or a piece of celery. She liked to cut them all up for me, and we'd just sit out there like that. I wonder sometimes what kind of memories Elizabeth's going to have of me." Judith cringed. "Probably me running around in a frenzy in the morning trying to get her, Mom, the house, me, the housekeeper and the nurse ready to go in thirty minutes. Or me screaming across an acre of land. You know, Melanie, I'd like Elizabeth to have the same kind of memories I do of my mom."

"Well, wouldn't you like to do it with a bigger budget?"

"Sure. And I could get an intercom throughout the house. I don't think so, Melanie."

"Chances like this don't come along too often, you know."

"I know. I'm just not corporate material. Even at its worst, I'd rather be where I am than where you are. . . . Sorry."

After lunch, Judith walked slowly back to her office.

Her heart skipped a beat as she entered the reception room.

Niki Crawford was waiting to see her.

Niki could not avoid the unavoidable. She could leave Engle behind, but not her conscience. What she had seen, what she had done, needed to be directly confronted.

"Mrs. Thornton . . . I need to talk with you."

37

Pike had been quickly summoned by Judith while Niki was escorted to one of the office conference rooms. Fearful Niki might disappear on them again, Judith arranged for a tape recorder to be brought in to them. On arrival, Pike couldn't resist the temptation to make amends.

"Would you like a Coke? Pepsi? Water?" he asked Niki.

Niki eyed him warily as Judith's quick glance brought an apologetic shrug and ended his inquiries.

"No, thanks."

"Ms. Crawford," Judith said, "I'm very sorry about your accident." Her expression of sympathy unacknowledged, she continued. "I've read a report prepared by Officer Martin back when he came to see you and you identified a photo of a car he showed you. I think you told him you saw one like it near the time Kelly Solomon disappeared. I also spoke with Mr. Eberle. I don't want to put words in his mouth, but it sounds like you've got an awful lot of anxiety about what you saw out at the field in Mission Valley. Are those pretty fair statements?''

"I guess so."

"Mr. Eberle tells me you aren't eating or sleeping too well. Have those conditions improved any?"

"Not really. What else does he say?"

"Well, he says you saw a man and a little girl out there. And he says there's something you saw that seems important to you, but you can't remember it.''

"I know there's something. But I don't know what it is.''

"I'd like to help you remember. Whatever it is could be very important to us.''

"I don't think anything's going to help. It's useless.''

"Well, let's see. . . . You saw a picture of a little girl when Detective Martin came to see you. Is that the little girl you saw at the turnout?''

"I—I can't say. Don't ask me.''

"Okay. Let's talk about your dreams, Niki. Mr. Eberle says they're a real problem for you. Have they continued to be a problem since you went to the turnout with him?''

"They're the same. I keep having these dreams over and over. Each time I see more of the picture, more details here and there.''

"Well, that's good! Really! The pieces are fitting together a little bit better.''

"I wish they didn't fit at all.''

"Niki, listen. I've been a prosecutor a long time. I've dealt with a lot of victims and witnesses who've had really bad things happen to them. And you know, the thing almost all of them say is, 'I wish it didn't happen.' So I understand where your feelings are coming from and why you might not want to remember.''

Niki fell silent, her head bowed.

"I don't know why it is you're having such a tough time remembering what you dreamed or what you saw, but whatever it is, I'm going to tell you up-front that you ought to get it off your chest. What can we do to help you? What do *you* want to do?"

"Leave town, leave the country and be able to stay away."

"Well, you know that won't work. Running away never does. Let's talk about this recurring dream. The last one you had—what was happening?

"I'll try. First, I s-see this particular individual and I wake up in a cold sweat, really edgy."

"When was your last dream?"

"Last night—this morning. Whenever I woke up."

"For my benefit, where did you start this dream?" Judith asked.

"I'm just coming back from Fashion Valley after I went shopping."

"What time was that?"

"Maybe seven or eight or so. It's dark."

"And then what happens?"

"I'm driving past the field kind of slow. I have my high beams on, seeing what's there . . . and I see this car."

"What kind of car was it?"

"Blue, with paneling kind of on the side. He doesn't take care of it very well 'cause it's all faded and scratched up. It's a two-door, and the two rear windows back toward the hatch are tinted black; you can't see through them. It's real dirty. Especially . . . there's a lot of dirt underneath where the back tires are and where the back tires would kick up dirt on the back."

"Is it fresh dirt?"

"I can't tell—it was just dirt."

"What else is there?"

"There's a guy leaning on the car. His car's pulled out. There's a line that comes around the turnout. His front tires are *on* the white line. I don't know if I see him or not, but I think I see him."

"What does this guy look like?"

"He's kind of thin. I think he has Levi's on and, you know, a white T-shirt. The Levi's have kind of dirt on them, and the T-shirt was all, oh, I don't know how to describe it. And he has shoulder-length brown hair."

"Can you describe the guy's shirt?"

"Well, it's kind of grimy, it almost looks like he's been in a fight, you know, kinda how it looks. . . ."

"Sure. Somebody's been struggling."

"Yeah. Like he's been fighting with someone."

"Fighting with someone. Okay, now, how would we know that? What in the dream makes you think he might have been fighting?"

"Oh, just the way the shirt looks."

"Is the griminess all over the shirt?"

"No, right near the belly."

"Was it a splash or a dot?"

"The whole area was kinda . . ."

"Full of blood?"

"No! Just dirty, but it wasn't dirt."

"Okay. And then where does the dream go?"

"That's it, I wake up, bingo."

"That's real important, Niki. Is it when you see him or when you realize that it's blood?"

"It's *not* blood!"

"Oh, I'm sorry. It's a stain that made you know he was fighting."

"It just . . . looks like he's been in a fight, I see that, and then I almost hit his car and I wake up."

"What are his eyes like? What kind of look does he have in his eyes?"

"Dark, beady eyes that look right through you like an I-dare-you type. You know how you get those people who look that way all the time? It's just the look that he has, like I don't really care because you're not going to get me."

"He almost challenges you?"

"Yeah."

"Anything else you want to tell us?"

"No, just . . . when *he* came over with pictures of the car and said have you ever seen this car and I said yes. Then the dreams got bad."

"Is it okay to say that when you first talked to Detective Martin, you knew this man with the dirty shirt had something to do with the little girl you saw walking across the field with a man?"

"No . . . I don't know. They're all pieces in some crazy puzzle."

"What about the little girl?"

"You mean the girl that got killed out in the field?"

"That's the one you saw in the photo. This is really important, Niki. Could you have seen that girl with the man in your dream? The man with the dirty T-shirt?"

"I don't know."

"Niki, I think you *do* know."

"I don't. . . . I want to go now."

"Niki, you know we'll need to bring you in to testify in the case."

"I can't."

"Why not? What are you hiding, Niki?"

"Nothing!"

"Get it out in the open, Niki. It's what's going to stop the dreams, don't you understand?"

"No . . . I . . . don't."

"Why did you come here today?"

"I thought if I talked with you I could get this whole

mess cleared up and put everything back the way it should be. . . . It's my last chance. I don't want to see him again. I want to have a peaceful life again.''

"Why do you think he comes back in your dreams?"

"I don't know."

"Do you think he'll come back at you if you see him in court?"

"Maybe. The way I understand it, they can get him on kidnapping and put him away for maybe a couple of years."

"Niki—Niki! We aren't going through all this so we can put him away for a couple of years! He's getting the death sentence. At the least it's life imprisonment. But the jury needs it all set out in front of them. We just about *have* to have an eyewitness."

Pike had been silent long enough. "And we don't have an eyewitness! So there's no guarantee this guy's going to get *anything!*"

Niki began to laugh.

Judith leaned forward. "I know how tough it is, but I also know you're trying, and that's the part of you I'm talking to. I'm not talking to your fear, Niki. I'm talking to the part of you that wants to do the right thing. You know what the right thing is, don't you?"

"Yes and no."

"Okay, what's the 'no'?"

"The 'no' is, I can't tell you anything else because I'm not sure of it. You can't say anything unless you absolutely, positively know it."

Judith placed her hand on Niki's knee, instantly stopping the bouncing. It was the same way she stopped the occasional reflexive bouncing in her mother's knees after she'd been moved into her wheelchair. The reaction was a nervous one.

"Niki, look, the trial's not far off. We're going to be

sending you a subpoena to appear. I want to leave you with one thought. When you're called, tell the truth. As hard as it might be to do, you have to do your best to tell the truth.''

"But I don't think I know what the truth is.''

"Then just tell the facts. And, Niki, I want you to call me every day and let me know you're okay. All right? I don't want to lose you.''

"You won't. I don't really think I can help you. But I need to try.''

"Niki?''

"Yeah.''

"One more thing. If you need some help getting through this, we can arrange for you to talk to someone, a psychiatrist.''

"I don't need anyone's help, Mrs. Thornton. This is something I need to deal with.''

"I know, but . . . just keep it in mind. If things start to close in on you, call me, okay?''

"Okay. I had a guy come to see me about the case . . . a defense attorney.''

"Did he tell you his name?'' Pike asked.

"Uh . . . Al something.''

Pike's face turned red. "Alan Larson? A thin, blue-eyed guy?''

"That's him! He lied to me and said he was the little girl's father. I felt so stupid . . . I should have known.''

Judith looked toward Pike and shook her head, signaling him again to silence.

"Miss Crawford . . . Niki, that kind of thing happens. It shouldn't but it does. Just remember, you're not under any obligation to talk to anyone.''

"I won't be talking to anyone else, Mrs. Thornton.''

When Niki had gone, Judith turned to Pike. "Well, what do you think?''

"About Larson?"

"No. He won't try any more stunts. It's too close to trial. I meant, what do you think about Niki?"

"I think we've got big trouble. A weird man in a grimy T-shirt? Cars pointed the wrong way? Sounds more like a bad dream she had than something she saw. And how's this fit with her seeing a man and a girl and a body? Was he digging, burying Kelly Solomon? Is that why he's got dirt all over him? It makes sense to me. It could happen. But she tells it as if it's a dream. The problem is, a jury might think everything she tells them is part of some bad dream she's having. Trying to get the truth out of her is like trying to nail Jell-O to the wall."

Judith exhaled loudly. "We put her on the stand and cross our fingers."

"She could kill us, Judith. You know that. And the defense is going to rip her to shreds. And if that happens . . ."

Judith finished his sentence. "We lose."

38

While the attorneys plotted their initial approaches to trial, Pike dug into Engle's history. It was there he would find the likely defense strategies. Unusual EEGs might produce the insanity defenses. A history of child abuse would certainly end up as a mitigation factor at the sentencing trial. If the prosecutors knew his history well enough, they'd be that much better prepared for trial.

It wasn't just the big-ticket items that interested Pike. It was the little pearls, as he liked to call them. That was what Pike was looking for. The bits and pieces of information you find if you look closely enough at the information in the files and you know what you're looking for and where to look. It was Pike's specialty. It was what he liked most about his work. Now he sat winnowing through a two-and-a-half-foot-thick dossier on Engle.

"What have you got there?" Pike could tell by the way Abrams asked the question that he knew what it was Pike had in front of him. "Where the hell were you able to get your hands on Engle's correctional file so fast?"

"Subpoena."

"No shit. Corrections didn't put up a battle?"

"Not this time."

Prisons throughout the state were regulated by the State Department of Corrections. Aside from its responsibilities to maintain the inmates, it was also the state agency whose responsibility it was to maintain the records, past and present, for each of them. And it guarded this responsibility zealously. Generally speaking, the department resisted requests to turn over its records, and it didn't matter who was requesting them and for what reason. It routinely turned subpoenas over to the State Attorney General's Office to examine with a fine-tooth comb and object where any objection lay: *the subpoena is too broad; too much a fishing expedition; not specific enough; not properly signed.*

"What were you able to get?"

Pike looked at the handwritten list he was in the process of preparing. "Let's see. To start with, I've got Engle's juvenile records from the Youth Authority. And the records from his imprisonment back in '79. That's the prior kidnap and assault."

"Anything of interest?"

"We have a real choice actor here. Some of these are real gems. He's been in and out of trouble since he could walk. Truancy, then theft, then assaults. He had a hell of a childhood. His family moved around a lot. He got into trouble everywhere they went. He ran away three times from the juvenile camps he was sent to. They finally picked him up in Colorado on a petty theft and tried to rehabilitate him by putting him to work for the Space Agency."

"The what?"

"No shit. There was a NASA program for minors in Inglewood, Colorado. Don't laugh. He was a bright kid.

When they tested him there, he checked out at an IQ of one hundred forty.'' Pike started to laugh. ''Look at this.'' He pushed the dossier on the desk toward Abrams.

''Let's see,'' Abrams said, ''he was put to work on the solid-rocket fuel program. What the hell kind of program was that?''

''It's great entertainment. NASA really put together a training program. Bobby worked in it. But he started cutting out little tiny pieces of the stuff and smuggled it out in hollow pencils. He'd roll the stuff up in cigarettes and pass them around to his enemies. He blew up a few noses and got transferred out. But they didn't give up on him. They put him to work in maintenance, tried to make a painter out of him. What does he do, he overdoses on the paint fumes. What's truly choice is that he does this the day before he's scheduled for his EEG. And wouldn't you guess, his EEG shows up irregular. It's right here. I've got a yellow tab on it. I'd expect this EEG's going to pop up somewhere in the defense case to show how mentally ill he is. But it's written right here that the irregularity is due to solvent ingestion. He was a real hellion. Loved to gas the guards.'' The reference was to the practice of throwing urine or feces at the guards when they walked past the cell.

Pike continued. ''The same guard got it in the face three times and on the fourth decided our boy needed to be matched up for his outside exercise with a guy named Frazier. It seems Frazier hated Bobby's guts. Bobby took a hit out in the yard from Mr. Frazier. The guy didn't know how to properly use the razor pen he'd made. It's made to slit the throat. He tried to stab Engle in the back with it. That kept Bobby on the straight and narrow for three whole months. That's when they sent him outside

to arrange a field trip to a baseball game, and he didn't
come back.''

"Nice history.''

"Yeah. Nice guy. After his escape, he made his way
to California, and that's when all this relatively lighthearted activity started to give way to the heavy-duty
stuff. After they picked him up on a couple of minor-
child molests, he kidnapped that little kid. That's when
the system took over. And it gets real good after that.
They sent him to Atascadero on the MDSO program.''

Abrams groaned.

"You got the picture. After assaulting the little girl,
he was found to be a mentally disordered sex offender
and was sent off to Atascadero. There's some interesting
information there too. His prison chart says he lost his
ground privileges. That's a pretty serious thing. So I
checked through the daily entries to find out why, and I
found a notation that he got caught stealing the sex education slides, the slides that show the inmates who are
being tested on the plethysmograph—that's the machine
they use to test whether an erotic photo's going to cause
the guy to get a hard-on. He was having a great time
with the slides back at his cell.''

"When'd he take the slides?''

"About a month before he was released. It's not mentioned anywhere in the release reports. They missed it.
They also missed the magazine that was found in his
locker. The one with the naked little kids in it. They
never mentioned this stuff at the release hearing. It's not
even in the closing reports.''

"Is there anything in the shrink reports themselves
that talk about whether he was okay to parole from
prison?''

"We got reports from thirteen shrinks. Twelve of
them say to keep this guy in or he'll continue assaulting

kids. One report says he'll make it on the outside and sets out Bobby's reform. He apparently became one of the spokesmen for the new prisoners' union the ACLU helped organize. He got the inmates better shower soap, a choice of two entrées once a week and a color television in the recreation room. This impressed someone, because they let him out.

"It's not hard to understand. Doctors see the results of their work when the patient recovers or dies. A carpenter can see what he's made . . . everyone looks for the result of what they do. Psychologists, psychiatrists—they can't see anything. They can only tell if they've been successful if the guy comes back to them for the same offense. And if your treatment program doesn't work, you see them all again.

Pike pushed the dossier off to the side of his desk. "You see what we've got on our hands here. We've got a sick kid with a bad family history and an abusive family life. Defense counsel's going to go right for the heartstrings, and hit us with that EEG. A bright kid destroyed by his stepfather. We need to pull out this stuff on the past offense and hit home with the idea that if this guy's let go, he's going to kill again."

39

Eight-fifty A.M.

The elevator was crowded as Judith rode down to the third-floor courtroom complex. There was nobody on it she recognized. She carried few files with her. There was no need for anything but the basics this morning.

A jury selection was about to begin, the part of the case no one ever saw on TV or in the movies.

Outside the courthouse earlier, Judith had seen the television vans. The local stations had requested and received from the court permission to tape the trial. They would undoubtedly be in the courtroom only for a brief time. They would film the opening statement of the judge; then, during the few minutes of the first morning recess, they would carry away the cameras and equipment they had spent the better part of the morning setting up. Despite the notoriety of this case, it was highly unlikely the attorney's opening moves today would get more than casual mention on the six o'clock and eleven o'clock news programs. The brief clips taken would make their way into the stations' film files and show up years from now to illustrate news stories on Engle.

Although Judith had subpoenaed twenty-five witnesses, there was no way they would be called to the stand today. They were all "on hold." They'd been ordered to appear for trial that morning "unless otherwise directed," and Judith had directed them to go about their lives but to be ready to come in on half an hour's notice, sometime between today and six weeks from now.

This morning the task of picking the jury, the voir dire, would begin. If the process followed the path of most capital cases, it would most likely be very long, tedious and gut-wrenching. Each of the two sides in the battle for the jurors' hearts and souls would have the assistance of experts sitting next to them to cull through the public in search of those individuals most susceptible to the arguments the respective attorneys would make. There were no hard-and-fast rules. There were, of course, some generalities. Prosecutors were, as a rule, wary of engineers and teachers. Engineers were nitpicky. Teachers weren't nitpicky enough—too much heart, not enough outrage, no such thing as a bad boy. The defense would want teachers, especially if it reached the second phase of trial, where life or death would be decided, where the quality of forgiveness was so important.

Even from the end of the hallway Judith could see a huge crowd gathered outside Courtroom 1, the largest courtroom. She could tell from the dress and groupings of two and three persons that this was the jury panel waiting to be called inside. It was Tuesday, so this was a fresh, new jury panel. Monday panels were the jurors rejected the previous Thursday from jury selection. They would have a higher incidence of unacceptability. But this new panel would have just been sent up from the jury lounge, where the group had been subjected to a forty-five-minute tape covering the duties and obligations of jury service. Every panel emerged from this indoctrination ready to wave the American flag.

Before she went inside the courtroom, Judith took a moment to observe the panel members. Her attention was drawn to one young man, who looked to be about twenty, sitting alone on the corner of the hall bench, reading a book. She took note of the man's face and the book title, *Soul on Ice*. She was wary of this potential juror. She was wary of anyone reading alone in the hallway. He was young; he probably had no children. And there he was, reading a revolutionary book. He was a maverick, and thus a potential holdout on the jury.

There was much to learn, much to control, even there in the hallway outside the courtroom. As the selection process progressed, she would visit the hallway many times, observing and making note of how the groups were forming, who were the talkers, who was being avoided. The dynamics of the group selected would be important.

Inside the courtroom the defense team had already moved into place. Engle was there. His hair had been neatly cut and combed. He was dressed out complete with white shirt and brown-and-gray-striped tie. Bennett, Larson, a paralegal and the defense jury expert were seated with him. Only Pike would be seated with Judith and Farrell.

Judith arranged her files carefully on the long wooden desk. She could smell the paper. She could also smell something else. Fumes of some kind.

"Do you smell something, Judith?" Bennett asked, stretching sideways across the walking space between their tables.

"It smells like diesel fuel," she replied. They were courteous to each other, but distance was important. Too much familiarity, too much fraternizing with the opposing party, could jeopardize your credibility.

"Come to order, please. The Honorable Roston L. Baker presiding," the bailiff said, emphasizing the *L*.

Baker was relatively new to the bench. The product of Vanderbilt Law School and eighteen years with one of San Diego's oldest, most established civil law firms, his penchant for red bow ties and ever-so-subtle southern drawl had already earned him a reputation as a soft-spoken gentleman. But the experienced civil practitioners in the city knew the man behind that exterior as a trial tactician who could vacillate smoothly between elegance and vicious cunning, a skill which ten years earlier had reeled in the largest award of punitive damages in a medical malpractice case the county had seen.

The Engle case was Baker's first capital trial.

"Good morning," began the judge. "Let the record reflect all counsel, the defendant, and jury panel are present. I know you're probably wondering about the odor in here. I've been informed it's the jail buses downstairs. They've been idling and the exhaust has sucked into the court's ventilation system. Now, I've been promised it will clear up in ten minutes or so. If it doesn't, we'll break for the morning. So unless you all hear further from me on the matter of the odor, or I hear from you that you can't stand it anymore, we will proceed."

Judith ignored the fumes. So did the defense team. No one wanted the physical condition of the courtroom to interfere with the flow this morning. Besides, this was one of the most comfortable courtrooms, and it was in better shape than the one next door, where a ceilingful of asbestos had fallen down around the heads of the clerk and the judge just a month before.

"Bring the panel on in. I see all the seats are taken in the courtroom. As much as I do regret the situation let's bring everyone in from outside."

Depending on the judge and the projected length of

the trial, as many as two hundred people might be interviewed as prospective jurors. Five to ten percent of those would be eliminated quickly for legal hardships, an ill spouse, inability to understand English. Another three to five percent would be lost during questioning due to illness. Maybe eighty to eighty-two percent would be left for consideration.

This morning eighty people had been brought up from the jury lounge. Their names had been picked from phone directories, motor-vehicle-department registration and electoral rolls. They were from all parts of the city, from Imperial Beach on the county's southern border to Rancho Bernardo, thirty-two miles to the north. Some of the people wanted badly to be on this case, and they would be rejected. Some wanted no part of it, and they might be selected. They would all be questioned about their childhood and criminal records. They would all be asked about their feelings on the death penalty. More than anything else, the process was one of dissecting their language. Every word of each answer would be diagnosed and examined and challenged. And the responses to the clarifying questions would be diagnosed and dissected.

As the courtroom quieted and they all waited for the judge to give the panel some general instruction about the case, Larson stood.

"Your Honor, the defense has a motion to make before the jury selection begins." His voice was loud and clear, intended for all to hear. "The defense wishes to sit at the counsel table nearest the jury box, where Mrs. Thornton is now seated. And we ask that the prosecutor yield to the request, which we don't consider unreasonable."

Judith had been writing, but looked up quizzically at the judge.

"I'm sorry, your Honor. I've never had to respond to such a motion before," she replied. "The People always sit at this counsel table." It crossed her mind that the motion should not have been made in the presence of the panel, but at side bar or in the judge's chambers. But it had been made, and it needed to be responded to in a like manner, so all could hear.

"Well, this is a capital case, your Honor," Larson said. "I haven't any authority to present to the court. We can't really find anything to support our argument other than the common-sense argument that in this most sensitive case, the People should yield. I'd be happy to look for additional authority. . . ."

So this was how it was going to be, Judith thought. Trial by obstruction. By nonsense and nit-picking. That was why Larson was there. This was going to be a battle for the courtroom. And for now, it wasn't as much between the defense and her as it was going to be between the defense and the trial judge.

"Your Honor, I'm not prepared to yield my table."

"But, Judge, the prosecutor—"

"The People have *always* sat closest to the jury box. I'm not entirely certain why, but . . ."

"Well, Counsel . . . Mrs. Thornton, perhaps I can elucidate on the subject." Baker paused, thinking. "The People sit next to the jury box because they have the burden of proof." He looked at Larson and grinned. "It sort of evens up the battle, if you will. Really, go out and look it up, Mr. Larson. It was first discussed in some case dealing with a fox, I think, in England . . . oh, back in 1823. If you want to verify it, Mr. Larson, I can give you, oh, say, ten minutes to run down to check the casebooks in the attorneys' lounge while these good people"—he waved his arm toward the crowd—"wait for you."

"Thank you, your Honor." Larson paused momentarily and glanced out over a courtroom full of the serious faces of people who had been sitting for the past two hours waiting to be called up to a courtroom. "We wouldn't want to keep the jury panel waiting. Our objection is on the record." He sat and had a brief discussion with Bennett.

"Thank you, Mr. Larson. Your request to re-move Mrs. Thornton is denied. Now, let's move on, shall we?"

Score one for the judge.

Baker's clerk read the information, the charging document, to the assembled panel, and the judge took over the initial explanation.

"From the reading of the information, you have been informed that the defendant, Robert Dean Engle, is charged with murder, which it is alleged was committed under certain special circumstances. The special circumstances alleged are set forth in counts two and three of the information and allege that the defendant personally, willfully and with deliberation committed the murder as set forth in the course of a kidnapping, and that the defendant committed an offense of murder during rape and torture.

"In this type of a case, the law of the State of California provides for certain procedures which I shall outline to you at this time, and after which, inquiry will be made concerning your personal views and attitudes with respect to this special type of proceedings as they apply to this kind of a case.

"It will be the duty of the jury to first decide the question of the innocence or guilt of the defendant as to each of the charges of murder. In California, there are two degrees of murder, definitions of which will be given to you when the jury is instructed on the law. It is sufficient at this time for you to know that murder in California may be in the first degree or in the second degree. In the event, and only in the event, that the jury finds the defendant guilty of a charge of murder in the first degree, and that finding must be a finding beyond a reasonable doubt, then the jury in the same proceeding will be required to make a determination as to the truth or falsity of the special circumstances alleged.

"In the event, and only in the event, that the jury finds the special circumstances to be true beyond a reasonable doubt, then the law provides that the jury in a second or another phase of the trial decide the punishment to which the defendant shall be subjected. In the event that the trial reaches the second phase of the trial—that is to say, first, that the jury has found beyond a reasonable doubt that the defendant is guilty of a murder in the first degree as alleged, and second, that the special circumstances as alleged are true, all of which findings must be beyond a reasonable doubt—then the jury must decide whether the punishment shall be death or life imprisonment without the possibility of parole.

"Now, let me ask you the question as to whether you understand the procedure that I have outlined to you and the possibility of a penalty phase. Please raise your hand if you have a question."

There were no hands. Judith knew that some understood not a word of what he'd said. This was for her to straighten out and keep the defense team from mushing up.

"Okay," the judge continued. "I want to tell you all that we expect this trial to last between six weeks and two months. Some of you may believe you have a hardship that will prevent you from doing your duty here. Please give us a show of hands, those who will not be able to sit through this trial as a juror."

Judith looked around. There were maybe five, then gradually fifteen or so hands raised.

"Okay, those who have raised your hands, please remain seated. Those who did not raise your hands, we will be bringing you into the courtroom for voir dire, questioning in two groups of about forty each. For now, please report back to the jury lounge, where you will be instructed which group you will be in. We'll be in recess for five minutes to let the panel leave."

The judge had wisely chosen to separate out the jurors who believed they had a hardship. It was strange, but when an excuse was publicly discussed, the number of jurors with the same excuse rose substantially.

By the time the panel members claiming an excuse from service had been questioned, and all but three excused, the remaining panel members had been sitting, waiting and reading. The court clerk called the jury room and instructed the jury commissioner to send the panel back up at one-thirty.

Promptly at the appointed time, the judge was ready to proceed with the selection. The clerk, following time-honored tradition, pulled the names of twelve of the panel members from a gray box she kept on her desk. As their names were called, they were each directed to one of the twelve chairs in the jury box. Now, as the remainder of the panel waited patiently, the court, and then the attorneys, would have a chance to question each of the potential jurors in the jury box to determine his or her views and biases. Any person who was found to have actual bias would be excused by the court for cause and be sent back to the jury commisioner's office for reassignment to another trial. But each of the attorneys also had the right to exercise what were known as peremptory challenges, challenges to a particular juror for whatever reason, which did not have to be divulged.

Because it was a death penalty case, the prosecution and defense would each have more than the normal ten allotted in criminal trials. Each would have twenty. Part of the challenge was to get those people you didn't want excused by the court for cause so that you didn't have to use up your peremptories. You'd want to save the peremptories and use them on the people for whom you had an intuitive bad feeling. Or use them to exclude whichever ethnic group, gender or any other individual you felt appropriate to the case.

As a group, the first twelve called didn't look all that bad. Generally middle-aged. Children or grandchildren, maybe. Five white males, four white females, two Mexican-American women and one black male. The court's own questioning of the twelve individuals consumed the better part of an hour and a half. Then it was the attorneys' turn to ask questions.

Judith questioned one of the white females, the one in jury seat six. She was a stunning young redhead with an expensive-looking, full-length red fox fur that matched her softly curled, shoulder-length hair. She belonged to a cocktail party, not a capital jury trial. She stood out like a sore thumb, just like she wanted to. She wanted attention. She wanted control. Not much give-and-take with that one. The women on the jury would hate her. Judith was glad when the court, on its own motion, dismissed her because she was a cousin of the judge's bailiff. As she left the courtroom, the bailiff cast a sheepish grin at Judge Baker, whose only acknowledgment was one raised eyebrow.

Marianne Blackburn was called to take the redhead's chair. She was a stark contrast to her predecessor. Approximately forty years old. Brown earlobe-length hair, and she was wearing a flowered dress with a white Peter Pan collar. Judith sized her up as a teacher or saleswoman. The court's general questioning confirmed the prosecutor's impressions. The woman was an unmarried kindergarten teacher who was active in her church.

It would be with the Marianne Blackburns that the war of jury selection would be waged and the case ultimately won or lost. This was true because, as Judith well knew, a capital case is not a fight for justice. It is a battle over the most primitive and paradoxical of human instincts: the passionate belief in the sanctity of life, and the overwhelming desire for carnal vengeance. Every person who sits in the death-penalty jury box in judgment of another human being must be able to reconcile these opposing instincts. Every attorney preparing a capital case must understand these instincts and control them if he hopes to prevail.

If you are a prosecutor, you deal with this cognitive dissonance by selecting jurors who will err on the side of societal vengeance and moral outrage, who will help form their own mini-society, who will exchange their individual norms and values and create a group norm. It may be different from society's norm, but it will be a norm. The prosecutor's goal is therefore the selection of jurors who can get along together, who can bond and form a cohesive unit, who in the end can forgive one another and thus themselves for ordering the death of another human being.

But if you are the defense attorney, you deal with the life-and-death paradox by selecting jurors who will, first and foremost, maintain their individuality and bend to the sanctity of life. And maybe, if you are the very best at what you do, you can identify one person who cannot deal with the paradox, who cannot reconcile man's duty to protect life and the juror's duty, where appropriate, to order its destruction. Only one such person is needed to bring in a hung jury and drive the prosecution to its knees.

Marianne Blackburn would likely be Judith's first skirmish in the war of cognitive dissonance.

"Miss Blackburn, have you served as a trial juror before?"

"No."

"From where you were seated in the body of the courtroom when you were first called for jury duty for this case, were you able to hear and understand the court's discussion?"

"Yes, I was."

"Have you read or seen or heard anything about this case before reporting for jury duty?"

"I recall it occurring when it did."

"All right. Do you now have any impression or state of mind as a result of those recollections that you feel would interfere with your ability to be a fair and impartial juror in this particular case?"

"No, I do not."

"And simply for the record, you understand that if you were to serve as a juror, you would have to conduct your deliberations and base your verdict only upon the evidence that was presented in court here and on the law as given to you by the court?"

"Yes."

"All right. Since the matter may proceed to the point where the death penalty is involved, it is necessary because of that possibility that we consider that at this time. Do you have any conscientious or other objection to the death penalty which would prevent you from voting for or concurring in a verdict carrying the death penalty in a proper case?"

"Yes, ma'am, I do. Because of my religious affiliation, I am—I believe that you cannot take a life for a life."

There it was. Turmoil. She had said she could follow the law and be fair but could not ethically take a life. How would she resolve it? Did she know what she'd said?

"All right. First of all, would you please identify for us the particular religious affiliation to which you refer?"

"I'm a Catholic."

"All right. And are you telling me, then, that you would just automatically and categorically vote against the imposition of capital punishment in every case without regard to the evidence that might be developed at the trial of the case before you?"

"See, that's really kind of a strong question, because I have my religious beliefs, but I'm sure—I would want to base my thinking on the findings here and what I saw as evidence. But I question if I might not have a conflict between my beliefs and what I would, as an individual, feel I should do in following your instructions."

"All right. If the case proceeds that far—and, of course, it may never get there—but if it does so that the death penalty is involved, evidence would be presented, evidence in aggravation, evidence in mitigation. You would be called upon to consider all that evidence and to evaluate and weigh it and then to make a determination."

"I see." She didn't really.

"And you would be called upon, then, to vote for either the penalty of death or the penalty of life in prison without possibility of parole. Would you be able to do that? Would you be able to make a choice between those two?"

"I just wonder if I can be a free agent when I'm

taught by religion that I'm supposed to follow that religion in faith and morals. I've been really deliberating this ever since last Friday, because, you know, it's kind of easy to say, 'Oh, I believe in the death penalty or I don't.' Until you're faced with a situation like this, you really—it takes a lot of thought, it really taxes you . . . I . . .''

She needed help.

"Well, that is the reason—"

"Here I am—I'm not trying to evade your question, really. It's just that I feel that, you know, I'm obliged to follow my religious feelings."

Judith, who had been standing near the jury box, blocking Miss Blackburn's view of Engle, had begun to back up slowly toward him.

"Is there some possibility that you might vote for the death penalty if the case were one that you thought should call for the death penalty under the court's instructions?"

"I guess this is where I would have the conflict, because I would want to follow the court's instructions. I guess—I guess I have not really come to a— I've just been thinking this over for all these days, and as an individual who believes in the death penalty, but I also believe that I have to follow my religious beliefs, which is in contradiction to—is contrary to the way I feel, but I think I would possibly be able to come to that judgment. I don't know . . . I'm in such a turmoil. I think I need to talk to my priest."

Now was the time for the bombshell question. Judith was directly in front of Engle. A side step would bring Miss Blackburn directly into eye contact with him. Judith stepped to the right and gestured toward Engle.

"Miss Blackburn, can you walk out of this courtroom and, on your way out, look the defendant here"—she pointed at Engle—"in the eye and say, 'You're going to die'?"

Marianne Blackburn froze, her brown eyes locked on those of Engle. Slowly, her brown eyes rolled back and she began to slide forward in a dead faint. Only the quick thinking of her neighboring jurors, who caught her arms, saved her from the ultimate indignity of hitting the floor.

Even in the midst of the ensuing turmoil, the court and counsel maintained control. Any physical action required toward anyone was carried out by the court staff only.

Neither Judith nor the defense team moved as the clerk and the bailiff scurried to retrieve the tissues and smelling salts kept in the side of the judge's bench.

Then Judith remembered her obligation to assure a proper record was being created.

"Your Honor, may the record reflect Miss Blackburn . . . has fainted?"

"It may, Counsel. Can Miss Blackburn be excused, Mr. Bennett?"

"The defense has no objection, your Honor. May we have a recess?"

"It's almost time to break for the day. I think this is an appropriate place to stop and regroup. Court's in recess until tomorrow morning at nine."

40

And so it went, the daily probing of words, thoughts and deepest personal beliefs, making the panel members think through, maybe for the first time, exactly how they felt about recommending the death of another human being.

By the fourth day, the jury panel had been fully examined and another panel of eighty sent up. Six days later, yet another panel was subjected and interrogated. No one else quite presented the conflict as visually as had Marianne Blackburn, but the struggles were there, left to be discovered by the attorneys and used to reject or keep the panel member.

By the third week of questioning, after almost the entire panel had been examined, the clerk called Eugene Matson to take the place of a woman Bennett had excused with one of his peremptory challenges. Matson was a thin, blond man in his mid-thirties. Bennett's questions were not particularly revealing of any significant internal struggles over the death penalty. He was an unmarried architect who had read little about the case and had formed no opinions about it. But Judith could tell without asking that Matson was of particular interest to Farrell, who had leaned back somewhat in his chair, staring intently at the man during questioning.

During the lunch recess, Farrell, Judith and Pike brown-bagged it in her office. As was their custom throughout the selection process, they met during the breaks to assess which panel members still seated in the jury box they wanted or didn't want.

By the time lunch was over, they agreed they could accept the panel as it was currently comprised. Over the brown-bag lunches in Bennett's office, the defense team had come to the same conclusion.

When court convened at one-thirty, Judith and Bennett announced they were willing to accept the jury as constituted. The afternoon session was taken up with selecting three alternate jurors. At five o'clock the jury was sworn in and the remaining panel members thanked and excused to go home.

After three weeks, the jury had been selected. Five women. Seven men. No one under the age of thirty-five. No one over the age of sixty-five. It was a good cross-section. No one admitted to opposing the death penalty. No one admitted to supporting it. All said they promised to uphold and apply the law, whatever their personal beliefs.

When the jury had been sent home for the day, Baker turned to the subject of the opening statements, which were scheduled for the following morning.

"At the outset, Mr. Bennett, I'd like to make clear who on the defense team will be handling the various parts of the trial. With two aggressive attorneys there at your table, I think it's understood there can be only one of you—whomever you choose, of course—conducting the opening statement and questioning the witnesses.

Trade off as you wish, but only one of you per witness, please.''

"We have discussed this, your Honor, and Mr. Larson will be conducting our opening statement to the jury and cross-examining the prosecution witnesses. I will be conducting the direct testimony of our own witnesses.''

"That sounds just fine. We'll see you all back to-morrow morning, let's say at eight-thirty in case there are matters to consider before the jury comes in.''

Court was adjourned. Only Larson remained, preparing his notes for the following morning, periodically glancing around the empty courtroom, into which the clerk returned from time to time.

He was wondering just how he could most effectively present his opening salvos to the jury, and just how quickly he would be able to take charge of the trial.

41

The jurors would want a story, a chain of information that flowed, that made sense. Judith didn't want any breaks in the chain. The more breaks there were, the greater the likelihood the jury would find reasonable doubt. Even in the most heinous crimes is this the case.

The jury would want to be able to follow along with the evidence and in the end take that body of evidence and have it fit the story. The difficulty was that large chapters of the story about what had happened to Kelly Solomon would never be revealed to the jury. They were tucked away in the evidence that had been ordered excluded. Judith's opening statement would be important. It would have to preview the story for the jurors and give them a device to hurdle the blank spots.

"Kelly Solomon was nine years old." She held up a picture of the child, her fourth-grade photograph, and handed it to a juror to pass along. "I'd like to tell you a little bit about her. She loved to dance. Most all little girls love to dance. She was going to be the Sugarplum Fairy in *The Nutcracker* at Christmas. Then one warm day in September she set out to Mission Beach with her friend, Tara Markham. Kelly never came home. Five days later, her body was found in Mission Valley. She had been brutally beaten, tortured and killed.'' Judith held up a photograph of the girl's nude, brutalized body. Then she allowed the jurors to absorb the first shock of the trial. Several of the women pursed their lips as Judith gave them the photo to pass down one row of the jury box, then the other. When the photo made its way back to her, she began again.

"Somewhere between the time Kelly went out to play and the horrible night her body was found, *this man* brutally beat, tortured and killed her.'' She had bridged the evidentiary gap. "We don't know what happened between the time Robert Engle picked her up and the time he left her body for the coyotes at the San Diego River. That is your job, ladies and gentlemen. You will be writing those chapters based upon the evidence introduced here in this courtroom.''

Judith realized something was happening behind her, as gradually all of the jurors' eyes shifted from her to her counsel table, where Pike had been taking notes. She stopped, turned and noticed immediately the water dripping from the paper cup in Pike's hand onto the table, dampening Pike's jacket cuff and notepaper. As she watched, Pike put the cup down and tried his best to mop up the water with the tissues left at each counsel table by the court clerk.

"Do you wish a break, Mrs. Thornton?'' the judge asked.

"No, your Honor. I'd like to continue.''

Judith completed the opening, carefully setting out in general terms what information the various witnesses would bring into the courtroom, her comments still geared to placing the jurors in the position of filling in the gaps that would surely be evident at the end of the trial.

Following Judith's hour-long statement, the court called the morning recess.

"I'm sorry, Judith," Pike began as she returned to the table. "Have a look." He handed Judith the now empty paper cup he had taken from the stack of seven or eight that were normally left at each counsel table, along with a pitcher of water. "Hold it up to the light."

She closed one eye and squinted into the small white, pleated cup.

"There's a hole in it. It looks like a pinhole. We've got a bunch of defective cups?"

"We've got *a* defective cup." Pike handed her the remaining cups that had been sitting on the desk. When she looked into them, she couldn't detect any holes.

"Someone slipped this in," Pike said, glancing toward the defense table. "It's a great way to disrupt an attorney's train of thought. And the jury's."

"Harley Bennett would never . . ."

"No, it's not his style, Judith." Pike looked over at the defense table, where Larson sat, working on his presentation to the jury.

Judith explained their finding to the clerk, who informed the court. Glass cups would replace the paper ones, and thereafter, the attorneys would not be allowed to remain in the courtroom when the court was in recess.

The battle lines had been redrawn. Judith knew she had now been drawn into Larson's war of the courtroom.

42

The note on Alan Larson's chair the next morning said, "Please see me," in bold letters he recognized as being the printing of his co-counsel, Bennett. He found Bennett in the coffee room.

"I got your note, Harley."

"Yeah, Alan. Can we talk over our strategy?"

"I thought we had a pretty good idea of where we were going. We allow the forensic experts some leeway and go for the throat with Niki Crawford."

"That's right, and we stick to that. But I want to be certain we're on the same wavelength with the amount of pushing we're doing with the court and prosecution." Harley didn't mention the pinhole in the cup and wouldn't. "I'm in general agreement that we push. I just don't want the jury to think we're in any way involved in questionable conduct in the courtroom. Push all you feel is appropriate, but let's not do anything that turns the jury off."

Larson was not surprised at Bennett's concern. He'd known, going into the case, that their approaches to death penalty trials were fundamentally different. Some of his techniques would appall Bennett, he knew. But Bennett knew that as well. As long as he trod carefully and didn't overdo the theatrics, they would get along fine.

"No need to worry, my friend. I won't do or say anything that's going to jeopardize the case."

"I know, Alan. And believe me, I'm not trying to alter your style or your beliefs. If I felt that I needed to, I'd never have asked you be assigned as co-counsel."

"How about this? I run with the ball the way I think I should, and if you see me stepping over the lines of . . . civility . . . you let me know and I'll back off."

43

As she got off the elevator, Judith noticed Abe Solomon standing outside the women's rest room.

"Oh, Mrs. Thornton, can you check on my wife? She hasn't been feeling well. Deborah's been in the rest room for fifteen minutes now. I'm worried about her."

"Of course. I thought you were going to come up to the office and meet me there. I waited."

"We were. But she went in there and she hasn't come out."

"Don't worry, Mr. Solomon. I'll check on her and we'll be out in a minute. The first day of trial and having to testify are always pretty traumatic. I'll see what I can do."

Judith entered the white-tiled bathroom area. Seeing no one at the sinks or in the small lounge alcove, she bent down, looking for feet in the toilet stalls. She saw what she had expected.

In her softest voice, she inquired, "Mrs. Solomon?"

A halting, broken voice responded from behind one of the stalls. "I . . . I'm here. I'll be out. Can I just have a couple of minutes?"

"Of course you can. I'll wait for you here. But we do start in fifteen minutes. Can I get you a glass of water?"

"No. Thanks." The toilet flushed, and the stall door opened. Deborah Solomon emerged, her eyelids black with mascara. As she passed the large mirror above the sinks, she looked at her reflection and stopped.

"Oh, my, what a mess I've made of myself." She lowered her head and started to cry again as she leaned against the sink nearest her. Judith quickly set her files on the shelf under the mirror and went over to her, placing her arm around the woman's shoulder. She could feel Deborah Solomon, still slumped toward the sink, lean back toward her, accepting momentarily that she was helpless.

Judith reached into the pocket of her suit jacket and retrieved a tissue.

"Here. Why don't you clean up your eyes with this tissue and come to the courtroom with me? You can stay outside and wait to be called, or, if you want, you can go up to my office, have a cup of coffee, and we'll call you when we need you. You don't have to sit through everything that's going to be said in there this morning. But you've got to come out now. We all have a job to do. And it starts this morning. Besides, your husband's pretty worried about you. Do you want to wait upstairs?"

"No, no. It's difficult, but Abe and I want to see it. We need to be there for Kelly. Every minute of it. We want to see the jury. And we want that animal in there to see us." Deborah Solomon blew her nose and wiped at the smudges beneath her eyes. Judith was unsuccessfully trying to think of something lighthearted to say, but nothing seemed appropriate. So she smiled and, touching her lightly on the elbow, led her outside to her waiting husband.

As hard as it was going to be for them, Judith was glad the Solomons had decided to make their presence known in the courtroom. They would be an asset to the case. The jurors would be watching them as intently as they would be watching Engle.

With the Solomons comfortable in the front row of the spectator section, Judith spread her files out across the table and premarked her exhibits. They were about to move into the thick of it now, and every question, every move Judith made in the courtroom, would be designed to convey her word against the defense's that Engle was a guilty man. Now all the little pieces of the case against Engle would be put on. She likened the procedure to building a house one little step at a time. Nothing was simple in the process. A matter as seemingly mundane as identifying the body would take the testimony of three people: Chin, Deborah Solomon and the forensic pathologist, who could testify that the tooth fillings Kelly Solomon had last summer were identical to the fillings in the mouth of the body.

Because Judith had decided to present the case chronologically, the better part of next week would be taken up with reconstructing the events between the day Kelly Solomon disappeared and the night her body was found. In the process, Judith would create a verbal portrait of the girl. Unassuming. Innocent. Bright. Gullible. Then scientific, forensic evidence would explain what had happened to her. It would substantiate torture by virtue of the mysterious marks on her body. Judith could not be certain how long this would take. It depended upon how willing the defense was to let such evidence go unchallenged. But with the preliminaries completed, the case would shift to identification of the perpetrator. Tara would be of little use. The fingerprint on the beer can accounted for some weight, but the case would rest on what they could get out of Niki Crawford. And if she couldn't or wouldn't testify to what she had seen, all the work, all the detail and ground laying, would be for nothing.

At the outset of trial, there might be the usual objections:

The photos are too prejudicial.

You don't need to show the sixty-five black-and-white glossies of the child's body.

The court would likely reduce the number to forty-five or so. Going in, Judith knew which ones she really wanted the jury to see; knew where she would compromise.

She decided to call Deborah Solomon first, both to get her on and off quickly so she could then relax somewhat, and because it was clear she had been crying and there would be sympathy engendered even if the woman maintained complete control on the stand.

Deborah Solomon looked particularly gaunt and her cheeks seemed more hollow than Judith had remembered. She didn't look well, and predictably, she cried when she was handed Kelly's photo to identify. She broke down completely when Judith asked her to look at Engle and tell the jury whether she had ever seen him before Kelly's disappearance.

Larson was silent throughout Deborah Solomon's direct testimony. He made no objections even when he felt they were in order. Any pushing would provoke an outpouring of jury emotion for her and enmity for him. And besides, she could offer no evidence against Engle.

In the several days that followed, Larson and Bennett chose to downplay the testimony being offered. Particularly as it related to how Kelly Solomon had died. They had decided to focus their energies upon all evidence dealing with who it was who had committed the crime.

Tara Markham's testimony went the way they had all expected it would. She was a better prosecution witness than she had been at the preliminary hearing, but she still could not make a positive identification of Engle as the man who had taken Kelly's and her picture at Mission Bay.

The fingerprint evidence from the can found at the turnout was well laid out by Judith over the course of two days. The procedures used to retrieve the can and the magic of the superglue in the fish tank, complete with in-court demonstration of the process, regaled the courtroom. But in the end, even Henrickson had to admit that the conclusion that Engle had left the print was a matter of probability. High probability. But still, probability.

Following the forensic testimony, Judge Baker ordered a two-day recess. When they returned to court, Niki Crawford would be called to the stand.

44

Larson wanted, needed, to eradicate Niki Crawford. Even a tentative identification from her would be devastating to the defense. He had read and reread all of the reports, especially Pike's accounts of his interviews with her and her retreat into the shower. He knew in his heart that she had seen the body. She would not testify willingly to it. She would not testify willingly to anything. She had lied to the police, evaded their direct questions and was blocking as much of it out of her memory as she could. The truth of the matter was that she had seen the girl with Engle. Maybe she had seen him kill her or had seen the girl's grisly remains. Whatever else she had seen, it had her running scared.

The question was, how could Larson use it to his advantage?

The solution struck him as he drank his morning coffee at his office desk. It just might work. And if it did, it would assure the young woman's complete destruction. The idea was so bizarre, even obscene, that he hesitated to share it with Bennett. But it was also ingenious.

He would destroy her with the truth.

The truth was already destroying Niki Crawford. Now all he needed was to ram it home in just the right way. If she was forced not only to face it but to do so publicly, on the witness stand, she might just fall apart, crumble away. . . . It would be very tricky, this truth angle. It could backfire. But the prospect had set his creative juices bubbling.

There was only one, sizable obstacle to this plan. He needed to find the truth.

Larson pulled his evidence lists from his file-cabinet files and called the evidence locker in the basement of the courthouse to see how soon he could look over the items collected from the field. First, though, he needed to talk to Engle. Although Larson's purposes were seldom served by having his clients describe the sordid details of their crimes, occasionally this was necessary. And now was one of those times.

45

Bennett had seen no need for his presence at Larson's discussion with Bobby, particularly since Larson had indicated he wanted to go through Bobby's account of the murder.

"Bobby, you're looking good today."

Indeed. Since the trial had begun, it seemed to Larson that Engle had actually become invigorated, his face less gaunt, his voice more assertive.

"Sleeping okay, Bobby?"

"Yeah. I adjusted to the noise pretty good and they have me isolated, away from all the fags."

They both knew the real reason he was isolated was because child molesters are not safe in the general jail population, where, strangely, there is a code of ethics even among the worst criminals. Almost any crime can be tolerated among inmates, but not the sexual assault or murder of a child.

Because of the potential for violence against him, Bobby was being housed alone in one of the two X cells located in the north corner of the jail's fifth floor. The cells had glass windows instead of bars. Each contained its own television, toilet and washbasin. A floor deputy checked Engle's condition every fifteen minutes. Food was delivered to him, and he showered alone, transported by two deputies. His special treatment showed.

"Bobby, I'd like to spend our time this afternoon talking about the charges against you."

"Okay, so where do we start?" Bobby clapped his hands, rubbing them together. Larson had read Evelyn Cross's admonishment to watch for suicidal tendencies. He saw nothing of such a threat. Just the opposite.

"How do you feel about the charges against you, Bobby? You've had a chance to read the police reports we sent for you. So you know how bad the crimes are."

"I really don't have any feelings about them."

Not once had Engle expressed any sign of regret, even though he had openly professed his guilt. Nor had he displayed any emotion about the murder or his own plight.

"Well, then, let's start with what you can remember about the day the little girl was killed."

"I can only remember pieces of it. I *supposedly* kidnapped the kid. That's what they say."

"Do you remember kidnapping her?"

Bobby shifted uneasily in his chair. "She wanted to come with me. Does that mean I didn't kidnap her?"

"It depends on why she came with you."

"I was drinking beer. I drank maybe four or five cans. And I smoked a couple of joints. I drink too much and then I can't remember. I can't seem to keep myself out of trouble with kids."

"You said 'kids.' Bobby, we're talking about *one* kid here. Aren't we?"

"Are we?" Bobby paused with an obviously feigned look of confusion.

"Bobby, please, this isn't a game and I'm not a novice. I'm not interested in trying to muscle through an amnesia of convenience—*and I do not like being toyed with.* Can we agree to just talk?"

"They won't find anything else, Mr. Larson."

Bobby was looking smug but resigned.

"Okay. For now, I want to hear only about the day this crime happened. Any detail you can supply would be helpful. You told me you drank beer and smoked joints. And then?"

"I decided to cruise into San Diego, to Mission Beach."

"Why Mission Beach?"

"No particular reason. I just wanted to drive around, maybe pick up one of those college girls who Roller-Blade around there in those little bikinis. I just wanted to talk to someone."

"The district attorney's reports said they have a photograph of one of the dead girl's friends. They found it in your apartment. Did you have a camera with you?"

"Yeah, I did. It's, how do you say, a conversation starter." Bobby started to snicker. "I tell the girls I'm a photographer for a fashion magazine. They give me their addresses, phone numbers, you name it—measurements. And you know something really funny?"

"No . . . what?"

Bobby looked around, as if someone were seated close who might hear. He lowered his voice to a whisper.

"I don't usually even have film in my camera!"

"But you did that day?"

"Uh-huh. But no one wanted to talk."

"How'd that make you feel?"

"Frustrated. Maybe mad. But I'm used to it, so I just went out and got more beer and started walking with my camera. And then I saw her." He leaned back, looking over Larson's head into space, his hands in the air, palms forward. "Long black hair. Big black eyes. I put film in the camera so I could take a couple pictures and keep them. Then she started to, like, really freak me out...."

"Was this the little girl?"

"No, this was a different girl, an older girl."

"What do you mean you freaked out?"

"Well, this older girl, she talked to me for a while, but I can't remember a lot of what she said. Uh ... I started daydreaming, like. I kept imagining things."

"Imagining what?"

"You want to know, really?" His eyes searched Larson's face. "You do. Okay. You see, I was wondering, what would she look like if I tied her up and cut off her clothes?" He paused, then added, "And pushed something real sharp up against her throat? What would her eyes look like if I *told* her I was going to kill her? Would her face get all twisted up and look ugly? I thought about what I could do to get her to scream ... really scream at the top of her lungs." His body was taut; his eyes were distant.

"Did, uh, did you write this girl's name or address down anywhere?"

"No. Oh, no. I let her go, just let her go." Bobby put his head down and shook it from side to side as if in disbelief.

"What's wrong, Bobby? Something important about this decision you made to let this girl go?"

"Yeah. She said she had this little dog, Flip. I had a dog once named Flip. Can you beat that? Two dogs with such a stupid name? I thought, God, if I killed her, who'd take care of Flip?''

"And so what happened then?"

"I just left. Said, 'Good-bye, beautiful. No sayonara today,' and headed for my truck." Engle was suddenly animated. "Man, I was on my way home. A minute later, I'd have been GONE. Then I heard this giggling and this kid just wandered into my eyesight, real sudden. And I thought, There you go! That's the one. Funny how things happen, huh? I walked right up to her and asked hey, could I take her picture. Jesus, she fell all over me. I guess the beer got to me after that.''

Engle proceeded to tell Larson how the girl was interested in posing for him, but the friend with her wasn't. He took one photo of the two of them and they left.

"I followed the girl in my truck, just watching her. She stopped to pet a dog; then she looked in a store window. Then she was in a kind of abandoned-like area and it was the right moment, you see, so I stopped ahead of her bike and hopped out to ask her if she wanted to come along with me to a photo session right then. She came with me, boy, really fast, but I'd already decided that if she hadn't said yes, I'd just keep following her and when the opportunity came, I'd jump out and force her into the truck.''

"Did you force her to come with you in any way?"

"No. Luckily, I didn't have to do that. We drove out east on Interstate 8 to the Cuyamaca Mountains. I promised I'd get her home in an hour. I was going to dump the film out there, but I didn't. I chased her around a lot, just playing. Then something happened. I don't know. I wanted her to fight with me. I wanted to chase her and make her fight. And we did, but when she started to fight, I got mad and I hit her. And I hit her.''

"Did you sexually assault the girl?"

"You know, I can't really remember much after I hit her. But I might have."

"Now, Bobby, there were marks on the body. Pinching marks."

"I got her with my alligator . . . with my pliers. After I taped her hands up, it . . . I pinched her. I wanted to see her eyes. I got a little crazy after that. Then she stopped fighting. I guess she knew what was coming. But I never said it was going to kill her."

"How long were you with her out in the Cuyamacas?"

"I don't know. I guess the rest of the afternoon. I drank another beer or two and had some joints; then I took the tape off. I gave her some beer. She wanted to be a model. I told her she was too skinny. She made me like her, you know. For a while I thought I'd bring her back to San Diego and leave her somewhere. But then she tried to run. I caught up with her and I guess I lost my temper. I hit her some more. Should've left her out there in the mountains. Try to do something good for someone and see? She was out of it on the way back. She slept. Must've been the beer. I was looking at her and I said to myself, Here's a smart girl. I got to thinking. She's going to turn me in. Then I knew I had to kill her. So I woke her up and we went to the river, near the shopping center. It was incredible. All those people right there, driving near us."

"How'd you kill her, Bobby?"

Engle was holding his hand as if it held something, as if he were looking at the girl's face before him. "I hit her a few times."

"There were bruises like heel marks on her body. Did you kick her or stomp on her?"

Engle was clearly amused. He knew what Larson was talking about.

"Nah. It was a s-s-snake got her," Engle hissed.

"What do you mean 'a snake got her'?" The explanation made no sense to anyone but Engle.

"I don't recall too much of it. Can I read the report?"

"No, not now. I'll leave a copy for you. You have any tools left, Bobby? In the truck?"

"No. I dumped them. You don't need to worry. They're gone."

There was no emotion. No inflection in his voice. He was casual almost, as if he were recounting an afternoon barbecue with friends.

Bobby was keeping the details to himself. And he was enjoying it. That was part of the gratification he was getting out of this.

Larson could continue to press Bobby on what else he could recall, what else he had done to the girl, but the attorney didn't ask.

There was, though, one more question he needed an answer to.

"Bobby, where are the photos you took that day?"

"I developed them, but I threw them all away. All but the photo of the girl's friend that I took out at the beach. It was the best one. I kept it with my snake's head."

"Bobby, you keep talking about this snake. Can you tell me about it? Is it a real snake?"

Bobby grinned. "Naw, it's not real. It's the friend I got for my alligator."

"Your alligator is your—oh, okay. The alligator is your pliers."

"No, the pliers, see, is my alligator."

Larson had no desire to engage in semantical jousting. Nor had he any need to do so. The pliers used to torture Kelly Solomon was what Bobby was referring to as his alligator. The snake had to be some other tool.

"Care to tell me where the snake is?" Larson asked.

Bobby looked sincere, even concerned. "I really don't know. Part of it got away from me and it's not the same anymore. I still got its head."

"You mean you left it somewhere?"

"I lost the little guy."

"Can you try to remember where he's run off to, Bobby? It's important."

"I'll try, but my mind's a blank on that one. Maybe he'll turn up."

"Can you tell me what the snake did?"

"It helped me."

"How did it help you, Bobby?"

"It made her stop trying to get away."

"How?"

"It bit her for me. Couldn't you tell?"

"It's a tool, isn't it, Bobby? Like the pliers?"

Engle smiled. "Can you find him for me, Mr. Larson?"

"I'm going to try my damnedest, Bobby."

As he gathered his files and was about to walk out the conference room door, Engle called out to him.

"Larson! The s-s-snake. It was the snake that really got her. It kept biting her." He was teasing the attorney. He started to laugh but stopped before Larson got out of the conference room. "Think how easy all this would have been if your friend Bennett had just let me plead guilty."

"Bobby, it's not our job to make your prosecution easier, it's to defend you. We'll do that whether or not it's easy."

As Larson walked back to his office, he tried to focus on what Bobby had told him. Several things in particular interested him. Kelly Solomon had wounds whose causes were unknown, the strange gouges. Bobby had been teasing him about the snake, but there was more to it. What the hell was the snake? Could it have anything to do with those gouges?

46

By the time Larson got to the evidence room in the courthouse basement, he had only the vaguest idea of what he was looking for. He had decided the best thing he could do was to just look at the evidence. Sit in the middle of it. Spread it out. See what happened. His request to the evidence technician seemed a bit strange. Could he have all the evidence collected at the scene so he could spread it all out right there on the floor? It was unusual, but given the sheer amount of evidence, the request would be accommodated.

Larson placed the items, one at a time, in no particular order, on the gray linoleum. Eventually he found himself sitting surrounded by an array of refuse. The process of examination took him three hours, including the time he stopped to eat the sandwich he'd brought and to review the notes he had taken on a small yellow pad. But he never tired, never felt frustrated or overwhelmed. He placed several photos of Kelly Solomon's body next to him and methodically began placing pieces of evidence next to the photos showing the mysterious gouge marks. Suddenly something Engle had told him made him pause. The photo of Kelly's friend. *I kept it with my snake's head.* That was what Engle had told him. Where was Tara Markham's photo? He'd seen it referred to on the evidence list.

Larson systematically culled through the evidence found at Engle's San Diego apartment and the items located near the child's body. At last he smiled, quickly scribbled his final notes and helped the technician replace the items in large brown bags that had the word "Solomon" scrawled across them in thick black felt-pen ink.

His last act of the afternoon was to visit the courtroom and inform the court clerk that there were items of evidence Larson would need to have brought up to court for trial the following morning.

He had found Engle's snake. He knew what it had done. And if his hunch was right, Niki Crawford had seen it too. Now, if he could confront Niki Crawford with this in the right way, Engle was as good as free.

47

━━◆━━

"Mrs. Thornton, are you ready to proceed?"

"Yes, your Honor, we are."

She really wasn't. Not with Niki Crawford, anyway.

"I can't testify, Mrs. Thornton. I'm having problems remembering."

Those had been the first words out of Niki Crawford's mouth when Judith telephoned to let her know she would need to be available in the approaching week.

"Fine. The record *will* reflect the reporter is present as well as the defendant, Counsel Mr. Bennett, Mr. Larson and Mrs. Thornton. The jury is out in the hallway. Let's bring them all in."

"Before we do that, your Honor, I would like to inform the court and co-counsel that my principal witness, Miss Niki Crawford, is present outside in the hallway, ready to testify under subpoena. However, she has essentially informed me that she will—well, I don't want to misstate what she said—that she has no recollection of the events of this case. I wanted to mention that on the record because I wish to test her memory in court and put the defense on notice that her mental condition is such that I hope she remains available throughout the trial.''

"You understand, Mrs. Thornton, that you're taking a calculated risk here?'' the judge said.

"I know, your Honor. But she is the most significant witness against Mr. Engle.''

Indeed she was. And Alan Larson was ready for her. First, he would not allow her to make an identification. After that—well, after that, he could deliver his final blows.

"We have no objection to what the prosecutor suggests, your Honor.''

"For the record, your Honor, it is the People's position that Miss Crawford may simply not *want* to remember,'' Judith said.

"Well, let's call her, shall we, Mrs. Thornton?''

Outside the courtroom, Niki had taken a seat on the bench, periodically pacing the hallway.

As the jury was brought in, Judith went to the door.

"I'm calling you next, Niki. Are you ready?''

"If a person can be ready for this, yeah.''

"Come in and just take a seat at the back of the courtroom for now.''

The judge was still on the bench. "The People ready to call their witness?''

"Yes, your Honor. The People call Niki Crawford.'' As the oath was being administered, Judith leaned toward Pike. "Watch her, and if you think she's having a real problem, get my attention.''

Judith took a few moments to look through her file. Niki could use the time to adjust to the feeling of the courtroom.

"Miss Crawford, you are a park officer for the city of San Diego, are you not?''

"I am.''

"How old are you?"

"Twenty-six."

"I'd like to take you back, if I can, to an evening in early September. You are familiar with a city-owned field near Freeway 805 and Interstate 8?"

"Objection, your Honor. Leading. The question assumes the answer."

"Your Honor, it's a preliminary question."

"Overruled, Counsel. I'll allow it. Mrs. Thornton is correct."

"Do you remember the question, Miss Crawford?" Judith asked.

"No. Can you repeat it, please?"

"Can you tell us if you were assigned to patrol the area including the field in September?"

"Yes. That was part of my patrol area."

"Can you tell us if your duties in September usually took you to the field?"

"They did."

"Did you drive there one evening in early September, when something unusual happened?"

"Yes."

"Were you alone?"

"Yes. After work, I was going west on the frontage road to Mission Valley."

"Now, as you drove along the road near the field, did you see something that caught your attention?"

"Yes, I did."

"Can you tell us what it was?"

"I slowed down to take the curve and I saw two people walking toward the river."

"Can you describe the individuals?"

Larson was on his feet again. "Objection. Calls for a conclusion."

"I'm sorry, your Honor," Judith said. "It calls for

information. If that's a conclusion, so be it.''

"Overruled, Mr. Larson. Continue, Mrs. Thornton.''

"Can you give us the answer to the last question, Miss Crawford?''

"Can you repeat it, please?'' Niki asked.

Larson was confident now that the first part of his assault on Niki was going to be effective.

"Yes, of course. Can you tell us what the two people looked like?''

"It was a guy.''

"What did he look like?''

"Medium build, dark brown hair—he had on a white T-shirt and Levi's. There was also a—a young child in front of him. And—well, all I remember seeing was this man sort of forcefully steering the kid toward the river.''

"Objection. The last part is nonresponsive to the question.''

"Sustained. Mr. Larson is correct. Strike everything after 'shirt and Levi's.' ''

"Let me ask it this way,'' Judith went on. "Was the child a girl or a boy?''

"A girl.''

"What did you do?''

"I kept going.''

"You didn't stop?''

"Objection again. I'm sorry, your Honor. That's leading.''

"He's correct, Mrs. Thornton. It suggests the answer. Rephrase it.''

"You didn't stop then?''

"No, ma'am.''

"How did it make you feel when you saw them?''

"Not too good.''

"Tell us about the truck you saw.''

"It was a blue Toyota.''

"Did you tell anyone what you had seen?"

"No, ma'am."

"Why?"

"I didn't."

Larson stood again, trying his best to look pained and uncomfortable.

"Objection. I hate to keep doing this, your Honor. But the witness is not answering the questions being put to her."

"Can counsel please approach for a moment?" the judge asked. "We won't need the reporter."

When all counsel, including Bennett, had assembled at the side of the bench, Baker turned to Larson.

"Mr. Larson, can we not compromise just a little bit here? Some of the answers are too broad for the questions. But so much of this is preliminary. The court can give a lot of leeway with this kind of questioning. I haven't. So far. But can't we just go through the introductory matters and get on with it?"

"I'll try, your Honor. But every step of the way in this witness's testimony is critical to the defense."

"I understand that, Mr. Larson. Just you understand that I then expect that the objections will be proper objections. Okay?"

"Understood, Judge."

The attorneys returned to their former positions.

"Can I ask you to step down from your chair and take this pointer and point out for the jury where the field is located on this map?" Judith had a long gray pointer in her hand. Larson noted that Niki's eyes were glued to it, watching it as she tried to answer the prosecutor's questions.

"I'm sorry, I can't." Niki had stalled. She bent her head. Her eyes closed.

"Well, Miss Crawford, can you look at the chart map

from where you are and tell us if you see the field on it?''

There was no audible response.

''Niki?''

''Your Honor,'' Larson began, but the court interrupted.

''Miss Crawford, do you recall the question?''

''I'm sorry, your Honor. I just don't think I can answer it.''

The judge leaned back. Judith set the steel pointer on her table.

''Niki, can you tell me why you can't answer it?'' Judith asked.

''I still can't deal with what happened there.''

''Did you see something there?''

''Your Honor, please, I'm going to object,'' Larson said.

Niki was still struggling with the question. ''I . . . can't.''

''What did you see there?'' Judith persisted. ''Can you tell us what you saw? Niki? This is your last chance to get it off your chest.''

Larson was on his feet again, his voice louder. ''Your Honor, I must adamantly object to this. That's not a question. It's a highly improper comment from the prosecutor.''

''I'll overrule the objection for now and allow it to stand,'' Baker declared. ''Go ahead, Mrs. Thornton, but please be careful with the personal comments.''

''Can you tell us, Niki, what you did several days later?''

''I stopped the car. I turned the lights off and I sat there for a while. I took the flashlight out of the glove compartment. And . . . I started walking up the path . . .

and it smelled pretty bad. I got to the point where it took off . . . to the left.''

There was silence.

"I stopped and I saw—I saw—"

More silence.

"I saw—I saw a blue-and-white tennis shoe and what I thought looked like a—a pair of shorts and a T-shirt. And I turned to my right and—"

Niki stopped. The courtroom waited. The jurors were getting confused. Brows were knitted. Juror number six had leaned forward, his arms folded across his chest.

When the silence had become uncomfortable, Larson stood and said, "Your Honor, I'm going to ask to step to the bench with the court reporter."

"All right."

The judge pushed his chair back and leaned over into the huddle of attorneys and court reporter.

This was better than Larson could have hoped for. His voice was above average in intensity for a bench conference. "I haven't been keeping track of the length of time between each question, but I think the record should reflect that we have been in session for approximately fifteen minutes, and for most of that time the witness has been rocking back and forth. Her eyes are closed, and, well, I'm not an expert in the field, but she seems to be undergoing some kind of psychotic episode. I move to strike her testimony. There's something wrong with her."

"Excuse me, your Honor. Can the court admonish Mr. Larson to lower his voice? I'm sure the jury heard that last comment."

"Well, okay. Lower, Mr. Larson. But now, Mrs. Thornton, do you believe she's still available as a witness? If she's not going any further in her testimony, she won't be legally available for the defense to cross-examine, and I will have to terminate her testimony.''

"Our thoughts precisely, your Honor,'' Larson stated.
"In fact, we would object to her continuing.''

"Your Honor, I think she is still available.''

"The motion to strike her testimony is denied, but
we're not going to let this go too much further.''

The defense attorneys resumed their seats.

"Niki, what did you see?'' Judith asked.

"I was just standing there, standing right next to *it*—
I just stood there. I couldn't move. *People just don't do
that to other people.*''

Larson become animated, rising and holding his hands
up. "Objection; I move to strike that last part. It's nonresponsive. Again.''

"Motion is granted. Strike 'People just don't do that
to other people.' ''

Niki hadn't heard them. She continued. "They just
don't.''

The court stepped in again. "Miss Crawford, I want
you to answer the questions of the district attorney as
they are asked of you, if you will, please. All right?''

Niki nodded her head.

"Niki, describe to us what you saw,'' Judith continued.

"I can't do it. I just can't. It was just lying there.''

"What was it, Niki?''

There was no audible response.

"How far away from you was it?''

"I was standing right next to it; I just couldn't
move.''

"How long did you stand next to it?''

"Just stood there and couldn't move.''

"Niki, what was it you were standing next to?''

"It was—it was—it was a—'' She began to rock
back and forth.

"It was a what, Niki? Niki, was it a body?"

Larson objected again, loudly. "Leading and suggestive."

"Overruled." The court allowed the question to stand.

"Niki, would you answer the question?"

There was no audible response.

"Niki? What was it you saw?"

Judith looked at the judge. He understood her silent request. Larson had too, but it was going so well he didn't want to lose the momentum.

"Ladies and gentlemen, we'll take a twenty-minute recess. May I see counsel?"

Baker led the reporter, Judith, Bennett and Larson into his chambers. He waited for the reporter to set up her machine, then obviously proceeded to make a record for whatever action he might decide to take.

"The afternoon session began at approximately one-forty-two. During the time the witness, Niki Crawford, has been on the witness stand, Mrs. Thornton has asked a number of questions of her. The witness has now failed to answer the last question, which has been repeated at least twice. The issue is this: has the witness imparted all of the testimony on direct examination that is going to be forthcoming? If you believe not, we have to then discuss what period of time can be further expended in eliciting the remainder of her testimony for direct examination. In short, Mrs. Thornton, do you think you're going to get anything more from her?"

"It's so hard to say, your Honor. I apologize for having to pull it out of her, and I know it is time-consuming—"

"Well, do you feel it will be productive to proceed?"

"I think it will. It's a question of how long it's going to take. Because I'm sure the court can observe she's giving us a little bit more with each response.''

"Well, she really hasn't given us much for about ten minutes—beyond saying that she was standing right next to something and repeating the words 'it was.' And that has consumed almost all of the time from when we had our conversation at the bench to just now, when we recessed.''

"What I would suggest is this, your Honor. I'll try one more time to see if she'll respond to the rest of my questions, and if not, I'll leave it at that. Your Honor, I would represent at this time our belief that this witness is suffering from a post-traumatic stress disorder and what we are seeing right now are symptoms of that disorder. We have an expert witness ready to testify after her, if necessary, to explain this to the jury.''

"Well, with all due respect, your Honor and Mrs. Thornton, I think it is highly improper to continue with her. She is sitting over there rocking back and forth, her eyes are closed, and I think that the whole scenario created by this examination is highly inflammatory. I frankly don't know why the prosecutor would *want* to continue with her.''

"Frankly, your Honor, it seems to me it's none of Mr. Larson's business.'' It was a peculiarity of the law that attorneys addressed one another through the court.

The judge interrupted. "Counsel, please. Let's keep this civil. I have not been looking at her at all times, but I have been looking at her frequently, and on most of the occasions that I look at her, she appears to be sitting with her head down. Her eyes are downcast, but, I believe, not closed. With regard to the assertions you are making in support of your motion, Mr. Larson, this witness has testified that there were things she observed but hasn't described yet for us. Mrs. Thornton says this witness is suffering from a stress disorder caused by what happened in this case. On that representation, I'm inclined to grant some latitude here. Take a ten-minute break and then let's get back out there, Counsel, and see if she is able to communicate better.''

During the recess, the defense team huddled with Engle, going over what, exactly, Niki Crawford had testified to. It wasn't much. She had seen a man and a little girl. She had seen something else sometime later. Whom she had seen, what she had seen, were still big question marks. Larson had observed a few other developments. He had disrupted her testimony just enough to test her ability to follow a consistent train of thought. What he had observed was that Niki's memory was impaired. And the closer Judith took her to the events she had witnessed, the more she was blocking, at least as badly as she had been when he'd talked to her at her house.

Things were proceeding along as he had planned.

Niki had gone to the second-floor cafeteria for a cup of coffee. She was shaking so badly her coffee had sloshed over the rim of the white Styrofoam cup more than once, falling in large tan drips on the white linoleum.

''Niki?''

She turned to see Pike Martin standing behind her.

''I don't want to talk with you.''

''I don't blame you. After today, you'll never have to hear my voice or see my ugly face again. But for now, you need to look at me. Because for today, we're on the same side.''

''What side is that?''

''Getting out of you what's inside. Whatever it is you've pushed down so deep inside you that you can't dredge it up. Getting it out to keep Bobby Engle in jail. You're all that stands between him and the door.''

''That's not fair—you can't lay that on me. Besides,

it's not that I don't want to help. I *can't* do it.''

"*Won't* do it."

"*Can't.* I just . . . can't remember it all."

"What was it you saw out there, Niki?"

"I'm not sure anymore. It's all so mixed up in my dreams now."

Fear welled up in Pike. If that was what she was going to say on the stand, they were in deep shit.

"Uh, Niki, it's important that you be able to separate the dreams from reality. Unless you can honestly say that they're the same thing."

"They're not the same thing."

"All you need to tell is the truth. Not your dreams. What you saw. You've been in the courtroom for a while. You must know how important your testimony is . . . your telling the truth."

"I can remember some of the big things. It's what happened at the same time and around the big things that I get mixed up about, and some of the things I . . . can't remember at all. It's like there are these gaps, you know? Time gaps."

"Well, why don't you just tell the big events you can remember? The things you know happened. After you saw the man and the girl, you went out to the field again?"

"Yes, I did."

"And what was it you saw? Be real general for a moment."

Niki looked into her coffee cup. "The . . . I saw . . . the . . . the . . . b-body."

"Can you tell the jury you saw that? Just try. That's all anyone's asking."

At the end of the break, Judith and Pike had a few moments to talk.

"How's it look, Pike?"

"She's disintegrating up there."

"I just want an ID of Engle. Any kind of ID. Even a bad one."

"Judith, I spoke with her. She told me she saw a body," Pike said.

"Good, great. But let's see if she can repeat at least that one simple thing."

The judge was on the bench, and Niki had made her own way back on the witness stand.

"Proceed, Mrs. Thornton."

"Thank you, your Honor."

"Niki, during the break, did you tell Detective Martin what you saw when you went back to the field the second time?"

"Yes, I did."

"What did you see?"

"It was a body."

Larson was surprised by the force of her answer.

"Okay, okay. Good. And what did you see about the body?" Judith needed to establish that the body Niki had seen was Kelly Solomon's. To do that, Niki had to describe it with enough detail to match the coroner's description of the body found out there.

"It was—it was—pretty cut up."

"Whereabouts?"

"The body itself."

"Was the head there? Niki? . . ."

"Part of it."

"Were there any clothes on the body?"

"Uh . . . clothes? No."

"What else can you tell us about the body?"

"I remember it was bloated . . . like an animal gets after it sits for a while."

"Anything else?"

Niki shook her head.

"Is that it?"

Niki nodded.

"After you saw the body, what did you do?"

"I think I ran. I don't remember."

"Where did you go?"

"Back into my car, and I left."

"Did you tell anyone about what you saw?"

"No one."

"Did you call 911 for help?"

"I don't remember doing that."

"Have you ever told anybody about this before today?"

"No."

"Why did you have so much trouble telling us about this, Niki?"

"It's just something that—it's just something I can't deal with. It's just not supposed to happen."

"Niki, now this is important. . . ."

Larson knew the identification was coming. "Objection!" He rose from his chair and walked quickly toward the jury box, knowing exactly what Judith's reaction would be, inviting her reaction. "Objection, your Honor, to the prosecutor baiting this witness. That was an improper comment."

By the time Larson had completed his objections, he was standing near the exhibit table. He placed his hand momentarily on the gray steel pointer there, pausing just long enough to see that Niki had followed his actions.

"Excuse me, your Honor! I wasn't aware Mr. Larson had the floor here! I object to his improper advance into the—"

"Counsel, please. Both of you, please take a seat for a moment."

Larson walked back, slowly, to the defense table.

"I'm sorry, your Honor—and Mrs. Thornton. I did

get a bit carried away. It won't happen again.''

"Okay. Let's carry on, shall we? Mrs. Thornton.''

"Niki, you testified previously that you saw a man and a girl, and the man was forcefully steering the girl.''

"Yes. That's what I said. I did see that.''

"Is that man in the courtroom?''

"Is that man . . . uh . . . yeah. I . . . there's a man that looks like him very much.''

"Looks like him'' were not the words Judith wanted to hear. A simple "Yes'' was what she wanted.

"Can you point to him, please?''

"He's there with those two attorneys at the table. He's wearing a white shirt.''

"Can the record reflect the witness has identified the defendant?''

Judith's request was a standard one which was seldom objected to. Larson, however, wanted a break between the question and the answer.

"Your Honor, may I, for just a moment, address the prosecutor's last request?''

"Can we do it at side bar here, Mr. Larson?'' The court asked, wishing now to remove as much of the cat-fight as possible from the already confused jury.

Larson and Judith approached the bench.

"Mr. Larson?''

"I hope this isn't too picky, but there has been no identification.''

"Well, Mr. Larson, I think the prosecutor's question goes to the witness's identification of Mr. Engle as the man she says looks like the man she saw at the field. Right, Mrs. Thornton?''

"That's correct, your Honor.''

"Then can the request to the court properly reflect that?''

"How would you rephrase it, Mr. Larson?" the court asked.

"The record can reflect that the witness has pointed to the defendant as the person who looks like the man she saw at the field."

"Is that okay with you, Mrs. Thornton?"

"No. But I fail to see how it's going to make much difference."

"I beg to differ with Mrs. Thornton. It could, your Honor."

The two attorneys returned to their chairs at their respective tables.

"Okay, Mrs. Thornton . . . can you rephrase?"

"Can the record, your Honor, reflect that the witness has looked at and pointed to the defendant, identifying him as looking like the man she saw at the field with the little girl?" She intended that her request differ from that articulated by Larson. She also embellished it with the gestures that Niki had used to accompany her answer.

"Yes. The record will so reflect."

"The People have no further questions of the witness at this time."

"Then, Counsel, shall we break for the day?" asked Baker.

No one voiced an objection.

"Court is in recess until tomorrow at nine."

Bennett leaned over toward Larson and whispered, "Excellent job!"

Tomorrow it would be Larson's turn. He had destroyed Niki Crawford's identification of Engle. Tomorrow, if what he had found was true, they'd have to carry her out of the courtroom.

48

Larson, bursting with energy, waited impatiently in the hallway outside the courtroom. The clerk usually unlocked the doors thirty minutes or so before the nine o'clock start-up time. This morning Larson wanted to be the first inside. He had his work cut out for him. His first order of business was to inform the clerk of the number of exhibits he would be using so that she could prewrite the evidence tags. Then he moved the portable easel as close to the witness stand as he could and still have it capable of being seen by Niki and the jury. He positioned it carefully so that Niki would have a straight-on look at it and he could point directly at it as he stood next to the witness stand. By the time trial started again, Larson had the implements of his presentation ready.

Even before setting down their files and notebooks, Judith and Pike gazed intently around the well of the courtroom.

"Jesus, get a load of that," Pike muttered. "It looks as though they've brought in everything we picked up out at the field." There were thirty-two items, to be exact; all were neatly laid out on two six-foot tables, and placed in rows at the sides and underneath them. "What do you suppose Larson's going to do with all of that?"

"Chaos, Pike. He's going to try to confuse Niki, maybe get her to admit to not having seen any of this stuff and shake her up."

"He doesn't need to confuse her. She already is plenty confused."

"But we have a tentative identification," Judith said. "That's all we need, and he knows it. Where is Niki now?"

"She should be in the hallway, at the far end. Yesterday I told her to meet us there."

The clerk's telephone buzzer sounded. It meant the judge was ready to begin the morning session. As the bailiff left to gather the jury, Pike went to bring Niki into the courtroom.

Niki was sitting, neatly dressed in a long-sleeved navy blue dress with a white collar. She'd make a good impression. This morning she walked more self-assuredly and spoke with more clarity than she had the prior day.

"I think I'm ready for this, Mr. Martin."

"Well, don't get overconfident. Larson is ruthless. Answer his questions as best you can and just tell the truth . . . as best you know it."

When they got into the courtroom, the jury and the attorneys were ready to proceed. Niki retook the stand. The clerk called out into the judge's chambers, and within a moment, it seemed, he was at the bench and the case was called.

"The record will reflect the jury is present, as is the defendant. Counsel are present as well. If I recall correctly, the People had rested and the cross-examination of Miss Crawford was about to begin."

"That's correct, your Honor." Larson rose and approached Niki. His pacing would be critical. He had spent the better part of last night thinking about how fast he should move through his planned lines of questioning and in what order the topics should be covered. Slowly at first. He would have some fun with her. Then move in for the kill. Not cat-and-mouse. More like bullfighter. The picture presented by the analogy pleased him.

"Good morning, Miss Crawford. You're looking rested."

"Thank you. I feel okay."

"Miss Crawford, I'd like to begin this morning by going back to this"—he paused, ever so momentarily—"this body . . . you have told us you saw."

"Okay."

"Now, it's been a while since you saw it. Certainly you told someone about seeing it before you came to court yesterday?"

"No, I didn't."

"You didn't. Well, now, Miss Crawford, is that because the sight of what you saw was *so* bad that you just *couldn't* bring yourself to talk about it?"

"That's correct."

"But yesterday, after the break, for the first time, you had the wherewithal to deal with it?"

"I could, yes."

"What did you do during the break, Miss Crawford?"

"I talked and visited."

"With whom, may I ask?"

"With Mr. Martin."

Larson walked to the prosecution table and stood behind Pike.

"Oh, you mean Detective Martin sitting here . . . next to the prosecutor?"

"Yes."

Larson moved back toward the witness.

"During the break, did he tell you what to say when you came back into trial?"

"No, it's all been building for a while. I wanted to get rid of . . . of the nightmares."

"Oh, yes, your dreams. . . . Let's see. You felt somehow you would be able to sleep better by testifying that way yesterday?"

"The only way I can find that out is tonight, when I go to bed."

"Well, now, besides the nightmares, has there been any other effect from seeing this body?"

"I'm not sure I understand."

"Well, did it cause you to become suicidal?"

"No!"

"Did it cause you to become emotionally disturbed or distraught?"

"I really don't understand what you're asking."

"Were you having mental problems after seeing the body?"

"What do you consider mental problems?"

Larson was holding a copy of the report Pike had prepared for Judith. He took a moment to examine it while the courtroom waited.

"Well, didn't you tell Detective Martin that you were uptight, that you didn't sleep at all, that you couldn't eat, you couldn't get your act together, you couldn't cope, you had a death wish and everything was falling apart?"

"I don't remember."

"You don't remember if you said those things?"

She shook her head.

"Do you remember if any of what I've said is true?"

"I can't tell you."

"Can't or won't?"

"Can't."

"Do you have *any* recollection of your first conversation with Detective Martin?"

"Vaguely."

"Now, that first time you talked with Detective Martin, you had a chance to tell him about seeing the man and the girl at the field, didn't you?"

"Yes."

"About finding the body?"

"Ye-yes! But I did tell them I saw the truck—the truck they showed me in the pictures."

"So you gave them a *little* information. Were you hoping that they'd put the rest of the story together?"

"That's not true."

"Well, you didn't tell them everything you knew, did you?"

"No, sir, I didn't. I told them that I had seen the vehicle near the field. They showed me some photographs and I said, 'Those don't look like anyone I have seen before.' "

"Was that the truth?"

"That was the truth."

"Tell me, did the girl in the picture have blond hair?"

"Yes, sir, but there are lots of people with blond hair."

"But you said, 'I have never seen anybody like this before.' Right?"

"I said I had not seen that particular individual."

"Was that true?"

"To the best of my knowledge, it was."

"Didn't you put two and two together?"

"Yes, but the question that was asked was, did I see *that* particular girl."

Larson stepped as close as he dared toward the side of the witness stand.

"You tried to deceive the police, didn't you?"

"No, I did not."

"Well, you knew they were looking for somebody to make an identification of that girl in the picture, didn't you?"

"No, I can't say that I did."

"Now, Miss Crawford, come on. . . ."

"Objection, your Honor. Defense counsel is badgering the witness."

"Sustained."

Larson did not react to the objection or the ruling. His eyes were riveted on Niki's face. He moved on, picking up the pace, as if there had been no objection at all.

"Well, let's go back for a moment to when you saw the man leading a little girl to the river, is that right?"

"No, sir. He wasn't leading her."

"Pushing her?"

"Forcibly steering."

"Let's talk about this forcible steering you say you saw. Was he touching her during this forceful steering?"

"I couldn't tell you."

"Did he have his hands on her?"

"I didn't see his hands."

"Did you see the girl's hands?"

"No, sir."

"What portion of the man's body did you see?"

"His back."

"Well, when you say 'forcibly steering,' was he touching the girl in any way?"

"I don't remember seeing his hands."

"Was he bumping her?"

"I couldn't tell you."

"Did he kick her?"

"No."

Larson paused here to let the rapid-fire "I don't remembers" and the "nos" sink in.

"Did you ever, ever see the girl's face?"

"No, sir."

"Did you ever see the front of her at all?"

"No, sir."

"And you saw the back of the head of the person who was behind her?"

"He turned around and . . ."

"And what? . . . And what, Miss Crawford?"

Niki started slowly rocking back and forth on her chair.

"It . . . it . . ."

There it was. She was on her way out. A rush of adrenaline surged through him.

"It what?"

Just when Larson thought he'd ground her to a halt, she started up again.

"It . . . it scared me . . . it was like . . . he looked right through me. Like I wasn't even there."

"Oh, you were afraid of him?"

"It was more like I was thinking it was all out of place, and you keep going and you just kind of think about it."

"What did you *think* was out of place about it? Did you *think* the little girl was in any danger?"

"It . . . it was just a general feeling something was wrong."

"Can you please just answer my question?"

Judith rose. "Your Honor, he's badgering the witness again."

"Well, Judge, if I could get her to give me one straight ans—"

"Stop right there. Approach the bench, please, Counsel." Baker got quickly to the point. "Back off, Mr. Larson."

Larson's voice was hushed. He did not care to have the jury hear this scolding.

"But, your Honor, I feel I must—"

The judge, cognizant of Larson's concerns, took his own voice up several octaves. "I have told you to back off. I expect you will, Counsel."

All the jurors' heads were turned to the bench. Larson's voice rose.

"I apologize, your Honor. In my zeal to defend my client, I lost control momentarily."

The attorneys returned to their respective tables. Larson picked up a file and carried it over to Niki.

"Let's see if I can get this right. You *thought* the little girl was being forcefully steered into the river area, right?"

"Yes."

"Why? There was *nothing* you saw that demonstrated danger, right?"

"You're wrong."

"Your Honor, can you instruct the witness to answer the question, please?"

"Answer if you can, Miss Crawford."

Niki was looking at Larson. She was pleading. He knew it. He could see the growing anguish in her eyes.

He could stop right there. She was teetering on the brink, and he had solicited enough ambiguity from her to argue to the jury that she had seen nothing improper, let alone threatening, between the man and the girl. But there was fight left in her eyes too. If he turned her over now to Judith, on redirect the prosecutor might be able to pull Niki out of this and rehabilitate her. He knew what Niki had seen. If the prosecutor could take her to this very break point, she might fall in the other direction and blurt it all out quite involuntarily. No, he would have to finish her off right here. Right now.

Larson walked over to one of the two tables lined with items that had been collected from the turnout. From the carefully arranged rows of evidence he selected a metal rod. Before picking it up, he glanced at Niki. She was watching him. Watching his hands.

Larson walked, rod in hand, to the easel. The rod would be his pointer.

"Now, Miss Crawford, yesterday you had some difficulty going to the map of the field when the prosecutor asked if you would. I'd like to draw a rough diagram of the area and ask you a few questions, if I may."

Larson took a black felt marker from the ledge of the easel and began to draw. First a large square.

"This is the general area, Miss Crawford."

Then a zigzagging line.

"Let's say this is the San Diego River here."

Finally he drew a three-inch line in the shape of a horseshoe, its two prongs pointed upward. When the rough diagram was complete, Larson picked up the rod-turned-pointer.

"And this," he said as he traced the horseshoe one end to the other, "this is the exact area, let's say, where Kelly Solomon's body was found."

As he stood directly in front of the easel, the rod came to rest at the center base of the horseshoe. "Can you see all this, Miss Crawford?"

Niki's widening eyes were glued to the rod and the blackboard.

Bingo. He had been right. He could tell.

Larson maintained the rod's position as he asked his question.

"Miss Crawford, if you saw a man abusing, about to mutilate . . . and *beat* . . . and beat . . . and kill a helpless little girl, why, *why* didn't you stop him?"

There was no response other than her leaning forward

enough for Larson to believe she was about to revert on them.

"Miss Crawford? Why didn't you stop him?"

The fetal rocking began.

Pike turned to Judith. "We're losing her."

Judith had a feeling of nausea in the pit of her stomach. "No, Pike. We *have* lost her."

Larson was still pointing at the area where the body was found, still trying to elicit from Niki the reason that she hadn't rescued the girl. Then she slumped forward, sobbing, still rocking back and forth. The court called a recess.

Judith rushed to her witness.

Niki spoke between the sobs. "I don't know what happened . . . I . . . I'm sorry."

"It's okay, Niki." Judith put her hand on the woman's shoulder.

At the conclusion of the recess, Niki sat in the front row while the jurors filed in, some looking at her, others avoiding her.

"Does the defense wish to further cross-examine Miss Crawford?" the judge asked.

"No, your Honor."

"Any redirect from the People?"

Judith and Pike conferred briefly. An expert could rehabilitate Niki by explaining she'd been traumatized. But that would get them nowhere. The questions remained. Just what had traumatized her? It was her identification of Engle that had become critical. No expert could help with that.

"No, your Honor. We ask that the witness be excused. We have no further witnesses. The people rest."

"Okay, Counsel. Does the defense have any witness they wish to call?"

"Can we have a moment to confer, your Honor?"

"Of course."

Larson sat down next to Bennett, and for a full minute the courtroom was filled with only the muffled whispers of the defense team and, occasionally, of Engle. Finally, Larson stood to address the court.

"Well, Mr. Larson, have you any witnesses?"

"No, your Honor, we do not." The inflection in his voice added, *We don't have to.*

"The defense rests?"

"The defense rests."

"Well, then, we can use our time at break now to finish going over which instructions on the law you wish me to give. The jury is excused until one-thirty. Counsel, take ten minutes and come back. We can wrap up all our loose ends right now."

During the recess, Pike and Judith consoled each other. Niki had been a disaster.

"What in hell do you suppose happened to her?" Judith asked in a rare display of mild obscenity. "I was watching her. She was doing fine. She said she saw the body. Then"—Judith snapped her fingers—"she was gone."

"Who knows? She's going to need some pretty heavy-duty psychiatric help," Pike said. "I can see if we can get someone out to talk to her quickly. I sent her home and told her we'd call her if we needed her again. All hell's going to break loose if the jury fails to reach a verdict."

They were all thinking the same thing. All hell would break loose if the jury brought back a not-guilty.

"Something happened," Judith said. "She remembered something. She got to that one point and there was a complete breakdown. But what could have caused it? We were sitting right here."

"It's not going to help us now. She probably doesn't

even know what it is that she remembered. The best thing we have going for us is her tentative ID of Engle.''

"I'll stay and go through the instructions with the judge. You don't need to stick around," Judith said, obviously fatigued. "We'll probably instruct in the morning and present closing arguments." She turned to the clerk. "Can I get a copy of the transcript of Niki's cross-examination? I'd like to take a look at it. I just have this feeling something . . . I don't know. I'd like to see it in print."

The reporter in most capital cases usually transcribes her notes from the day before and has them ready for the court and counsel should issues arise that require going back over the record. These transcripts—"dailies," as they were called—were easily obtained if the reporter had sufficient time to prepare them. Now they had a break in the trial while court and counsel went over the instructions.

"I can see if the reporter can get it to us. She probably can, but it'll have to be in the morning, is my guess," the clerk said. "Is there something in particular you want to take a look at?"

"I don't know. Like I said, I just have this feeling, is all. That there's something she knows that she isn't saying or can't say and . . . I'd just like to take a look."

"I'll ask, Mrs. Thornton. Check back in an hour or so."

49

Judith returned to the courtroom at four o'clock to find
Margaret, the clerk, seated at her desk. Judge Baker was
going over the instructions which would be given to the
jury the next morning before it would begin its deliberations. The clerk had been instructed to tell Judith that
a reporter's transcript would be available for her in the
morning at eight-thirty and she should pick it up in the
courtroom directly from the reporter.

Judith stood there, taking in the courtroom scene. Garbage. It was all garbage that was so carefully laid out
and marked for exhibit. What could possibly have been
going through Larson's mind? He hadn't used any of it.
Had he even intended to? Had the display been just for
posturing, to throw Judith or Niki off guard? It was all
useless, really, to the defense case.

As Judge Baker's clerk worked on the court's business at her desk, Judith tried to pinpoint exactly what
it was that Larson had done. She walked over to the
first table of exhibits and looked at the steel rod. She
picked it up and examined it, one end to the other. It
was just a steel rod. Something had at one time been

screwed onto one of the ends. What was it Larson had done with the rod while he cross-examined Niki? He hadn't threatened her in any way with it. Judith had been watching, and she would have seen that kind of shenanigans pretty quickly. No, he had used it. That was right. He had used it. But only as a pointer. When he was talking about the turnout. He had used a felt pen to draw a picture of the turnout and he had used the rod to point.

Judith moved toward the easel. The diagram Larson had drawn was gone.

"Margaret?"

The clerk looked up from her work. "Uh-huh."

"Did you mark the diagram Mr. Larson drew during Niki Crawford's cross-examination?"

"No. It was never marked for evidence. The defense attorney took it with him."

Diagrams were usually marked as exhibits, even if they were never admitted as evidence. Sometimes, though, counsel for the prosecution and the defense would agree, stipulate, not to use them and they would be taken away. But in Judith's mind, everything Larson did was suspect, and she could not recall stipulating to the diagram's removal.

"Do you remember what was on it, Margaret?"

"Gee, not really. But I'll bet it shows up on the transcript, because I recall he did say what it was he was drawing."

"See you tomorrow, Margaret. I'll try to be here by eight-thirty."

The following morning when Judith arrived at the courtroom, Pike was there, reviewing his notes. Argument was scheduled to begin at ten. She would get the first chance to address the jury and then Larson or Bennett would respond, and because the prosecution carried the burden of proof, she would get to make the final argument.

"Mrs. Thornton, good morning," the clerk called out upon seeing her. "The transcript's ready for you. It isn't all of the testimony from Niki Crawford. I asked the reporter to prepare just the last part of cross-examination."

"I think that's going to be enough."

"There's another problem," Pike put in. "I've been trying to call Niki since last night. She's not there, or she's not answering her phone. She looked so bad yesterday that I'm worried about her. She can't disappear on us now. She's still a critical witness, especially if the jury is hung. If we can't get a verdict because the jury is split, we're going to have to do this all over again, God help us. We still need her."

"Well, if you don't mind, Pike, could you see if you can track her down? Go out to see her if you have to. I don't really need you to sit through the closing argument. We're hanging on a thread. As it stands now, I think we've got a fifty-fifty shot at a guilty verdict. I'll settle for that. Give him life imprisonment."

"I'll check back with you, Judith, at noon and let you know what I come up with."

As he started to leave, Judith began to accompany him out the door. The clerk called her back.

"Oh, Mrs. Thorton, the transcript." Margaret rose and handed Judith what looked to be fifty or so pages, neatly bound in a thin black notebook with a clear plastic face.

Pike first tried to telephone Niki. There was no answer. Although he hadn't discussed it with Judith, he had some concerns that Niki might do something irrational.

It was ten-thirty by the time Pike arrived at Niki's house. He rang the doorbell nine or ten times, and after leaving plenty of response time, he knocked hard on the door. There was no response. Pike then walked the perimeter of the building, trying to see what he could through the windows. When he got to what was obviously the bedroom, he stopped. It was in complete disarray. Vanity drawers were open. Clothes hangers littered the floor.

Suddenly fearful for her safety, Pike quickly sought out a neighbor, a man of sixty or so, and explained his mission and his concern for Niki's safety.

"Oh, there's no cause for alarm, Officer. She was in this morning."

"Did she say where she was going?"

"No," the man said, shaking his head.

"Can I ask if you have any idea if she has any friends or family I can contact?"

"None that I know of. She was a real quiet person. She kept to herself and didn't talk a lot. In fact, I don't recall her ever having any visitors that I saw."

"Do me a favor. If she calls or writes to you, can you get some indication of where she's gone? I can't fill you in on details, but she's a witness in a very important murder case."

"I promise I'll do that."

Pike handed over his business card and left, determined to find something that would lead to Niki. He had to do it as fast as possible. The farther away she got, the more likely she'd be gone for good.

His next stop was the Parks and Recreation Department office. No one could help him. She'd given her notice shortly after she'd had her accident. No one knew where she had gone. Even Paul Eberle, who Pike thought might have been contacted by Niki, had not heard from her.

By the time Pike had finished talking to the staff and several of Niki's past coworkers, the morning had slipped away. It was eleven-thirty. He needed to get back to Judith and report the grim details.

Court was in recess, and Judith was in the courtroom when Pike arrived. He didn't wait for her to ask the questions.

"She's gone, Judith. I think she might have packed up and left. I talked with her neighbor and went out to the Parks Department. It's clear she's just run away."

"Stay on her, Pike," Judith said, glancing at the notes she had compiled of Bennett's closing argument.

"How's it going?" he asked.

"It's going as predicted," she replied, looking up at Pike. "Bennett's done. He did a great job in his closing argument. I've got my closing argument, and then the jury will be instructed. That'll probably take us through this evening. Baker said he might keep us later than four o'clock. We may go till six. I think he wants to get this to the jury today. We'll release them, and they can come back and jump right into deliberations first thing."

"Have you had any chance to get to the transcript?" Pike asked.

"Not yet. I'll look at it this evening."

By four o'clock the arguments had been made and the jury instructed and released to go home. Pike telephoned Judith to say his leads had never materialized. Niki Crawford had vanished.

Judith wandered back to the courtroom after trying unsuccessfully to contact Pike. He had gone to an early dinner and wasn't expected back until morning. The clerk was still there, still working.

"Margaret, do you mind if I sit down and work for a half hour here? I'd like to take a look at the evidence again before you start to pack it up."

"Sure. That's not a problem. I'm going to be here until six."

Judith made herself comfortable at the prosecution table. Her first order of business was to read the transcript she'd been toting around most of the day. She read it quickly, then went back and carefully reread the parts dealing with the diagram.

The record reflected that Larson had drawn a square for the entire area, a zigzag for the river and a horseshoe for the specific area the body had been found.

Square.

Zigzag.

Horseshoe. And he might have used the steel rod to point at the drawing. He had. The transcript was specific. In parentheses in at least two places the typist had inserted "Points to diagram."

Judith got up and went over to the easel.

There was nothing unusual in what Larson had drawn. Except the horseshoe. She'd never seen a horseshoe line used to depict location. Squares, yes; X's, yes; circles, yes. Horseshoes, no. But she couldn't say there was anything illegitimate about that. Still, it bothered her.

Before she left the courtroom, Judith carefully looked at every piece of evidence one more time. Just to be sure there wasn't something, some one little thing, she was missing.

Judith spent a sleepless night. The image of a grinning Bobby Engle leaving the courtroom a free man, accompanied by his shrill laughter, woke her more than once.

By the time Judith had arrived at her office, it was seven-thirty. At her desk, she began the process, the ritual, of organizing and clearing away the mounds of paper and files she had collected in the past months of trial. Pile by pile she sorted, some of the material dropping in smaller piles into the two cardboard storage boxes she'd set up next to her desk.

By eight, Judith had worked her way through most of the paper mounds on her desk and credenza. She kept the newspaper articles on the case and her personal notebooks off in one corner. Those she would hold in her personal files in her office. The only other items to be stored were those on her walls. First the aerial photo of the field where Kelly's body had been found came off, then the layers of photos and memos she'd thumbtacked up, some haphazardly, some with great purpose.

When she got to the last layer of material, she froze. A wave of dizziness and nausea swept over her. The last photograph to be removed was of Kelly Solomon's body. It was one of the torso photos she'd thumbtacked up months ago, when she'd sat inspecting the black-and-white pictures taken at the scene and at the autopsy. It was the one on which Pike had used a fluorescent green pen to circle the strange, semicircular heel marks on the girl's body.

The strange *horseshoe*-shaped marks on the girl's body.

Judith lost her breath.

Where had she seen a horseshoe?

Grabbing the photo off the wall, Judith ran out the door of her office with it, almost hitting Farrell in the process.

"Judith, where the—"

Judith was too immersed in propulsion of thought to

stop. "I've got something, Larry," she called over her shoulder. "Something big!"

At the court evidence locker, out of breath and panting, Judith asked the evidence-storage clerk to bring her the list of evidence in Engle's case. Her finger ran down the handwritten list until it stopped at the subtopic "Items Found at Engle's Apartment—Subject to Search Warrant." The typewriter case and the photos were listed. Along with the crucifix and ... horseshoe ... found in the case. When the horseshoe was brought out, Judith held it against the picture. Its shape and size were almost identical.

"I'd like to check this item out of court, please. Can you have it sent up to Judge Baker's courtroom? ASAP. And I mean ASAP." Parties were not permitted to check out the evidence across the counter. Baker's clerk would retrieve it.

Photo still in hand, Judith went up immediately to the courtroom and found Margaret, Judge Baker's clerk, at her desk.

"Can you bring up evidence item number sixty in the Engle case, Margaret? Please? And it's a matter of critical importance."

The surprised clerk looked at Judith's wide eyes, and realized at once that something important was, indeed, unfolding.

"I suppose so, Mrs. Thornton." Then she offered, "You know, the jury hasn't yet started deliberation. Is there some reason they shouldn't? They're down in the jury room."

"I think there just might be. I need to talk to Judge Baker, with defense counsel present."

Sensing urgency, the clerk did what good ones are expected to do. She took over.

"Let me call Mr. Larson and Mr. Bennett. I'll tell

them to be here at eleven o'clock. I know the judge is available then.''

"Thanks, Margaret. And have you picked up that steel rod yet that was marked as evidence?''

"Uh . . . no. It's in the back.''

"We'll need to see it.''

"Well, now, I've got a lot of things to do here. Let me call defense counsel, get the evidence item from downstairs and retrieve the rod. Somewhere in there, I'll ask my judge to hold the jury.''

Margaret disappeared into the back hallway. Judith used the courtroom phone to summon Pike, then waited for what seemed a terribly long period of time, fifteen minutes.

Then it seemed everything and everyone arrived at the same time. The rod, the horseshoe and Pike.

"Pike! Look here. I think I found something.'' Judith inserted the rod into the hole on the back of the horseshoe. With one mechanical movement, her left hand turned the rod, and her right turned the horseshoe. Two more twists and they were one—something that looked like a branding iron. She triumphantly handed Pike the tool and the photograph of Kelly Solomon.

"Son of a bitch!'' The expletive was emphasized as Pike set the photo on the prosecution-counsel table and held the horseshoe to the photo, recognizing at once the similarity in shape. He lifted the rod above the table and with one powerful thrust smashed it down on the wood, forming a perfect semicircular indentation very much resembling a heel mark.

There were shocked gasps from the two women at Pike's seemingly wild actions.

"I'll pay for the damage, Margaret, I promise!'' he yelled, mesmerized by the mark he'd just made in the table and blinking fiercely.

"Thank goodness my judge isn't here!" the clerk fretted, wringing her hands.

"Don't you see what that brilliant little bastard did to Niki?" Judith's tone was almost reverent. She took the tool from Pike's hand and removed the horseshoe, placing it in Pike's hand. Then she went over to the court easel. On the paper tablet she drew a horseshoe-shaped line. Then she stood directly in front of it and pointed the rod at the center of the base of the horseshoe-shaped line she had drawn.

"Look. What do you see?" Judith asked, still a step ahead of her observers.

Pike and Margaret moved to Judith's side.

"When I hold the rod right here like this," she continued, "and look at the diagram from this direction, it forms the same configuration as the branding iron when you screw on the metal horseshoe. Don't you see?

"Larson figured it out. He figured out that Niki had seen it. Then he told her he'd figured it out. And he did it without saying a word, without communicating with anyone. There was just a silent understanding between the two of them. He destroyed that girl just by re-creating the image of what she'd seen out at the field. Maybe she saw Engle use it to hit Kelly Solomon; maybe she just saw him poking at her as they crossed the field. We'll never know. But she saw *this*," Judith said, reattaching the horseshoe to its rod. "And one more thing we do know, Pike, is that this rod was found near the body, and the horseshoe that goes with it was found in Engle's apartment. And . . . the marks on the body match that semicircular mark the horseshoe just made there."

"So now what the hell do we do?" Pike asked. "The trial's over."

"Not yet it isn't. We see if Baker will let us reopen."

"Can the judge bring the jury back?" Pike asked.

"It's unusual. But it's possible. The California rules of criminal procedure allow it. The court, at its discretion, can reopen the evidence at any time, even during jury deliberations."

Within thirty minutes Judith had written a three-page request to reopen evidence and filed it with the court. Larson and Bennett were notified that a special hearing would be held at eleven o'clock to determine if additional evidence would be admitted. The jury was excused until 1:30 P.M.

Back in his office, Pike shuffled through the first police reports filed back when the body had been found. They were now in chronological order in a heavy black plastic binder. The one he wanted was two inches from the top.

Pike reviewed the report for anything that might relate to the metal rod, rereading page after page of what he'd read thirty, fifty times before. Then, twenty minutes later, down in the corner of the personal employment history on Engle, he found a notation that caught his attention. *The man moves around, working temporary jobs.* What kind of temporary job could Engle have found in Santee that would allow the use of a branding iron? Pike's body jerked upright, a smile spreading across his face.

"Well, yahoo," he murmured. "It's our cowboy. . . ."

Pike left his office and drove at breakneck speed east on Freeway 8 to the rodeo grounds down the street from Engle's Lakeside apartment. The manager tentatively confirmed what Pike already suspected. Employees had access to branding utensils, and yes, Engle, whose photo Pike had brought, had worked at the rodeo during the week Kelly Solomon disappeared and was found dead.

The manager of the rodeo grounds agreed to appear in court that afternoon without a summons being served on him.

The evidentiary link had been forged, but the legal battle was just beginning.

At eleven o'clock both sides brought out the big guns. For the prosecution, Judith, Pike and an appellate specialist, Wayne Madigan, sat in a row at their table. Bennett, Larson, and their own appellate advisor were lined up at their own table. The hearing lasted forty-five minutes. Judith, periodically receiving whispered advice from Madigan, outlined the new evidence, pointed an accusatory finger at Larson and summarized the impressive body of law which would allow Baker to reopen the case. Bennett argued eloquently against allowing new evidence, and in favor of avoiding the prejudice that would befall Engle by having his trial start up again after argument and instruction had been completed.

In the end, Baker ruled the trial be reopened, and the newly discovered evidence, all of it, came in through the testimony of Pike Martin and the rodeo manager, to whom Engle smiled and nodded when he took the stand.

As Pike demonstrated for the jury how the horseshoe found in Engle's apartment and the rod found at the field near Kelly Solomon's body fit together, Engle turned to Larson, grinning affectionately at him.

"Oh, my, will you look at that, Mr. Larson. They found my snake."

Bennett did his best at damage control, but that was all he could do. Emotionally prepared as he had been from the outset to move into the penalty phase, Bennett had already begun preparing for the second part of the trial, so sure was he that a jury verdict of guilty would be returned. Larson, too, was resigned now to defeat, and when the jury was reinstructed and began deliberating, he began working on the automatic appeal to the California Supreme Court.

50

It took the jurors four days to bring in a verdict of guilty.

Not until the trial was over would Judith learn that one juror, Paul Matson, had held out for a not-guilty vote for three of those days. Finally, tears trickling down his cheeks, he had gone off into the corner of the jury room and had sat, head bowed, obviously deep in thought or prayer, or both. His fellow jurors respected his need for silence, although, due to physical constraints, they could not give him the privacy and solitude his personal torment warranted. But at the end of the three days, he emerged from his dormancy and voted guilty.

The jury never asked a question of the judge, never asked that testimony be reread. By all accounts, even with Paul Matson's ethical struggle, the verdict had been a quick one.

A week later, the penalty phase of the case began. Judith carefully detailed the horror of Engle's crime, his past offenses and his dangerous nature. By the end of the penalty trial, half the jurors would have been willing to drop the pellet for the gas chamber. Not even the

341

poignant testimony of Penny Reynolds, Engle's half sister, could diminish the outrage. In the end, Engle's time in the closets of his youth accounted for little. After six days of listening to witnesses, a punishment of death was announced by the jury foreman as three jurors searched the audience for Deborah Solomon while others sobbed openly.

51

The maître d' at Mr A's restaurant ushered Judith to a small table at the window. The deep burgundy velvet covering the walls and dining chairs gave the rococo decor an air of elegance the new, trendy, noisy restaurants in the Gaslamp Quarter of downtown San Diego lacked. She was far more comfortable here.

The view wasn't bad either. The restaurant's perch atop an office building just north of the downtown high-rises gave it an unobstructed view of the airport and brought diners eye level with the planes making their landing approaches at nearby Lindbergh Field.

"Mr. Farrell hasn't arrived yet, ma'am."

"Can I get a cup of coffee while I wait?"

The black-jacketed waiter—there were no waitresses in the restaurant—offered a slight bow and backed away.

The view was dazzling tonight. The tiled roofs of the Balboa Park museums were lighted and protruding from the tops of the trees ringing the park. In the distance, the Coronado Bay Bridge, traced in lights, arched across the bay.

This was the first relaxing meal of any kind Judith had had in months. It was a chance to unwind from the stress of the trial. And it was compliments of Farrell, with his wife's permission, as he had put it to Judith when he issued the invitation. With her mother's nurse spending the night, Judith didn't much care if they stayed until the place closed. But the dinner tonight was also a debriefing, a chance to kick around what had happened and why.

"Larry! Hi."

Farrell had arrived, unnoticed, and was standing next to her.

"You look rested," he said.

"The two days off helped. Have you heard from Pike?"

"Not in the last day." He chuckled. "When they led Engle out the back door after the death sentence came in, Pike took off out the front door, wrapped up the case and called the next day from Rosarita Beach down in Mexico. He made some noises about retiring or some such silly thing. It won't happen. He won't leave until they push him out the door—or carry him out. Tell me, Judith, was I right about him?"

"I admit he's good. Almost too good."

"What do you mean?"

"Good God, Larry, he almost single-handedly drove Niki Crawford into permanent hiding."

"He was just doing his job."

"To excess."

"I wouldn't say it exactly that way. We all push to the limits, Judith. Me. You. Larson. And Pike. The whole lot of us. We're supposed to. That's what the system's set up for. The rules, the judge, they may not keep us ethical all the time, but they keep us balanced. And as long as we do what we're supposed to, and they do what they're supposed to, something approximating justice should squeeze out at the end.''

· "This one was too close for comfort."

"Well . . . sometimes it *is* close."

"And sometimes it's a complete miss. Look at the times Engle slipped through, got back to the streets.''

"Maybe it was the system's fault. But only because someone wasn't doing what they were supposed to be doing. Some psychiatrist, the judge—maybe even our office.''

"And the Niki Crawfords?"

"They get ground up, Judith. They start up the process and get devoured by it.''

A waiter appeared next to the table, silently handing them heavy brown leather-bound menus with none of the prices listed inside.

"You know, she came back again, Larry, but she's a mess. If we get a reversal somewhere along the line and have to retry Engle, we may not be able to get her to cooperate and testify again. If we can't, we'll have her declared an unavailable witness and read her testimony from this trial into the record.''

"She's that bad?"

"We've had a psychiatrist take a look at her. And our victim-witness trauma counselors too. She saw Kelly Solomon's body when it was in a pretty bad condition. And she saw Engle pushing that kid with that branding iron. It's her guilt that's ripping her apart—her knowing something was wrong when she drove by and saw Engle with Kelly out at the field, and not taking the time to stop it. She could have prevented it. In her eyes she killed that girl.''

Farrell stared at Judith. "In a way she did, though, didn't she?''

Judith fell silent as a white china cup and saucer

slipped next to her on the table. The waiter poured from a silver coffeepot. As he turned to walk away, Judith spoke.

"And Alan Larson puts it all together.

"It's an irony, you know: the defense puts the truth together. Truth by accident. I like that. At least the Solomons have had a day in court."

"You're being sarcastic, of course, Judith."

"I said they had *a* day in court, Larry. They're going to be marking their calendars with Engle's court dates for the next decade at least."

Farrell reached for the cracker basket and opened the plastic wrapping on the rye thins he'd pulled from it. The paper no sooner had landed on the tablecloth than the waiter's hand darted between them and removed it.

"Parker's announcing his retirement tomorrow, Judith."

She was unruffled. "That's not a real surprise. The gossip's been heavy in that direction for months."

"I got word today that the Board of Supervisors will be meeting next week to discuss his replacement. I can't predict the future, but I suspect—"

Judith interrupted. "When's he leaving?" Then she realized Farrell was about to tell her his own plans.

"Two months. That doesn't leave a lot of time. There's no way the board's going to be able to take nominees through the replacement process in such a short period. I'll be stepping into Parker's spot as acting D.A. Don't mention it to anyone. It'll all be public tomorrow afternoon, when Parker calls a press conference."

"Have you decided who's going to take your spot?"

"I was hoping maybe you'd consider it, Judith."

"I wouldn't be doing trials, though."

"Not necessarily. You could pick what you wanted. We haven't ever had a woman fill a major administrative position. You're senior, and . . . hell, I trust you.''

"I don't know. I don't want to leave the task force dangling. There's a lot of unfinished work on a couple of real big cases."

"There's two potential candidates for your position." He smiled. "You are expendable."

She reached for the crackers.

"I like it, Larry. I do. I'll let you know in the morning."

"And, Judith, I want you to think about this for a moment. I'm not going to be at the post, assuming I were to take the D.A.'s position, forever. We've never had a woman fill the seat."

This was the first mention of his own candidacy.

"Well," Judith said, "what's to say I shouldn't go for it now?"

"Why don't you?"

Judith paused, teasing, "No, I'm going to hold out for a good judgeship; then I can supervise you."

He grinned. "Be quiet and order your dinner."

The waiter appeared again. "The lady is ready to order?"

The next day Parker Hunt, his press secretary, Farrell and Judith assembled in the district attorney's personal office for the press conference. In Hunt's style, it was a short speech. He thanked everyone who had worked for him over the years, spoke of his love for the office and with affection for the close friends he would leave behind, and, with a tear, looked into the audience for his wife, Agnes, with whom, he said, life was now going to be restful and filled with travel. At the end, he announced Farrell would take his position temporarily until the Board of Supervisors could make an appointment to the spot before the next election. And he also announced that for the first time in the history of the office, a woman would be filling the second-highest position, that vacated by Farrell's reassignment. Judith smiled, and when the press conference broke up, she made herself available for informal questions from the reporters.

Among the assembled press was Jon Kolker, who waited patiently until the majority of his colleagues had packed up their notebooks and cameras and left.

"Mrs. Thornton, I haven't had a chance to talk to you since the trial began. Is your faith in the system shaken any by the near miss in the Engle case?"

"Not mine, Mr. Kolker. How about yours?"

"I can't say I haven't had some interesting thoughts about the process in the last couple of months."

"If you can get them all into a nice paragraph or two, I for one would love to see it," Judith said, smiling.

"I don't think a paragraph's going to do it," Kolker replied.

"It won't, Jon. But my offer still stands."

Judith's secretary appeared through the dwindling crowd.

"Mr. Farrell's asking if he can see you for a few minutes before he leaves."

"Tell him I'll be right there."

Judith turned to Kolker. "How much of the trial did you see?"

"Enough."

"Good luck, Kolker. You've got your work cut out for you."

"Can we talk about it sometime over coffee?"

"You can count on it."

52

Bobby's hair was slicked back and his face was clean-shaven.

"Bennett!"

"I'm sorry, Bobby. We tried our best."

Bobby shrugged. "Why be sorry? I enjoyed this, especially watching your friend Mr. Larson. I told you a long time ago I did it. This was all pretty useless."

"I disagree. But you know that. I wanted to talk to you this morning about what happens now. There's an appeal to the California Supreme Court."

"Do I have to appeal?"

"You don't have a choice. It's an automatic review by the court."

"What do we appeal on?"

"Well, I won't be handling the appeal. The appellate attorneys are appointed by the court. They're all excellent, excellent. It's possible Alan Larson will handle it for you."

"You know, I've been contacted by three reporters. One's a real good-lookin' blond chick. She's doing a story on me and wants to interview me."

"I would think a lot of reporters might like to talk to you. Just remember what I said the first time we talked. Don't trust anyone."

"When will they gas me?"

Bennett smiled. For the first time, it seemed to Engle.

"We've only had one in this state in the last twenty-five years. Your case will go to the State Supreme Court, then the federal courts. With a good attorney like Alan, that'll take—oh, ten to fifteen years." Bennett smiled again. "You still have time to write your memoirs, Bobby."

"We'll talk again?" Bobby grinned. "I may need to interview *you*."

"We'll talk again."

EPILOGUE

San Diego Union   Part A State and   page 3
June 2, 1993   World News

The California State Supreme Court yesterday upheld the death sentence of convicted murderer Robert Dean Engle. Engle was convicted in 1992 of the mutilation torture murder of nine-year-old Kelly Solomon in San Diego. A closely divided court, led by conservative Maxwell Augustine, held the San Diego Municipal Court did not commit error when it rejected Engle's attempts to plead guilty, forcing him to go to trial.

Appellate specialist Alan Larson, representing Engle on his appeal, vowed to take the issue of Engle's guilty plea to the federal courts. "Given the close nature of the evidence in this case and my client's horrible, distorted childhood, the jury should have been permitted to see the remorse he would have displayed had he been allowed to enter a plea of guilty." Municipal Court Judge Henry

L. Moore, who rejected Engle's plea of guilty, was not available for comment.

Larson received the Criminal Defense Bar "Trial Attorney of the Year" award earlier this year for his work defending Engle. The award is the highest honor the statewide organization of trial lawyers can award a member of the defense bar. Interviewed following the Supreme Court's rejection of his appeal, Larson vowed there would be a lengthy fight in the federal courts to vindicate his client's constitutional rights to speak in his own behalf and represent himself at trial.

San Diego Union   Part E Obituaries   page 6
July 17, 1994

Deborah K. Solomon, a thirty-two-year resident of San Diego County, died yesterday at home following a lengthy battle with cancer. Abe Solomon, her husband of twenty years, was with her when she died.

Mrs. Solomon is survived by her husband. A daughter, Kelly, was murdered in 1992. The man accused of her murder, Robert Dean Engle, is currently awaiting hearings in the federal courts. The hearings are scheduled to be heard later this year.

Graveside services will be private.

FAST-PACED MYSTERIES
BY J.A. JANCE

Featuring J.P. Beaumont

UNTIL PROVEN GUILTY	89638-9/$4.99 US/$5.99 CAN
INJUSTICE FOR ALL	89641-9/$4.50 US/$5.50 CAN
TRIAL BY FURY	75138-0/$4.99 US/$5.99 CAN
TAKING THE FIFTH	75139-9/$4.99 US/$5.99 CAN
IMPROBABLE CAUSE	75412-6/$4.99 US/$5.99 CAN
A MORE PERFECT UNION	75413-4/$4.99 US/$5.99 CAN
DISMISSED WITH PREJUDICE	
	75547-5/$4.99 US/$5.99 CAN
MINOR IN POSSESSION	75546-7/$4.99 US/$5.99 CAN
PAYMENT IN KIND	75836-9/$4.99 US/$5.99 CAN
WITHOUT DUE PROCESS	75837-7/$4.99 US/$5.99 CAN
FAILURE TO APPEAR	75839-3/$5.50 US/$6.50 CAN

Featuring Joanna Brady

DESERT HEAT	76545-4/$4.99 US/$5.99 CAN

Coming Soon

TOMBSTONE COURAGE	76546-2/$5.99 US/$6.99 CAN

Buy these books at your local bookstore or use this coupon for ordering:

....

Mail to: Avon Books, Dept BP, Box 767, Rte 2, Dresden, TN 38225   C
Please send me the book(s) I have checked above.
❑ My check or money order— no cash or CODs please— for $_____is enclosed
(please add $1.50 to cover postage and handling for each book ordered— Canadian residents
add 7% GST).
❑ Charge my VISA/MC Acct#_____Exp Date_____
Minimum credit card order is two books or $6.00 (please add postage and handling charge of
$1.50 per book — Canadian residents add 7% GST). For faster service, call
1-800-762-0779. Residents of Tennessee, please call 1-800-633-1607. Prices and numbers
are subject to change without notice. Please allow six to eight weeks for delivery.

Name_____
Address_____
City_____State/Zip_____
Telephone No._____   JAN 0195

Meet Peggy O'Neill
A Campus Cop With a Ph.D. in Murder

"A 'Must Read' for fans of Sue Grafton"
Alfred Hitchcock Mystery Magazine

Exciting Mysteries by M.D. Lake

ONCE UPON A CRIME 77520-4/$4.99 US/$5.99 Can
Jens Aage Lindemann, the respected Danish scholar and
irrepressible reprobate, has come to conduct a sympo-
sium on his country's most fabled storyteller, Hans
Christian Anderson. But things end unhappily ever after
for the lecherous Lindemann when someone bashes his
brains in with a bronze statuette of the Little Mermaid.

AMENDS FOR MURDER 75865-2/$4.99 US/$5.99 Can
When a distinguished professor is found murdered, campus
security officer Peggy O'Neill's investigation uncovers a
murderous mix of faculty orgies, poetry readings, and some
very devoted female teaching assistants.

COLD COMFORT	76032-0/$4.99 US/ $6.50 Can
POISONED IVY	76573-X/$4.99 US/$5.99 Can
A GIFT FOR MURDER	76855-0/$4.50 US/$5.50 Can
MURDER BY MAIL	76856-9/$4.99 US/$5.99 Can